CW00855411

After Valour

CA Eccles

Published by KDP

For my children and grandchildren

Author's Note

This book is the story of what happened to my grandfather during and after the First World War. Where I knew the facts, I used them, and that is particularly true of the beginning and the end. But where I did not know I have had to imagine, so many of the characters, places, and incidents portrayed here are either the product of my imagination or, if real, are used fictitiously. I have also changed most of the family names.

Contents

A time of Innocence   4

Still Scoring Bullseyes   28

No Hysterics in this Ward   60

Sick for that gal   82

Dreadful Deeds   97

Oh! We'll never tell them   123

Je t'aime   150

A Second Chance   175

Towards a New Life   202

Wollabungo   228

Squalls   248

Clearing the Way   284

Some Things to Sort Out   309

During a Nightmare   333

It's My Turn   359

Prologue

Was it just a matter of luck, he thought, who fell and who remained upright? Eruptions of earth, stone and jagged pieces of hot metal were still slamming into the ground and into the bodies all around him. The allied gunfire continued but was having little effect on the Boche. The air was so thick with smoke and grit that he could have eaten it. The din reverberated under his feet; rising through his soles and along his veins and arteries. It occupied his limbs, climbing and smashing inside his head. He shivered as if an electric current had whisked through him. The cacophony travelled on beyond, into the air that was already reeling with noise. Was it the pandemonium that was propelling him forwards? He did not hear the individual bodies falling, being ripped apart, nor the final cries and whimpers of the lost, but he saw their remains. His stomach flipped, acid burned in his throat, and somewhere between his heart and his belly was an emptiness.

The allied bombardment was not halting the enemy's withering machine gun fire. His limbs moved of their own accord. He was running as if being chased by whips of lightning. He leapt, he ducked, he zig-zagged. He bounded over the shuddering ground and through the dirt-laden air until he stumbled into a deep furrow that ran left and right about thirty yards each way. Visibility was slightly better in the hollow. He recognised his Lieutenant scrambling along towards him on all fours, the expression on his face and his graphic gesticulations urging those still upright to be ready for hand-to-hand combat.

There were about twenty British soldiers down in the ditch – several already injured - when a group of men in grey uniforms and helmets fell upon them. Shots were fired at close range from rifles and revolvers, but knuckle dusters were out too; blades of all sorts; clubs and sticks. Khaki and grey twisted and struggled in the narrow channel. Edward had a fixed bayonet in his left hand, while in his right hand he swung a piece of wood studded with nails. He shifted his stance for better balance as another grey soldier jumped in, and the bayonet went straight through the German's face.

Lord Street Stockport

Early 1900

A time of Innocence

Lord Street, enclosed by cotton mills, hat manufacturers, a busy railway station, a saw mill, a tin works and scores of terraces, seldom had clement weather. Respite came at the end of June 1914, when Stockport's grey mantle was temporarily replaced by a canopy of azure blue without clouds pulling at the sky. Usually, tall factory chimneys belched filth throughout the year and often made the dreariness of cloudy days heavy and impenetrable. In cold weather, the hundreds of house chimneys thickened the sooty atmosphere to smog that coated the back of throats. It had to be washed away with strong tea or alcohol.

After dusk, in winter, the tightly packed rows of terraced houses looked like menacing fortresses.

Flickering gas lamps did little to improve the scene, so that people were generally reluctant to venture forth, even to their neighbours, except in an emergency. Identifying one's house on return from the pub was difficult, unless someone had painted white the three steps to the front door. Frederick Holmes, who was a decorator, had done this at number 62 and the steps were kept scrubbed by his wife - Rosa.

Those later June days, of 1914, banished thoughts of winter and the day's curling dirty ribbons. The unusually hot weather opened doors and windows, and neighbours waved, smiled and crossed the road to chat and share a glass of homemade lemonade. Women left off their corsets and petticoats; men abandoned their stiff collars and undid shirt buttons. Some even followed the younger boys' example; happy in just a vest or bare-chested. Children played hop-scotch and skipping games. A favourite game was 'Catch me if you can' on the pavement or in between the large flapping sheets stretched across the road. Children ran in and out of each other's homes. Babies were left outside in their perambulators or box carts and slept, unaware of their siblings' excitement. It was a precious time.

The three brothers from 62 Lord Street; William, Edward and Joseph - each bare chested and carrying towels for the baths, bubbled with laughter as they tumbled outside. Joseph was already dribbling a football before he reached the door. He aimed it through their legs, so they fell over each other. Then, jostling along the pavement, they were soon on the road.

Here some of the other kids joined in a kick-about. Joseph, showing off, kicked the ball too fiercely and it became a serious undertaking to stop it before it reached the end of the street. The main road of Wellington Street ran across the bottom of Lord Street, and trams passed every ten minutes.

Chasing down Lord Street, music trilled from open windows and front parlours. The children playing outside joined the variety show with choruses of their nursery rhyme games;

'The big ship sails through the ally ally oh, the ally ally oh.' Mrs Lanesboro's gramophone was whirring out Caruso, singing 'O Sole Mio.' Passing another house, they heard a brave trumpeter trying the accompaniment to Alexander's Rag Time Band. At number 6, the ivory keys were plonking out 'Daisy, Daisy'.

"Blimey, that's worse than you on the accordion, Eddie," teased William as he nudged Joseph to join the banter. Edward, the middle brother and the fastest, did not retaliate. He raced forward, jumped over the ball, twisted around and gathered it up. His brothers cheered before Joseph shouted, "The last one in the pool is a sissy!" and they set off at full tilt again.

There was no mistaking them for brothers, whose faces at ten, thirteen and sixteen almost mirrored each other. They were tall and strong with wavy black hair above hyacinth blue eyes caught from their mother. Their smiles revealed engaging dimples that their mother teased them about endlessly, especially when she noticed girls looking at her sons.

William, at sixteen, was already apprenticed at Crossley Motors in Gorton and mad about engines and the future of motor vehicles. Life was great, and there was a girl he liked. His biggest worry was his efforts to grow a beard to hide the dimples he thought were babyish.

Joseph, still at school, hated it and often received the cane for arriving late or for shoddy work. His thoughts were all about football and dreams of playing for Stockport County one day. His brothers scolded him every time he moaned about being in trouble at school. Their parents, however, always suggested that he had taken enough punishment from the teachers. His dad, Frederick, would say, "N'er mind lad. I were nowt at school. Look where I am t' day, 'Tis ya ma has the brains. We'll get thee sorted."

In Edward's eyes, his younger brother got away with murder; his older brother – only just three years his senior - was allowed to smoke and drink ale, while Edward felt continuously nagged about his progress and thoughts for his future. The day for leaving school was drawing near for Edward - just a few more weeks before school finished for the summer holidays. With his birthday in September, there was no point in him returning the following term. He was bright enough to try for a Grammar School, but as William had started work at fourteen, his parents decided that Edward was to follow suit; learning a skill and earning a living.

His teacher, Mr Crabtree, had said that he was a clever lad but liked nothing better than drawing or whittling away at a piece of wood. Recently, Edward, who was desperate to become a carpenter, had presented his mother with a mahogany bowl. It was made from an old newel post his father had brought home. Mr Crabtree had mentioned Millington's, only a ten-minute tram ride to Bredbury. Edward had been to have a look around. On the bus returning home, elation swelled inside him like a celebratory balloon. "They make all sorts, Mammy," he said. "Proper grand furniture and that. It's what I'm good at," he added hopefully. She said nothing but smiled and gave him a hug. Edward suspected that she was thinking of his dad, who had other ideas.

He had a few weeks' grace, but it was evident that Frederick had set his heart on Edward helping in his decorating business. The subject kept coming up at mealtimes, causing Edward to lose his appetite. He did not remember his dad pestering William in the same way.

Today was for fun though, and when William dashed into the grocers on the corner of the street and emerged with a bag of broken biscuits, they stuffed their mouths till their cheeks bulged. Trying to chew and swallow and not laugh at the same time, they dodged the traffic on the main road, still in competition to be the first to reach the baths. Joseph began to cough; too many biscuit crumbs. Edward stopped to slap him on the back, which let William be the winner.

By the time they had finished chasing, diving and water bombing each other, it was early evening. A cloak of cloud was evident with a faint chill and mizzling rain. They regretted leaving off their shirts and their soaked towels offered no comfort. Another race followed, back to the house. A few dawdling children remained on Lord Street, but the babies and the hanging sheets had been taken inside. Now the doors and windows were shut against the strains of music. Only the clatter of the boys' clogs echoed down the street.

Edward, a natural athlete, should have won the race easily, but he stopped momentarily by a lamppost and grabbed hold of William, before urging Joseph to get ahead.

"Ger off!" his elder brother snarled. "Don't let the kid win," and he pulled his arm away.

"Give him a chance," Edward said. "Needs stronger legs for his precious football game."

"You're soft, you," William rebuked, "I'll beat thee now," and the chase continued until they stampeded into the back yard and through the kitchen door, with seconds between them, like quick flashes of the same image.

Rosa, their mother, grinned as she continued slicing rounds from a loaf. Their father, comfortable in a chair on the far side of the range, emerged from behind his newspaper, "Good day, lads?"

"Swimming, dad. Near drowned our Joe," said William.

"Not likely!" Joseph threw his sodden towel at his brother. "I can beat thee any day."

"Dream on, kid."

"Enough, enough. Get 't table. Not sure how much fun we'll all be 'aving soon. Stuff in papers is right bad today."

"Fred, let's eat," interrupted Rosa. "No need to bother the boys with all that."

"All what Ma?" asked William.

Putting down the bread knife, she paused then turned to face them. "That Archduke and his wife, murdered - right out on the street. They had children you know."

"It's not right ma, but what's it to do with us?" asked Edward.

"Could bring war in Europe. That's what," their dad replied.

"That's all very well," Rosa said, and her voice was brittle, "but thank God our boys are not soldiers. Shan't affect them."

The boys glanced at each other, recognising a tremble in their mother's voice. They moved silently to the table.

There was sliced ham, cheese, lettuce leaves, scallions, tomatoes and relish all laid out ready on a crisp red-checked table cloth. Frederick had been to his allotment at Flowery Fields; a half hour's walk up to Woodsmoor. Something sweet was also cooking in the range – probably a fruit pie or crumble.

Rosa pulled the rack down and hung up their swimming suits and towels, before sitting down with a pot of tea and the plate of bread. Her thick black hair was worn up in a bun and already decorated with delicate streaks of silver-grey. Some of these strands that had escaped, during the hustle and bustle of her day, framed her small face with its apple pink cheeks.

The house was spick-and-span. The kitchen cum living room was comfortable, but practical, with smells of home cooking and fresh washing. The back door was never locked, and the kettle was always on the boil. Their mother could make scones in minutes when neighbours popped in for a chat or a favour. She knew how to listen and put people at their ease; and offering a bite to eat was always welcomed.

"Woman tha heart is t' big," Frederick would often tease her, "Tha wants to 'elp t'ole world," he'd say. But he was proud of her willingness to attend to the trials of her neighbours when he would absent himself to the front parlour or the pub. "I dunno abaht these tuther lasses, makin' all this fuss in't papers for voting, but I'd give thee that vote any day, duck."

Although not so gifted with words as his wife, Rosa valued his judgement and usually let him have the last say. The boys lived by his rules: good manners at the table and to all, no matter what their station in life; attendance at church every Sunday and total respect for their mother. They brought in the coal, hung out the washing and washed up when it was their turn.

At the tea table, after the swimming adventure, the subject turned to Edward's future again. "So, Eddie, shall we be kitting thee out soon?" His father's words were uncomfortable to swallow. Edward was sure his dad was picturing white overalls for decorating and not the blue ones he'd seen worn at Millington's' Bespoke Carpenters. His breath was trapped and there was a drum measuring quick time behind his ribs. Everyone had stopped eating. They were waiting on his answer. The silence was choking him.

He managed to catch his mother's eyes. He did not want his face to betray his feelings. Any moment there would be the blush, he thought, just like when the girls next door tried to engage him in conversation. He saw a glow in his mother's eyes, but couldn't work out if it was an encouragement for him to say what he had told her recently, or if she was willing him to say what his dad wanted to hear. He could not look at his dad but took a sip of his tea and coughed before saying quietly, "I'm not sure dad. Mr Crabtree thinks I'd make a good…"

"I can't see what business 'tis of his." His dad leaned back and folded his arms, "but no doubt thee 'll please thee self like William did." His voice dropped and all Edward could hear was the disappointment. Another silence.

His mother got up to refresh the teapot. Edward looked up, and she beamed at him, but what it meant he still could not fathom. His father reached across the table and nudged Edward's plate, which startled him and caused him to look straight at his dad. "I'm really good at woodwork," he spluttered.

"And tha still can be, but we'd make a great team, son. You're patient and thorough. Could be a master painter like me. Ah knows it."

Edward felt dizzy. The hope that had billowed in his chest deflated as quickly as the blink of a wink. In its place was a blockage, as if he had swallowed his food too quickly. His dad's eyes were glossy, and Edward panicked at the thought his dad might actually cry. Taking a sip of his tea, he swallowed hard and said, "Can I try it for a year, dad? Then I won't be too old to do the apprenticeship in carpentry if I change my mind."

"'Tis good enough for me!" His father's face looked like he had won the first prize.

Knives and forks resumed clattering and scraping on plates. Rosa poured Edward another cup of tea and stirred in an extra spoonful of sugar. William slapped his brother on the back, and Frederick asked for more cheese and continued to grin as he buttered a piece of bread. Edward drank his tea quietly.

The following morning, the weather was a blessing once more, and after church, the family went with a group of friends from Lord Street to Vernon Park for a picnic. Everyone brought food and drink to share. The Silver Band warmed up on the bandstand. Kids floated boats; some made from newspaper. Youngsters caught tadpoles in jars, and some showed off their brand-new nets and tried to capture sticklebacks. Mothers helped their infants to throw crumbs to the ducks.

William chatted to a girl who worked in the office at Crossley's. Joseph found a group of boys equally eager to play football while some of the older ones played French cricket. Edward was not keen to join in anything but wandered over to the bandstand with his mother. "I'm sorry about Millington's son, but your dad will be so proud to have you with him." She took hold of his hand.

"I know mammy, I'll try," he promised. Looping her arm through his, she gave him a squeeze, and they noticed a cluster of girls promenading, including the three from next door at 64. They were busy chit-chatting and laughing but kept looking towards the boys playing cricket. A volley of provocative looks passed between certain boys and girls, but Edward turned away.

Later, an enterprising young man with a Vesta Pocket Kodak offered to take people's photographs for a small sum. He took down names and addresses and arranged to call round the following week with the pictures. Frederick agreed to a family portrait, then his sons bunched together with a group of friends. They were promised a special rate if each bought one.

***

On the 31st August, a few days short of his fourteenth birthday, Edward started work with his father. At breakfast, he wriggled and scratched in his pristine white overalls. William chortled, "Look like yous dressing up for something." Edward hissed between his teeth and grimaced at his brother. William's brown overalls for Crossley's, although freshly laundered, had evidence of wear and tear and faded stains. Frederick's might have been white once but were now ash grey and the material softened after many boilings.

"Give it a week son, and you'll be more comfortable after I've washed them," his mother said. She winked at him, passing him the first piece of toast. William was ready to snatch it, but Edward anticipated his move and turned his back quickly. He stuffed it in his mouth so that he struggled to chew as he tried not to laugh.

Frederick worked with an old mate of his, Tommy Taylor. The previous summer, they had taken on Cyril Kent, as their apprentice. He was a couple of years older than Edward, as their apprentice. Frederick had commissions for pub and shop signs and Tommy could not manage on his own. Frederick supposed that his son and Cyril would work well together.

Their current decorating job was a large detached house near the park in Bramhall. It belonged to a Mr Blunt, the owner of one of the hat factories in Stockport. Mr Blunt's parents had died, and he wanted to replace the dark colours he had lived with all his life with a brighter look, both inside and out. He moved himself and his family out to the Grand

Hotel in Manchester for the duration of the work, which would take many weeks. He called to check on progress once a week.

On the first day, it was the best part of an hour's walk while pushing the laden handcart and trying to keep the contents steady. It took Edward and his father to manoeuvre it. On the way, they met up with Tommy and Cyril, and Edward was introduced. He knew Tommy so well, he referred to him as Uncle Tommy, and they both beamed at each other and shook hands heartily. Cyril, however, barely touched Edward's hand and avoided his eyes. He took Frederick's place with the cart, which Edward though was kind, but Cyril strode out and increased the pace vigorously until he and Edward were trotting. Some of the contents slipped and slithered about, and Edward wondered if Cyril was showing off for some reason.

Once around a corner, and out of sight of the other two, Cyril said, "'Opin' not to spoil tha' new outfit are thee? Goin' to be a soft job, wi' thy ol' man, is it?" The tubs, buckets and ladders rattled. Some of the equipment skated towards them, so they were forced to tip the cart and slow the pace.

"I'll work as hard as any of you!" The words were out of Edward's mouth before he realised, he had risen to the bait.

"Ah, but outside, where I'm working, is for proper decorators in any weather, and high ladders in 't wind. Not for patsies."

"I'm sure you're right, Cyril." Edward paused and looked straight at him. "You take care of yourself today then."

"Are you threatenin' me?" Cyril let go of the cart and jumped back, leaving Edward to grab both handles, which was quite a stretch, to bring the cart to a standstill, just as Frederick approached.

"Woah, lads! What tha playin' at?" Frederick ran towards them.

"We're fine dad, just Cyril had a sneezing fit."

***

Frederick thought that because Cyril was closer in age to his son, Edward would prefer to learn from him. He asked Cyril to work inside and show Edward how to mix the distemper with linseed oil, emulsified in water, using borax. Then the measured application of turpentine. He was to demonstrate the art of applying a smooth coat of paint, and the difference between the brushes for internal work and external painting. Edward learnt how to measure a wall for paper; to match up lengths of wallpaper; how to position the ladders safely and how to tidy up after himself and store all the equipment.

Over several weeks, nevertheless, Frederick had cause to find fault with his son's work. "Ah knows tha did'ne want to decorate son, but 'tis basic stuff. Are thee not listenin'?"

"Dad, I follow all my instructions, honestly."

Frederick studied Edward's face for a moment. "Ah think I compre'end thee, son. 'Appen someone's scairt o' loosin' out."

Edward raised his eyebrows and shrugged his shoulders. From that day forward, Frederick took over instructing his son, which should have been an end to any cause for complaint.

One morning, however, Mr Blunt was waiting for Frederick when they arrived and pointed to a broken china vase. It had been on the grand piano near the French Windows but now lay in pieces on the drawing room floor. Edward had been the only one working in that room the previous day.

Edward was perplexed. He wanted to protest that he knew nothing about the smashed vase. Instead, he said, "I am so sorry, Sir. When I went to shut the windows, at the end of the day, I brushed against it." He flexed his elbow to explain how it had occurred. "I thought it best to leave it for you to see rather than dispose of it," and he looked hard at his father as Mr Blunt paced up and down the room.

"I appreciate your uprightness," Mr Blunt replied but his tone gave away his anger.

"Yous should ah told me last night, son," Frederick said.

"Sorry Pa, but I forgot - with it being our Joseph's birthday and all." He shook his head and frowned at his father, hoping Frederick would let it go.

Fortunately, his father got the message and went along with the explanation. He also apologised to Mr Blunt, who took a lot of appeasing. The vase had been in the family for many years. Reluctantly Frederick agreed to reduce his fees by ten pounds. Afterwards, he was furious at the cost and injustice, but although they suspected Cyril there was no proof. They said nothing to Cyril, but Frederick made sure each evening that there were no other unexplained mishaps.

***

The day the job was finished, they were all in The Buck and Dog celebrating. Frederick and Tommy soon settled in the dominoes corner, while Edward and Cyril were asked to make up teams playing darts. Edward had a steady hand and a good eye. As the competition ended, he sat down with a couple of old school friends to catch up on their news. He learnt that Reg's brother, Sam, had decided to volunteer for the war. Mr Asquith had been calling for another 5000 men. Lord Kitchener promised that the volunteers would be better treated than any soldiers before them. They would receive two shillings a day for board and lodging as well as their one shilling pay.

"Our Sam says he's on a winner," Reg told Edward.

"But they say it'll all be over by Christmas."

"When it's all over though, he can stay in the army if he wants to. We've never had no soldiers in't family before."

Edward was distracted by loud laughter from the bar, and turned to look. It was Cyril, who was chatting up the pretty barmaid and drawing attention to himself. He hoped Cyril knew that Nora was the landlord's girlfriend. He turned back to his friends, "Do you know, I don't think I'm brave enough to fight in a war."

"Well if you're not, we aint!" laughed a fellow called Clive and he slapped Edward on the back as he got up for another drink.

As the bell rang for time, a chap called Gerry, from William's year in school, said, "It'll all be done with soon, anyway. No need to worry."

Realising his dad had already left, Edward decided to take the short cut through the back yard of the pub to Bridge Street. The gate there was rarely locked, but that night it was wide open and swinging. As he approached it, he heard some scuffling and raised voices on the pavement. Although it was dark, but in the shadows from the gas lamps he could see two men were kicking and beating someone on the ground, who was begging them to stop.

"Leave off, will you?" Edward called as he ran towards them.

"Want some y'self?" one of the men shouted.

"Reckon he's had enough," said Edward.

"Maybe, but you've had none yet!" and it looked as if they might move towards Edward. He stood his ground and raised his fists but luckily, they changed their minds and went back through the yard and into the pub.

It was Cyril. Edward crouched down to try to lift him, but it took ages because every movement made Cyril exclaim again.

"You've got to try and walk so we can get you to the infirmary. It's only up the road." He gave Cyril his handkerchief to mop the blood dripping from his nose and a cut on his face. After a few minutes, he became calmer. Between them, Cyril manged a half-standing position, and Edward supported his weight as they hobbled towards the hospital.

Cyril had two broken ribs, a badly bruised back, and needed stitches above his right eye. His nose was not broken but bled for several hours, despite the doctor's efforts to stem the flow. The doctor suspected that there might be a problem preventing his blood clotting. He had to remain in the hospital for a few days, and Edward visited until he was discharged. Frederick was puzzled. "He ain't done you no favours lad, what you bein' so friendly for?"

"He only has his mam, and she struggles with bad legs; can't walk so well."

When Cyril returned to work a few weeks later, he went straight to Frederick. "I'm sorry, Mr Holmes," he said, holding out his hand, "I acted up. I thought you'd let me go once Edward started with you."

"Reckoned on that lad, but I'd allus be straight wi' thee." He shook Cyril's hand and continued, "Let's be a good team goin' forrads."

Edward was more relaxed at work, but his enthusiasm for the job did not grow. He would not let his dad down but longed to be more creative. It was one thing to turn someone's home into their little palace, but it was always according to their choice of colour and wallpaper. He would not complain to his father though, who proudly introduced his son to new clients. "My lad, Edward 'as joint wi' me now," he beamed, "and is doin' a right grand job."

***

Christmas came and went with no sign of the war being over. Thousands had been reported killed or missing since the outbreak. But the newspapers at the end of December 1914 reported that the war had come to a halt in no man's land on Christmas Day. It seemed crazy that for a few hours the allies could swap chocolate or jam for German sausages, share cigarettes and sing together, but the very next day, the fighting began all over again. Fighting escalated throughout 1915 on land, at sea, and in the air. The number of volunteers had declined since the initial rush, and by the following January of 1916, a Military Service Act decreed that men aged from 18 to 41 were to be called up for service. Anyone applying for a certificate of exemption had to do so before March 2nd. Frederick escaped conscription by one year.

William was already eighteen. He was not a conscientious objector, but he had not rushed to volunteer. Crossley's had opened a branch in Stockport. The company was heavily into war production, making the 20/25 chassis, which could carry a variety of bodywork for ambulances, light trucks and staff touring cars. William enjoyed his work. He hoped he might get an exemption but got short shrift when he spoke to his boss. Mr Wyatt had lost his only son at the Battle of Neuve Chapelle. He told William, in no uncertain terms, that it was his duty to go, and by the end of June the necessary papers arrived at 62 Lord Street.

Rosa was already anxious about William having to sign up. When Edward said he was going to volunteer at the same time, she screamed. "No, no, no! You're still a child. Only sixteen come September." Her face crumpled, she collapsed on a chair and wept.

"Ma, we've had two Christmases, and it isn't over like they said it would be." He put his arm around her. "Us young men should show we care. Besides, I think I need to do something important with my life apart from decorating. No disrespect, Dad."

"Nowt taken," Frederick said, shaking his head. "'Tis fine son. I get it."

"Edward, you might be killed! Two of your cousins are buried in a God-forsaken place I can't even pronounce," his mother pleaded.

"Yes, and if I do nothing, it'll be like ignoring their deaths, and all the deaths reported in the papers. Think about all the posters, ma, everywhere. I see them in my dreams."

"You're barmy Ed," William exclaimed. He drummed his fork on the kitchen table then pointed it at Edward. "Ma's got the point; you don't go until you have to!"

"That's daft," Edward said. "I know lads my age who are already out there. Thousands are needed to volunteer. Not everyone gets accepted. Anyway, they won't send me to fight until they think I'm nineteen. It might really be over by then, but at least I will have tried."

"But there's no need to go yet, son, please." She bit her lip and tears rolled down her cheeks.

Frederick reached out and took his wife's hand on his left and grasped William's fist on his right. He held on to them. "Ah knows thee is only concern't for our Eddie, Will, but I'm right proud of him. He's a strong un and determin'. If he's a mind to 't, then he should go. Nowt goin' on at work reet now that can't be fixed wi' me and Tommy." He looked hard at William. "You should go t'gether." Yous like twins anyroad."

William tutted loudly, wrenched his hand free, scraped his chair back and left the room. "He's mad; just showing off!"

"Come on, duck. 'Tis reet," Frederick told Rosa. "Happen they'll look after one an' 'tother," and he leant across, kissed her cheek and stroked her hair.

She dissolved into deeper sobs so that she struggled to get her words out, "He's not like William and only a child; could still be at school."

"Ah dun think we can stop the lad, now he's a mind to it."

***

The sergeant major in the recruiting depot at the Armoury on Greek Street did not ask too many questions. A birth certificate was not required because many people at that time did not possess one. Noticing the sergeant's flat mousy hair but surprisingly bushy moustache with intense flecks of red, some of the lads who were queueing up, began to snigger. Edward studied the man's face, which was pale and weak-looking under horn-rimmed glasses, and he noticed the man's eyes looked lifeless. When he spoke, however, he sounded tougher than he looked. As he walked up and down the line prodding each of them in the chest, his profound limp was noticeable. Edward thought he must be a casualty of the war.

The sergeant's task was to authorise for military training as many trainees as possible; though two shillings and sixpence per new recruit provided a strong incentive. Each candidate had to pass a fitness and medical test. In practice, the only ones he dismissed were those less than five feet three inches tall and those who blatantly looked too young, or under-nourished; no matter how hard they stuck out their scrawny chests. A thirty-four-inch torso was the minimum requirement. Having ordered those who were rejected to leave the premises, he growled at the remainder, "Get rid of the cigarettes! Line up and shut up! Call me, Sir."

Edward recognised quite a few of the young men reporting or volunteering that day from the same neighbourhood. His pal Reg, from school, was there; also, Gerry, Clive and Eric from William's year and several neighbours. Edward exchanged nods with some of them. No one remarked on his presence. A doctor gave them all hearing, eye and dental tests.

He put a stethoscope to their chests; gave a few prods then stamped their papers with a grade from one to four. Edward, at five feet ten, with obvious strength, was given a grade one.

The pasty looking recruitment officer gathered the successful men and boys into groups to swear to, "faithfully defend His Majesty, His Heirs and Successors – against all enemies." They made promises to obey the authority of all Generals and Officers and to serve for the duration of the war.

Edward and William were hoping to serve together in the same local regiment. At this stage of the war, though, recruits were allocated to where there were the highest regimental casualties. The sergeant major deliberately separated brothers anyway, in the hope they would not be killed together. William was to go to a Yorkshire regiment; Edward, to a Lancashire one. For all his valour, Edward admitted to a lurch in his stomach when they heard they were to be separated.

When the day came for the brothers to leave, they had to travel in their own clothes because their uniforms were not ready. They stood side by side in the kitchen, as their parents and Joseph admired them in the new suits that their father had bought. He thought the army would regard them more highly if they looked smart and clean when they arrived. Rosa had starched their white shirts and collars, and Frederick had a tie to give each of them.

"Look like you're going to a funeral," Joseph sniggered.

"What a stupid thing to say, our Joe. If you can't say anything nice, don't say anything at all," said Rosa.

Frederick shook their hands and said, "Proud of yous, son," with a slight croak in his voice. Rosa sniffed and blew her nose and continued to clutch her handkerchief, which she worried into a ball in her fist. She hugged her sons and whispered, "Stay safe. Come back to us."

Edward held her tightly and said, "Ma, the training will take months, and we'll get leave before we're posted."

Still Scoring Bullseyes

Only a five-minute walk to Stockport station, from Lord Street - the whole family proceeded across Wellington Road South and up Greek Street. Rosa's could not hold back her tears, and Frederick linked her arm, holding her close. For once, Joseph had not brought his football. "Be good for ma and Pa, eh?" Edward said and put his arm round his younger brother's shoulders. "Need to be the man about the house now, our kid. No more truanting."

Joseph chuckled, "Shan't have yous to nag me no more." He escaped Edward's hold and skipping ahead pretended to dribble his missing football.

The older brothers laughed, and William said, "I hope we both get leave at Christmas. I'll be dreaming about Ma's feast!"

"Aye, I bet the grub will be foul at camp." Edward said. He scowled as if he'd just been forced to swallow something putrid. "You must write to the folks, Will."

"I'll try. You're best at that."

"Ma will worry more if you don't write."

As they entered the station, Edward could not catch William's further comments. The station was fizzing with huffing engines, clattering trolleys, the clunking of trains - moving off or coming to a standstill - clanking doors, whistles and chatter. The sulphuric taste of coal dust and steam clogged in people's throats so that some men growled and spat.

Many young men were leaving that day, and a depleted brass band had been gathered. They were playing 'Keep the Home Fires Burning;' at platform 2a, where Edward and his family waited. He noticed a young cornet player had to stop for breath and to shake the moisture from his instrument. The platforms ran parallel with each other at the station and each one teemed with young men and their families. The young men with luggage far outnumbered parents, siblings and sweethearts they were leaving behind. There were older soldiers in full uniform with kit bags, indicating that they were soldiers returning to the front. People smiled at them; wanted to congratulate them and some folk even clapped as they passed by. The babble of conversations was fast and urgent. Occasionally shouts rose above the hullabaloo, making people stop for a second and look up. Families and sweethearts said their goodbyes, made promises, hugged, kissed, shook hands and slapped each other on the back. Tearful faces were easy to spot.

Both brothers had to change trains en route for their camps. Edward had to leave first for his connection at Manchester for Burnley training camp, while William's train was half an hour later for Leeds then Ripon, from a different platform. A shrill whistle rose above all the commotion. Edward's train was about to leave. He shook hands with William and wished him well, hugged Joseph and his father and shook hands with Frederick.

"Right proud of thee, son," his father said, with a ruckle in his throat. Finally, he turned to his mother, who clung on to him and said, "I love you, son," and she tried to sniff back her tears. A second whistle screeched. Edward leapt into the nearest carriage and hung out of the window at the door. As it began its chug-chug away from the platform, his family and many others were all focussed on the moving train. They ran alongside it as far as the platform end, where they were all bunched together - a mass of frantic waving handkerchiefs like a flurry of snow. Their blown kisses and shouts of goodbye were swallowed under the chuff-chuff of the steam and woo-wooo of the train's whistle.

Edward pushed his way into the first available carriage and claimed a seat by the door. He was pleased to see a group of lads from William's class; Frank Stockett, George Matthews, Rodney Fletcher, Harry Pearson, Gerald Thompson, Rowland Chester and Cyril. Also, his pal, Reg, and Frank from his own class, who grinned at Edward and stuck up their thumbs. Reg Parkinson was the only other lad from Lord Street. He drew out a photo from his wallet and passed it around; most of them were in the group photo taken at Vernon Park in June 1914.

***

Ripon August 3rd 1916

Dear Mammy, Dad and Joseph,

I am hoping this finds you all well. It is really not so bad at camp. It's a huge place – more like a small town of its own. We have our own railway station, a hospital and cinema, church, library and shop and we play all sorts of sports. There are hundreds of blokes, and mostly we all get along. Some of the officers are a bit la-di-da, but I think they mean well.

Each day starts with a trumpet call at 5.30 am. It's called Reveille. We are allowed a brew before we have to tidy and clean our quarters until 6.30 am. Then we have to do parade and fitness work till 8.00 am when we have breakfast. I'm starving by then, and the food is OK, but not like yours, Ma. We work on the parade square again until lunch, learning to march, form fours and about turn and more after lunch. Even if it's pouring down, we are outside most of the day. All of the kit we will have to carry is not ready yet, but they make us practice with weighted sacks on our backs.

We always have to keep very clean and all our kit and uniforms in perfect order. Our boots must shine, so they catch the light. You even have to make your bed in a particular way. None of the training is too hard yet, but the Sergeant is very strict and notices the tiniest mistake. He gives out rotten punishments. Reg had to clean the latrines with a toothbrush the other day because one of his tunic buttons was loose. So far, I've not done anything wrong.

We do have some time off when we can do what we want for a few hours. We play a lot of football, cricket and even boxing, and I'm quite good at that. We are allowed a couple of hours at the local pubs on the weekends as long as we behave. There's serious bother if anyone gets drunk and causes trouble. If you are on a charge, you don't get to go again.

Missing you all. Send me another parcel, please.

From your loving son,

Edward.

***

October 25th 1916

Dear Mammy, Da and Joseph,

Thanks for the cake. It went down a treat with the lads.

The training has stepped up a gear now. We do a lot of field movements, route marching (even at night) and have been learning to dig trenches and handle our weapons and equipment. Most of our kit has now arrived. Our uniforms are full of pockets and straps, and something has to go in each space. We have to carry everything from our weapons to ammunition, to a water bottle, field dressings and an entrenching tool. Altogether our kit will weigh 70 pounds.

I ache in places I didn't know I had muscles. We all have a rifle with a bayonet fixed to kill and have practised marksmanship and running at dummies, that look a bit like scarecrows. Turns out I'm a right good marksman too. We have competitions, and I regularly come top. We have to practise reloading our rifles blindfold. Then dropping the blindfold, we have to keep our eye on a target and let our hands do the work without looking down. I regularly get off over 20 shots a minute. The lads have nicknamed me Bullseye, and the Sarge says I'll be very handy, and I'm to have some extra training.

I still don't know where they are sending me and won't be able to tell you anyway, but I think I'll be home for Christmas. Write soon and send some more cake please.

From your loving son,
Edward

***

William's leave was to be at New Year, but Edward did get home for Christmas that year. Rosa took a step back as he entered the kitchen and gasped aloud when she saw him dressed in khaki trousers and jacket with shoulder straps and glistening buttons. She said the hobnail shiny boots looked too big. Edward still had smooth cheeks and dimples but his mother said, "You look more grown up, for sure. Not my boy who left in the summer."

"Ah, uniforms do that, ma. It's still me," and he smiled and hugged her. Joseph laughed at his legs covered with puttees and mock-boxed him, saying, "Bring us a German helmet from one you've killed. 'tis called a pickled somat!"

Frowning at him and biffing him gently across the back of the head, Edward said, "Nearly right – a pickelhaube is what you mean," and they dissolved into play fighting.

The house was cosy, welcoming, with its usual comforting smells. The fire was lit in the parlour. Frederick had swapped a sack of potatoes for a small fir tree which was now decorated with tinsel. Candles stood in shiny brass holders shaped like holly eaves on the window ledge among a collection of real holly and red berries. Although food was more expensive than before the war, Rosa had still managed a feast. There was roast chicken with homemade stuffing and Yorkshire puddings. Heaps of roast potatoes were spilling out of their deep dish, and carrots, turnips and cabbage – all from the allotment. Her special pudding had been prepared well in advance, with silver threepences hidden inside. It was a banquet to come home to after Mass on Christmas morning.

Edward wore the suit that his father had bought for him when he enlisted. Once his uniform had arrived at camp, he had sent the suit back home. His mother had pressed it carefully for him. After the meal they sat in the parlour and the boys each received a knitted jumper, socks and a scarf from Rosa. She had prepared a tin for Edward with homemade biscuits, jam, Oxo cubes, chocolate, cigarettes, a candle and matches in their own tiny tin box, to keep them dry, and some socks.

"The papers tell us what the men at the front like to get in their parcels," she said, "but I'm hoping you won't have to go through all that." She avoided his gaze as she tried to stifle a sob, but he felt it when he hugged her once more.

"Oh, Ma, I've been trained well. Most of the time I'll be hidden - watching the enemy in secret. There isn't a battle every day, and they stagger the troops who go to the actual front line. Each company only spends a few days there before being relieved."

Frederick produced a bottle of brandy and they toasted William, whom they had heard was to be posted to somewhere in France, after his leave at New Year. Joseph was allowed a small amount of brandy, but watered down, which he moaned about, until Edward gave him a carved toy replica of a Webley Mk4 pistol.

According to his military records, Edward had turned nineteen in September 1916 – in fact he was still sixteen. He had expected to be posted somewhere in France, like William, but he was surprised to find, on his return to camp at the beginning of January 1917, that his division was being shipped to more distant foreign parts. He wrote to his parents telling them that he would be travelling for a while and not able to write. He did not correspond with them again until he arrived in El Quantara – the headquarters of Eastern Force.

February 20th 1917

Dear Mammy, Dad and Joseph,

I'm in luck this once, I think. Our officer has said he won't be too strict censoring our letters. Maybe, because we've had such a long journey, when we couldn't write.

There's more training to be done here – so nothing to worry about, Ma.

The trip took almost a month and was not much fun. Nearly everyone was seasick at some stage of the journey, and we all of worried about torpedoes. We did have practices to evacuate the ship, but we were very crowded on board. It wasn't very orderly when we all had to put on life jackets and jump into life boats. It was not so bad during daylight and calm weather, but we had to imagine disaster at any time of the day and in all conditions. Anyway, thank God we were not hit.

There weren't enough hammocks to go around, but they're dreadful bits of canvas; not like a bed at all, so I just kipped on the floor. We didn't get much grub and a lot of us, including me, got the runs then couldn't eat for a few days. There were mules on board too. They didn't half stink the place out, and some died on the way and were chucked overboard.

We came by train to the place we're in now and we're all in tents. The Royal Engineers built the track. We were so glad not to have to march in the heat. Fortunately, it was not too hot the day we arrived. Water is rationed and some days we are not allowed to drink until after mid-day. Flies are a darned nuisance too, and you get sweaty and parched just swatting them away. You can't escape the blighters. We have to be careful of the mosquitos; even a struck match at night invites the buggers.

We had a sand storm the other afternoon when we were out in the desert doing trench work; much worse than rain. The wind blows the sand up in the air like a thick wall of grit. The grains of sand feel like needles and get up your nose and in your eyes, mouth and hair. We cover our faces immediately, but it doesn't help much. Afterwards, you have to shake the sand out of your uniform. Somehow, there is always some in a pocket. Sand is hard to march on as well because it's often very dry and soft – not like Blackpool. But when it rains, it's sludge.

We can go into the town and explore when we're off duty. It's quite dazzling at times and the smells are unusual - all sorts of spices I've never heard of for the local food. It burns your mouth at first but it's so tasty, and I think I'll get used to it. It's a welcome change from camp provisions.

Some of the girls are very pretty and wear long dresses in bright colours – not like posh stuff for a wedding or a ball at home, but softly draped from their shoulders to the ground. Often the top is different from the skirt part, and I think they call it a sari. Some wear black only, and all of them tend to cover their hair. Those in black look like nuns. The surprising thing is that a lot of the men wear what looks like a long white shirt to below their knees.

I've seen men being rough with women and beating their little kids and animals in the street. I don't know if they are just showing off how tough they are or if they are worried that we might steal their women or kill their animals. It's like they want us to know who is boss.

We call them gyppos. They do look like gypsies at home and they are always trying to sell us something and can pester you, and even the kids run around begging and will steal off you, given half a chance. I think the kids come from poor families and are just trying their best to help.

There are hundreds of horses out here, but you should see the camels. Most are a lot grander than those straggly beasts we once saw at Belle Vue Zoo in Manchester. They can carry very hefty loads and folk out here race them like we do horses. They had a kids' race the other day, and these nippers, aged about eight, were skilful and fearless. We all had a bet, and it was quite thrilling. The camel I chose came in second, and I won a shilling.

We are still marching and practising manoeuvres and digging trenches which is sheer murder because the ground is rocky and sandy here. I am doing some special training most days, because I am accurate when I shoot. Gerry, a pal from William's class is with me too. We spend hours at Company Headquarters, which makes us miss the banter with the other guys in our section, but we have to learn more skills to catch out the enemy.

There's a bunch of Aussies here, who are a great laugh. They call us chooms, and we call them diggers. They keep chirpy all the time and don't seem to mind the heat much either. Most of them are big chaps. They take the mickey out of some of our skinnier lads and usually beat us at all the sports. They don't respect rules and regs much and make fun of la-di-da officers. They think the Brits in charge are idiots, with no common sense, and say they won't salute an officer unless they respect him. Things can get pretty heated, but they don't care what kind of pickle they get in. They are punished but take it and start over again. We'd be crucified if we answered back. They drink plenty too and when they're drunk, fights start in the town between them and us. Then everyone gets it in the neck. They seem to think I'm OK, cos they know I can shoot *straight. I beat them all in a competition the other day, and they all slapped me on the back and wanted to buy me a drink. Now, they are calling me Bullseye too.*

Must close now, before the light goes. Can you get me cocoa and some toffee and always cigs? The ones out here are evil. Might take ages, but I'll live in hope.

Your loving son,
Edward.

***

Towards the end of March, Edward's platoon moved up to reserve trenches, but still carried on training. It felt like they were waiting around for ever and would never see action. Then the word went out that it was definitely their turn to move forward. Once they knew they were about to engage in their first battle, there was a frisson of mixed emotions and few short tempers. They learnt some more realities in the last few days before the engagement. The veterans told the youngsters that there would be no swinging their rifles in an enemy trench because the seventeen-inch blade of the fixed bayonet could snap or get stuck. They were encouraged to find or make small weapons for hand to hand combat. They all carried grenades, knives, clubs or bits of wood with hammered-in nails.

"But the bombardment and the cavalry will do most of the work, Sarge. Won't we just be collecting prisoners?" asked a young soldier.

"Don't be bloody stupid, son. It'll be fucking chaos, loud, brutal, bloody messy and fast." Sergeant Billy Smithers was in his eighteenth year in His

Majesty's Service. He was lean but broad with a strong neck and a large bald head, set off with unusually thick eyebrows. His face was swarthy but there was usually a sparkle in his eyes that could show fury at times but also humour and shrewdness. He swore better than any of his men, who sometimes thought him a bastard in training, but generally had respect for him and considered him fair.

Another veteran, Corporal Syd Moss, advised, "Whatever happens in the bombardment and the cavalry charges, we will be called on. Don't stand still; keep your eyes peeled but run like the devil in a zig-zag line. Your eyes and second sense must be everywhere. And shoot to kill. No second thoughts." The new recruits including Edward and those in his section, nodded vigorously, but Edward swallowed hard, feeling his mouth dry. He saw the same anxiety in the wide eyes of some of his pals. Others were fidgeting and looking at the ground.

Their officer, Second Lieutenant Hugh McDonald-Innes, who looked not much older than Edward, paced up and down the trench as the men gathered for their first engagement. Finally, he called out Edward and Gerry. "I know you were not expecting a sniping assignment so soon, but I've been watching from first light. The enemy machine guns are not heavily protected here." He showed them an X marked on a map. "See this outcrop, only yards from this trench. I want you to move out there when the rest of us go over; there'll be plenty of cover from our artillery." Edward thought of the fancy camouflage techniques they had been learning at company headquarters. There would be no time to dress up like trees or build a hide that looked like innocent rocks. "Reach that outcrop," McDonald-Innes continued, "and take anything in your sights, but a machine gun as a matter of priority." He gave Edward his field glasses. "You are number one, Holmes."

Rum was passed around and zero hour was upon them. The heavy barrage, under cover of which the troops would advance at a measured pace, had already started. Edward and all the other recently trained young men looked smart in their unstained uniforms. All their buttons were in place and fastened correctly. Edward noticed how very clean shaven most of the soldiers were. He and Gerry smeared their faces and hands with some boot polish and sand.

As McDonald-Innes fired, the sound was repeated in other sections along the zigzagging front line. Several sections, including Edward's, scrambled up the ladders and over the top into no man's land like ants following the scent of food. Edward was immediately aware of rattling machine-gun fire; the whistling of shells before they burst and the crumping and thudding of explosions. Between thundering bursts and booms from both sides, came yells and screams. Overwhelmed briefly by the speed of the action and the augmented racket, he and Gerry slithered slowly forward on their bellies. They hoped the action of the other men would keep eyes from them. It was about fifty yards to the outcrop. When they reached it, they lay low like stones but breathed heavily.

From the shelter of the rocks and a grassy mound, they searched the enemy line. In just those few minutes blasting shells had already quaked the earth and blown apart bodies as they had stepped into the fray. Many had fallen when they had barely made it out of the trenches. Scraps of bloodied uniform and body parts spattered across the ground. Pools of blood blotted in sand. "Shit and more shit, Gerry! Let's find that fucking machine gun," Edward yelled through the din.

He swept the glasses across no man's land. Right to left and back again before passing them to Gerry. There was more than one machine gun, but the Lieutenant was right; they were not hidden. He had done a good recce. One was almost opposite their hiding place - about three hundred yards away. It was not the distance that bothered Edward but the lack of clear visibility because of the smoke. He took the glasses back and shouted in Gerry's ear that they would have to be patient. They watched for several precious minutes without speaking.

Edward knew he would have to use every instinct and memory of his training to measure the distance accurately and perfect his aim. He passed the glasses again, keeping his eyes on the target all the time. They were aware that they might be being watched themselves. Making himself as flat as possible, he threaded his left arm twice through the canvas strap of his rifle, creating a rigid platform and making him one with his weapon. Showers of sand, muck and the drifts of smoke continued to hinder. He tried to block out the uproar in front of him and focus just on the target. He knew Gerry would be alert too, ready to kick him in the leg twice if his shot was successful. He wanted to fire and keep firing, but dared not risk more than a couple of shots, or it could reveal their position.

Making a deliberate effort to breathe more calmly, he edged the gun into just the right position. Poking the rifle, a mere trace, through some loose stones, he prayed that no one was watching on the other side through enemy glasses. Their outcrop was an obvious place for a sniper to hide, but Edward forced himself to think only of his shot. He was about to fire when the wretched smoke obliterated any chance of the perfect shot.

Just as quickly the air cleared, and he was sure an enemy soldier was moving close up on the right-hand side of the machine gun. He fired immediately and saw the figure fall. The enemy gunner twitched with this action, and Edward fired again. He was confident he'd got Fritz in the neck when he saw him drop. Edward released a deep breath but remained watching and motionless when someone out front lobbed a Mills bomb at the machine gun. The explosion allowed him to move and pull at Gerry to follow. He jerked his head to indicate that they should edge back to their trench. The Lieutenant had warned them not to stay too long in the same place but had not explained what they should do next. It crossed Edward's mind that maybe McDonald-Innes had not expected them to survive.

Sliding on their bellies and thrusting themselves along using their elbows, they barely raised their heads. They wriggled towards the trench they had set out from. Dust and grit stung their eyes. Edward wanted nothing more than to lie still and cling to the ground, but the land shuddered under the rumbling and roaring exchanges of artillery, offering no comfort.

The impacts of the friendly creeping barrage were moving further away – but those of the enemy were coming closer, and the air was full of bitter and choking smells. A shell-hole allowed them to rest for a few moments and take stock. Through the thickened air, they could identify men moving, but their actions looked fractured and haphazard. They did not look as if they were moving fast enough. Edward and Gerry agreed that the enemy fire did not appear to be aimed at the trench they had set out from. They had been warned, however, that vacated trenches were often blown to pieces by the enemy, to prevent survivors taking shelter. A Lewis gun on their right that was still firing, gave them the confidence to begin moving more quickly, risking a crouching run. Adrenalin helped them leap over sandbags like practised gymnasts and land safely in their old trench.

As soon as they were on their feet, Edward suggested that they try to knock out a second machine gun. This meant approaching a fire step that was possibly opposite another enemy gun. In order to pinpoint the next target accurately, they would have to risk revealing themselves briefly. Moving cautiously slowed them down and then at the second fire step, they came across their first fallen comrade. A section of the trench wall had almost collapsed under the Turks' opening bombardment, and a soldier was sprawled face up on a mound of wreckage. It was George Mathews, who lived on Colliery Road, two roads down from Lord Street. The very top of his skull was missing. Part of his brain had been ripped away and the rest was oozing out. Edward and Gerry puked then they grabbed hold of each other. Edward realised that Gerry was screaming and shook him and yelled at him to stop. George was still holding his rifle; his legs at an awkward angle beneath him. His eyes were wide open and his mouth slack, but his face did not look like his last thought had been about pain. He looked peaceful. Flies had already been drawn to the bloody mass and mess beyond. "Reckon the poor sod was dead before he hit the ground. Let's move him to the side," said Edward. He placed his fingers on George's eyelid, but they would not close.

The fallen soldiers gave Edward an idea. "They don't need their helmets or rifles any more. Look for another helmet. Let's balance the helmets on top of the rifles then raise them up to rest on the sand bags." They waited in this position for several minutes. No close-range shots came in their direction, so they climbed more positively onto the fire step.

They manoeuvred some sand bags to stand on and give them greater height, then tunnelled out a narrow passage through the bags lining the top of the trench. There was just enough space for each of them to use the glasses and Edward to position his rifle.

The land fell away gradually to the left. From the noise of the action, the battle was obviously more in that direction than straight ahead. As the miasma thinned, it revealed a machine gun over to the left. Edward was also aware of the many fallen allied soldiers scattered over a wide area. Like George, some had evidently been mown down in the opening seconds of the action. Their remains lay close to the trench in heaps, like bundles of discarded clothing. Scraps of bloodied uniforms, equipment, bodies and sometimes just flesh muddled the land. Soldiers were snarled up in the wire and, only about twenty yards away, was a single upright black shiny boot. The remnant of a leg above the knee was sticking out; the bloodied puttee like a useless bandage. "God above!" yelled Edward.

Gerry had slid back down to the fire step and was shuddering. Edward followed, "It's shit, I know," Edward shouted, "but we have to keep going. We're getting these buggers!" They concentrated again, passing the glasses as before. Edward strained through the commotion to detect the tell-tale pattern of firing and pauses that would indicate, even in the haze, the position of the gunner. He slowed his breathing; fixed his eyes on his chosen spot; his body motionless and his trigger finger as steady as time. A sudden clear view showed him – just underneath the machine gun and slightly to the right – the barrel of a rifle peeping through a heap of stones. It could not have been anything else. An enemy sniper was too much of a risk for Edward to make a shot. "Fucking sneaky bastards!" Edward yelled. He knew he must not draw their fire. He dug Gerry in the ribs and gave him the glare and jerk of the head that meant they should move fast. When they were down, he told Gerry to run back along the trench to collect a couple of rifles no longer in use. He left one where they had been positioned in the hope of confusing the enemy sniper.

Edward ran to the next fire step and began ripping open sandbags and emptying their contents. "We're gonna wear these, and then we're going over," he explained, "while the bastards concentrate on that gun we've left."

"You sure?" Gerry looked alarmed.

"Make a tunic and a hood, quickly, like we practised." Gerry frowned but followed Edward's actions. They made peepholes in the hoods and, when they had dressed, Gerry laughed and said, "We look worse than scarecrows."

"I want you to shoot immediately after I do," Edward said. Gerry had been selected to work with Edward because he too was a good shot and had to be prepared to take over, if Edward fell. "I'm going for the machine gunner," Edward told him, "but you watch for the soldier who will stand up the instant their gunner goes down – see if we can get the whole bunch!" His plan was to get over the top as fast as they could and drag some more sandbags around themselves; hoping that they had not been spotted. They counted down from five together before leaping up a ladder like chased foxes and began scrabbling with the sandbags.

Then they lay motionless; following the rules they'd learnt; waiting; making judgements. Eventually having checked the emplacement, Edward decided they needed to wriggle forward a little to gain a better angle. It seemed the Turks had not spotted them. There was still no firing coming directly at them. They exchanged the glasses for the last time, and Edward stuck his thumb up, above his barrel.

They fired almost simultaneously. Seeing the machine gunner slumped, Edward remained still. Gerry's shot smashed into the soldier who was clambering up to take over the gun. Edward was aware of an echoing shot and believed the decoy rifle had in fact attracted the earlier Turkish sniper. He aimed again and took out a third soldier. This was followed by a retaliatory shot back across no man's land, but Edward concentrated on the gun emplacement. There should have been one more enemy soldier, but he could not spot him. "I wanted the whole bloody lot," he said to himself and cursed mentally, but he knew they had been fortunate and should get out of there fast.

As he shuffled backwards, sweat was trickling under the hood; his eyes prickled, and his head felt like he had been hit with a flat iron. Stabbing pains irritated his right arm; his firing arm. He nudged Gerry but got no response. He tried again harder, but Gerry did not move. Edward no longer thought about enemy fire.

He wriggled backwards then grabbed Gerry's legs, he pulled him towards himself. Blood was soaking into Gerry's makeshift hood. Edward took his own off, heedless of the danger, so he could better locate the ladder. He threw their rifles into the trench. He had to get Gerry down one rung of the ladder at a time. He placed one arm around Gerry's waist, with his friend's legs, more or less, in front of his own. The first few steps were fine, but then the weight of his friend knocked him off balance and Edward missed his footing and slid off. He landed on his back with Gerry on top of him.

It felt like his chest had been steamrollered and his right shoulder and arm were screaming at him. He had to summon up the strength to push Gerry off, and it took him a few minutes before he could examine his friend. The left side of Gerry's head above his ear was oozing blood, and the upper section of his ear was gone. His cheekbone was damaged too. A cut continued around the back of his head, but Gerry was groaning – so alive at least – "Come on, Gerry. I've got you," Edward urged. There was no response, but Edward kept speaking to him as he struggled to extricate a field dressing. This was when Edward realised that his right arm was too painful; useless, so he had to give up. The Aid Post was Gerry's only chance. It was only two blocks back in the dugouts.

Edward found a discarded trench coat in a nearby dugout and arranged it on the ground, then rolled Gerry on to it. With great difficulty, he fastened some of the buttons and managed to tie the belt around Gerry, using his left hand and his teeth. It was all taking too long, but he dragged him, by holding on to the sleeves of the coat with his left arm. He walked backwards to keep Gerry's head off the ground.

Progress was slow over the fifty yards to the first support trench, which connected to a communication trench, but at least the boardwalks were reasonably level. Edward had to stop to rest several times but within reach of the support trench he called out, "Password – sightseeing - Private Edward Holmes here. Got one wounded here!"

Two soldiers came rushing out to meet him, with fixed bayonets, but stopped and stared at Edward's blackened face and sacking tunic. Edward just managed to say, "We're snipers," he barely gasped before he collapsed.

When he came to, he was on a raised stretcher next to Gerry, who was still being examined. He watched as the doctor cleaned away congealed blood from Gerry's face and head; gave him an injection and bandaged his head. "Is he going to be all right?" The doctor stared at Edward before saying, "That's anybody's guess. Now shall we have a look at you? Can you get that sack off?"

The doctor had to cut it off because Edward couldn't raise his right arm. "Ah," - the doctor was murmured, "You've been shot through the top of your arm – corner of your shoulder. The blood has soaked into the back of your shirt, so not so obvious to you. Not much more than a flesh wound but badly bruised already – no bullet. The gods were on your side today."

"I don't remember it happening, but it's bloody sore now."

"I'm sending you to the clearing station. No Blighty. Some stitches, morphine and exercises and you'll be right as rain in a few days."

Gerry was carried to an ambulance, but Edward had to clamber onto a truck with a group of others who could walk. They followed the ambulance for about an hour and when they arrived, a label on Gerry's chest told the medics precisely what was needed and Edward watched him being taken straight to an operating tent. His own wound was not urgent. He waited in line for another two hours as each soldier shuffled forward to be patched up.

Afterwards, Edward should have joined the line waiting to be transferred to the hospital, but he decided to look for Gerry. He lingered outside the operating tents until a nurse came out, and he asked about his friend. He described the wound and told her Gerry's name. "I'm afraid I don't know anything about him. Not one of mine." She looked about to turn away but must have picked up on Edward's anxiety. "Wait here. I'll find out what I can," and she went back inside.

She returned within minutes and told him that the surgeon had removed a bullet from the back of Gerry's head and he was currently in the surgical tent. From there he would be sent to the field hospital and then home if he survived. "Is it that bad?" asked Edward. "Did I make it worse by moving him?"

She looked at him kindly, "Head wounds are always bad."

He felt sick with guilt. He needed a cigarette and wandered away from the tents to some trees. He watched a group of nurses washing bandages and hanging them out to dry. They had their sleeves rolled up above their elbows, and their once white aprons were smeared and blotched. The many long ribbons, some far from white, stretched across pieces of rope between trees, like curtains flapping in the soft breeze. The girls were young and attractive and, under better circumstances, he would have liked to talk to them.

Tired and hungry, his stomach snarling, he saw it was past mid-day and he had probably missed out on anything hot. The smell of cooked food was still lingering though, so he followed his nose to a likely tent. Sticking his head through the flaps, he saw tablecloths, cruets and decent cutlery. A voice bellowed, "Who the hell are you? Out – before I put you on a charge!" A couple of officers were sitting at a table with a bottle of whisky and full glasses in front of them.

Behind them, the cook was tidying up, and he gave Edward a friendly smile and jerked his head a couple of times indicating that he should go around the back of the tent.

Edward scooted out of the tent and followed the cook's instruction. At the back was a swill bin of leftovers and large cans of water for the washing-up station and others for drinking. He was considering picking out the least slimy lumps of food and taking some water when the cook turned up and said, "'ere, wash yurr 'ands un face furst, an I'll fetch ye some scran." He threw a rag at Edward and showed him which water container to use. By the time Edward had finished, doing the best he could with his left hand, the cook had returned with a tin mug full of sweet tea and a mashed biscuit in warm condensed milk. "Sorry, I cannee give thee nowt else today." Edward smiled, sank to the ground and relished his snack as if it were a feast. He was licking the dish when the cook returned with a bottle of rum. "Tek this; tuk it in yurr wee sling; shan't be missed. Best scarper now, afore yus caught." Not understanding everything, but grasping that he should take the bottle; Edward thanked the cook several times as he was helped to his feet and sent on his way.

The first generous swig emboldened him to approach the surgical tent and ask again after Gerry. He pleaded with another nurse, "Just a quick wink at my mate, Gerald Thompson, before I have to go, please." She looked straight into his big blue eyes and said, "You may look, but don't disturb him. Leave him a message," and she passed him a pencil and a piece of paper from her note book and pointed towards the far end of the tent.

Lighting was dim and a potent smell of disinfectant combined with a sickly decaying odour came in waves as Edward passed through the tent. He coughed first of all, and then tried blowing short breaths out of his mouth to avoid the odour. All forty beds were occupied with bandaged men. Some had most of their bodies covered, and blood seeped in more than one area. Some were missing limbs. Some had their faces completely covered, and others were ghostly pale and lying so still, they seemed dead. Edward began to worry he would not recognise Gerry and had to resist the urge to run out. He had already approached several men with head bandages, before noticing that most men had a name-tag attached to a hand, foot or pinned to a dressing. Finally, he spotted Gerry, his head expertly bound with what looked like a tight cap. He said his name, but Gerry did not stir. A chill ran through Edward; his friend was so still and barely breathing. Surely Gerry wasn't dying. He knelt down at his side and took hold of his hand. It was cool but not cold. "Come on, mate. Get well, now." He took Gerry's hand in both of his and held it awhile. "I can't stay Gerry. You did so well, and this is shit, but get well, and you've a ticket home." He scribbled a note – *Came to say good luck and cheerio. Just you get better,*

and I'll see you back home sometime. Your pal, Edward.
"I've to go now, mate. There's a nurse looking like a thunder cloud marching down the ward Hang on in there." He squeezed Gerry's hand once more and was sure he felt the tiny pressure of a response.

He moved away quickly deciding not to look back. Outside, he checked around him, before taking a second gulp of the delicious golden liquid and went to find the queue of walking wounded, ready to be transported to the hospital. Twenty soldiers piled into a wagon, and he wanted to share his good fortune, but there would not have been enough to go around. Bumping along the road for a few miles, he could hear the rum swishing temptingly inside his sling. The bottle would have to be disposed of before they arrived; it would be presumed that he had stolen it. When the nurse sitting at the front with all the paper work, shouted, "Almost there now chaps," he dragged it out, took a long gulp then passed it to those nearest to him. There were no refusals, and he tossed the empty bottle in the bushes.

Unfortunately, although he had not swallowed a significant amount; with little to eat during the day, he was a bit too chatty and his breath smelt. He told most of the truth to the nurse who first questioned him. "A lad I'd never met before, at the clearing station, gave me a swig after I'd been cleaned up."

"I'd say it was more than a swig, and against the rules. I'll have to report it." Edward shrugged. He knew he was not drunk, and he had not caused any trouble, and who was going to do anything about it in the hospital? In the meantime, not being a patient in need of a bed during the day, he was escorted to the rehabilitation area and given a programme of exercises and advised that a nurse would change his dressing each morning. A time table of available daily activities was scribbled on a blackboard. He thought he might be able to kick a ball about a bit, but there would not be much he could do with his hands while he still wore a sling.

During the evening, Edward watched as a sergeant entered the room where the walking wounded were playing cards and dominoes. He was limping, with a walking stick, but moving energetically as he came right up to Edward. Everyone was staring at them. "Shun!" the sergeant shouted as if addressing a whole platoon. Edward shot to his feet. The sergeant continued to bellow, "Eyes front!" and "Mark time!" while Edward felt confused and incompetent. He had never been in trouble before. He felt like a showman in a circus, with all eyes on him. "Forward march!" He had the whole length of the room to cover and a long corridor before reaching a small office, when he was told to halt and, "Stand at ease."

"I've checked who you are, Private Edward Holmes," pointing his walking stick at him before prodding him in his stomach. "This is your first offence – but a serious one. As you have been wounded in action, your punishment will not take place here, but when you return to camp." Cold sweat trickled down the back of Edward's neck, and a leaden weight dropped in his stomach. He cursed himself silently.

"Never take more than your daily allowance of alcohol again." The sergeant paused, and Edward sensed he should respond. He was about to salute and fumbled with which arm to raise and tried it with his left, as he said, "Yes, sarge." Now, Edward felt like a foolish child.

"Dismissed!"

***

The doctor at the first aid station had been right. It didn't take long to recover from his wound. Edward cast off the sling on the third day and found it much easier to do the prescribed exercises, and others he made up himself, to relieve the stiffness in his arm and shoulder. Apart from worrying whether he would still be such a good shot, and what would happen when he met up with Sergeant Smithers, the rest of the time was like being on holiday. Once the sling was gone, he could draw, read, play cards and more football. After a few days, he asked if there was anywhere in the grounds where he could do target practice, and if there were any spare rifles. The same sergeant came to supervise and enquired after Edward's own gun. He had to explain what had happened to him and Gerry. The sergeant observed as Edward took time checking and cleaning the rifle; loading and unloading it, and taking aim. Although his shoulder did ache, he was pleased he was still scoring bullseyes, but his speed had dropped slightly.

Five days later the stitches were removed, and although still bruised, he was taken back to the front and sent to report to Sergeant Smithers, but not at the front line. The remnants of his unit had been merged with another broken unit because they had lost their sergeant, senior officer and three first-timers. Edward's platoon was not even in the reserve trenches but further back again, with plenty of room for marching and manoeuvres and nearest to company headquarters. Edward learnt that four from his own section had not returned on the day when he and Gerry were wounded. He knew it would be foolish to think everyone had made it – especially after what he had seen in no man's land that day. Still he felt his stomach contract when he heard that Rodney Fletcher and Frank Stockett were lost and wondered if they had been in the messy carnage, he'd seen that day. Just thinking about it brought something between an emptiness and a pain in his guts.

"You bloody fecking fool," Sergeant Smithers yelled at him. "Not much point in you coming back here if I've put you on a charge. What possessed you?"

"I was given it sarge."

"Given what?"

"A bottle of rum, sarge."

"Did you drink the lot?"

"No, sarge, it wasn't full, honestly – I shared some."

For the next three days, after fatigues, Edward was escorted to a gun wheel - his wrists and ankles shackled in irons and fixed to the wheel for three hours. The punishment was known as crucifixion. There was neither shade nor water and he was increasingly aware of insect attacking him. His face, neck and hands stung with a combination of sweat and the mosquito bites. Following his release on the third afternoon, he collapsed with a high fever and was taken back to the Aid Post.

No Hysterics in this Ward

Someone threw a mug of water over Edward, but there was no response. Sergeant Smithers ordered two men, in Edward's section, to carry him straight to the Aid Post. "Just go!" he bellowed. "Stretcher-bearers are busy elsewhere." When Edward came around, he complained of a severe headache. He felt his wet shirt. "Why am I soaked?" The effort of speaking and trying to sit up made him dizzy, and he retched then clutched his stomach, "Bogs! Quick lads," he pleaded. They had to carry him again. Despite sweating, Edward was shivering from head to foot.

The doctor only glanced at the collection of insect bites on Edward's body, before saying, "Probably malaria. Sip water for a few hours, then we'll see." By tea time, Edward's temperature had risen alarmingly, and he complained that his arms and legs were stiff and sore to move. The diagnosis was confirmed. His first dose of quinine was administered and he was labelled to by-pass the Advanced Dressing Station. He was going, immediately, to the Casualty Clearing Station then on to the base hospital in Alexandria.

Edward had little recollection of high peaks of fever, vomiting and delirium, he experienced during the early days in hospital. He was hardly aware of the concerns of the doctors and nurses, as he drifted in and out of delirium for days. Quinine doses were increased, but when his urine turned black, the doctors feared for his life. They had seen this before - Blackwater Fever. They agreed between them to stop the quinine. A doctor Alladi, from India, had an instinct to try to flush out the drug from Edward's body and persuaded the other doctors to try a new procedure called blood transfusion. The process was repeated three times. Edward was given daily doses of Aspirin and Veronal and made to drink as much water as he could keep down.

In moments of consciousness, Edward was listless and could speak only in a croaky whisper. He was too weak to raise his arms or hold a cup of water. He felt like his bones had melted leaving him only floppy flesh, and supposed he was dying. For the first time, he wished he had listened to his mother, when she begged him not to enlist. He prayed to be made well again, and for forgiveness in causing her so much distress. A nurse told him that his parents had been sent a postcard informing them that he was in hospital, but not wounded. He knew this would not prevent his mother from worrying and supposing the worst. He wanted desperately to go home but this would not happen unless he was declared unfit for the front line but fit enough to travel. He wasn't able to sit up unaided, and could not imagine ever being strong enough to either hold his rifle or travel back to England.

Lying for hours, completely incapacitated, he thought of the kitchen at home and his family. Although he had no appetite, he imagined his mother's hot-pot and apple pie with steaming custard – unusually, the images made him nauseous. He thought of the banter at the table that might involve teasing William about a girl he had mentioned too often, or mocking Joseph about how badly Stockport County were doing that season. He recalled his father's deep belly laugh, making them all hoot once more. These were bittersweet moments.

A dream sometimes took him to the park at home. There were flowers, smiling faces, and kids playing chase. A band was making music - something light and lilting, but the pleasing harmony suddenly transposed to a discordant screeching of strings, blaring trumpets and booming drums. He wanted to run from the cacophony, but he was as lame as a drunken fool. Once, when he awoke, his bed was pitching and veering. He needed to yell for help as he clung on to the sides. His fever had risen again and he felt as if ants were marching up and down his body.

The nurses moved him daily, and bathed him gently. Their touch made him long again for his mother's hugs. His strength had all but evaporated, snatched away like an escaped kite. His body had surrendered the muscle tone he had gained in training, and his drastic loss of weight reverted him to a helpless infant. He believed, though, that if he could just go home, he would recover.

Several weeks passed before he could put his feet to the floor and totter a few steps with assistance from two nurses. Molly Entwistle, from Australia, made a little bird flutter inside his ribcage every time she smiled. He did try harder for her, loving her accent and the way she spoke to him as if he was a valued human being, who was bound to recover and lead a normal life. He wondered if normal meant returning to the boy he had been before he joined up, and doubted that possibility, but he appreciated Molly's kindness. When he finally made a few independent steps, he flung his arms around her and she returned the hug.

The matron, however, who did the rounds of the ward every other day, was only concerned with correct procedures, medication and good order. Never breaking into a smile, she looked down her nose and never met anyone's eyes as if she was permanently disgusted with life. In Edward's ward, there were plenty of soldiers who were sick, but none had been wounded. She spoke abruptly to each patient, "We'll soon have you back at the front," and "Are you making enough effort to recover?" or, "I trust there is no malingering going on here." The men pulled faces and made rude gestures behind her back, triggering giggles. With a face as stiff as a sculptured statue, she would say, "If you can laugh, you are neither ill, tired nor bored. In which case you shouldn't be here."

One night, as black as obsidian, Edward found himself shivering under his bed with no recollection of how he got there. The first of his orchestra of nightmares – he was unable to stand up without help. He tried to recollect images and told the nurses, "There were lots of us; my section and more – all shooting together – then they all fell down like a bunch of skittles - but the enemy popped up after each one of my mates like a row of sneering jack-in-the-boxes, and my sodding (pardon) rifle wouldn't work."

One of the nurses must have relayed the story to matron because she did an extra round that day, "There will be no hysterics in this ward. We'll have none of it," she declared. Walking slowly up and down the ward, eyes straight ahead, she continued, "Cowardly behaviour will not be tolerated. Concentrate on eating to gain strength. Get plenty of fresh air and do your exercises. Do not discuss your weak-minded thoughts with one another, including your nurses."

When she left, Edward sank under the sheets. The ward became very quiet, and all he could hear were the nurses' footsteps. He thought that if he looked up everyone's eyes would be on him. He was silently cursing his wretched nightmare when he heard,

"Jeez cobber – nobody would want to have a bluey with her." It was his Australian companion, in the next bed.

Edward had already met some Australians, and realised his new companion was trying to put him at ease. The dialect made him grin. He pushed his head out from under the blanket and asked, "How ya goin?" like an Aussie himself.

"The legs are crook, but I'm grand otherwise. I'm Ross Hooley," the man said and he leant over to shake hands. "Nightmares trouble you much?" he asked.

Edward frowned and looked around.

Ross tutted, "Well, she's talking through her arse. Have you had many?"

"First one." Edward tried to laugh it off, "Must be missing the action."

"I reckon you'll have more of that."

"Action, or nightmares?"

"Oh, both."

"I'm not a coward. It was just a dream."

"Course you're not. I've seen men bigger than you fall down with night terrors."

"But I've only been in one battle."

"That's enough. No fucking glory, is there?"

"No… I saw men blown away like they were no more than dandelion seeds."

Ross nodded and grimaced. "I get that." He had a strong angular face and tight blond hair that you could tell would have been curly if it had been longer. His hazel eyes sparkled despite their recollections. His arms were muscular and he appeared too bronzed and healthy to possibly be in a hospital, but his legs were ulcerated from infected mosquito bites.

Edward felt childish as his eyes began to prickle, and he turned away from Ross.

"Come on cobber; you won't be on your ownsome with the nightmares and I'll look out for you in here. That drongo needs a sense of humour"

Ross chatted up the nurses. He took a particular fancy to Betty Price and could make her blush. When Edward admitted that his favourite was Molly, Ross persuaded the girls, that when they were on duty together, they should make it their job to wheel them both outside. He promised them some goodies from the tucker he was sent from home, but they didn't need much persuading.

Every day, Ross told jokes, sang and whistled *Waltzing Matilda, Bravo! Boys of Australia* and *The Kaiser's Boast* and encouraged the whole ward to join in. Matron was furious at the noise but, nevertheless, sniffed and pinched her lips together when the British boys sang, *There's a long, long trail a winding.*

Ross mimicked matron outrageously, who told him he was a show-off and should mind his own business. Yet, everyone liked him, including the nurses, who tried to persuade matron that he was

66

good for morale. She made her usual poker face and reminded them sternly, "There'll be no consorting with patients."

The hospital had been a grand hotel before to the war. Once they were well enough, the patients were encouraged to explore the grounds. Edward was amazed at the unusual trees; tall palm trees laden with dates, others with coconuts and more with leaves like beautiful outstretched fans. He was surprised, however, to see sycamore and willows; "These are English trees," he told Ross, "but there aren't many trees where I live."

"How come?"

"Industrial. All gritty and smoky."

"Sounds grim. No bush?"

"Bush?"

"Countryside?"

"Ah! Derbyshire's not far. Beautiful green fields. Hills, valleys, sheep, steep gorges and caves that my brothers and I like to explore."

When the nurses arrived to clean the ward, Ross called out to Molly and Betty. "Take us down to the lake. Ed 'll love the blue water lilies." Ross laughed when Edward shouted about the beds of roses; walls of hibiscus and delicate poppies in red, yellow and white, mingling with blue cornflowers. "I like those the best." He pointed to flowers with a heady scent that looked like hanging trumpets and others that resembled exotic birds. "I need to get drawing," he said. "We've nothing like this at home. Have you seen those birds with their long beaks and stretched out skinny legs? It must be paradise here!"

Ross, from Western Australia, enjoyed the lush gardens but said, "We have beautiful flowers and birds and animals in my country." He talked about the bush and the outback and the enormous distances between places and where he had travelled. He described kangaroos, koalas, emus, platypus, numbats and dramatically colourful birds. His parents owned a sheep station with at least a thousand sheep, and Edward tried to imagine how many fields in Derbyshire they would fill.

He told Edward about the sheep-shearing season. "I never miss it – the competitions and parties. Most of the sheilas who come to help with grub are beauts." His descriptions were like fairy stories to Edward who began to think that Stockport had to be the ugliest place on earth. Ross chuckled as he recalled times when too much grog was drunk, and petty fights broke out, usually over the girls, with everyone teasing one another. "There's rarely any proper bother. Any real mean blokes are told to shoot through, and we don't take them on again."

Edward gradually began to recuperate. His appetite improved and he walked a few steps further each day, unaided until he was able to get out in the garden himself. He made sketches of all the unfamiliar plants and birds and sent them home. He asked for some wood and a chipping knife to carve one of the birds for Joseph. He hoped to have time to paint the carving before he was moved on.

The stronger he felt, the more he began to dread hearing the news that he was to return to his unit. His thoughts were occupied with who else might be gone for ever, and he told Ross what had happened to Gerry. "I wasn't supposed to take him back to the aid post, and I might have made his injury worse, but how could I leave him when he was right next to me?" He explained the consequences and the crucifixion. "It's not like I was even drunk," he complained, just warmed up a bit."

Ross was loud in his criticism of the British Army's ruddy rules and regulations. He declared, in his Australian way, that Edward was lucky not to have carked it. "Your so-called superiors have got kangaroos loose in the top paddock. Anyone with half a brain can tell you're an ace guy." He told Edward he had to stay alive to spite the bastards and gave him his address in Australia. "When it's all over, I'll teach you how to be a farmer, and you can get rid of some pesky roos for us." They shook hands on the deal.

The ward was steadily emptying. Men suffering from malaria, influenza, skin infections, venereal disease, diabetes, rotting feet, dysentery, tuberculosis, concussion (later called shell shock) and even mumps, were expecting to be sent back to the front after their final medical review. Rumour had it that the senior Medical Officer, a Captain Cornelius Hitchin was a jolly decent chap, but well versed in spotting someone who was faking continuing infirmity.

"Are you up for war again, Private Holmes?" the medical officer asked.

"Sir, it's not up to me," he replied – a little flummoxed.

"Ah, but I happen to think it is, on the whole. Are you as strong and fit as you were this time last year?"

Edward stared at the Captain, wondering if this was a trick question, and then at the nurse who had accompanied him. She just smiled back at him.

"Let's sit down and go over a few things about your illness," the doctor suggested, pouring Edward a glass of water. "You're lucky to be alive with what you've had. There are likely to be long term consequences."

Edward opened his mouth to speak, but the Captain continued, "You may have recurrences of malaria, and I think your blood is going to be – shall we say, weakened - is the best way I can describe it."

Edward managed to interrupt, "But I'm getting better and stronger every day."

Captain Cornelius Hitchin sat back in his chair and paused, looking at Edward. "These iron pills will have to be taken for a long time, and at some stage I hope you get another blood transfusion. I'm going to recommend it again, to be on the safe side, as this is what saved you, I'm sure."

"A blood what?"

"We literally put fresh blood into your arm from a healthy man. It works its way around your body, improving your blood."

"Blimey, that takes a bit of getting used to."

"Well it did the trick, and I'll be writing detailed notes to send to your company headquarters."

"So, where am I going, sir?"

"One thing at a time. What is the level of your physical strength? I know you've been doing training in the gym, but you are still underweight."

"I want to do my duty, sir."

"Not what I asked. What do you feel about returning to the front? I know you've had a couple of the night time episodes we'd associate with a concussion that some other men have been getting in his war – probably from the overwhelming noise of bombardment."

Edward blushed and looked down. Thoughts of further battles sickened him, but if he told the truth, this Captain would think less of him. He felt he should say he was quite well and ready to return to the front but instead, he blurted out, "I'm not as fit as I was. Lost all my muscles, but I'm out every day and eating better now."

"Hmm. What about aches and pains and sleep?"

"I do have headaches frequently."

The doctor turned to the nurse, "What's your assessment of Private Holme's physical and mental health?"

"He's not a malingerer, sir. Has often to be asked if he needs medication for pain. He is genuinely trying to build up his strength, but there has been a little troubled sleep."

"It's the headaches, sir," Edward interrupted, "and sometimes I have weird dreams."

"Bad dreams? Nightmares?"

Edward nodded, "But not every night, Captain."

"You're not ready to go anywhere yet, Private Holmes. More exercise and plenty to eat, and I'm going to prescribe Heroin Hydrochloride for the headaches at night. Aspirin as usual during the day. Report back in two weeks."

***

At the end of the two weeks, Edward asked the Medical Officer to watch him do his exercises. "I know I haven't put on much weight, but you can see how strong I am."

"All right, I am going to send you home - but recommend a return to duties no earlier than the New Year. I'll be contacting your regiment, as I said, with details of your medical problems."

"What problems?"

"I did tell you, the last time we met, that the after effects could be with you for a long time. Your malaria may recur."

"But I'm better."

"Remember, Edward, you had the worst type of malaria, and there are the headaches and restless sleep to consider. You will have to continue to take medication, but I think you will be fit to serve your country again fairly soon."

Edward studied his feet for a few minutes. He was tongue-tied. Home, he had been looking forward to for weeks, but he was puzzled about his health and anxious that he might have lost his nerve for active service." The room fell silent. Edward realised that the Captain had finished. He looked up to see the Medical Officer smiling at him, "All things considered Private Holmes, you've done remarkably well. Go and enjoy some home time."

Edward stood up and saluted, "Thank you, sir." The MO walked him to the door, shook his hand and patted him on the back. "Stay brave Private Holmes," he said.

***

Dear Mother, Father and Joseph,

The best news! I'm being sent home for Christmas and the New Year. I am well now but need to build up my strength. Your home cooking, ma, and some bike rides in the Dales will do the trick.

I'm a bit skinny, so don't be alarmed when you see me. Ma, you might have to alter my uniform, but don't get the scissors out yet. I have to wait for the next ship and it took a few weeks to get out here so it will be the same coming back to Blighty.

The hospital has been 'bonzer' as my Australian pals say. I'll miss the friends I've made here, especially Ross from Perth in Australia, and some of the nurses, who work long hours and look after us really well. I'll be sorry to leave the beautiful garden with its exotic flowers and birds, but happier to be home again with all of you.

I'm glad you've liked all the sketches I sent. Thanks for the last parcel too and the Manchester Evening News. It made me think a lot about home. The casualty lists in the paper were shocking. I hadn't heard about Billy Cornwall nor Jack Duggan, but thrilled that Gerry got home. Tell him I'll be seeing him soon.

73

I wonder how you are all managing. There was talk in the paper about possible rationing. Hope dad is still managing the allotment. The apple jam, Oxo and fags were very welcome. Can't wait to see you. I'll send word as soon as I know my dates.

Your loving son,
Edward

Ross organised a party for Edward's last afternoon in the gardens. "No sketching today, cobber." He spoke to all the blokes, and everyone was up for a bit of fun. "A few of us have a drop of grog. Not enough to get mouldy, but it'll keep us lively."

The singing started before everyone had finished lunch. The Aussies were in full swing with Waltzing Matilda, until someone shouted, "Who's this effing Matilda anyway?" And all the Aussies fell about laughing. A British soldier, with a fine tenor voice, started a new version of *If You Were the Only Girl in the World:*

If you were the only Boche in the trench
And I had the only bomb
Nothing else would matter in the world that day
I'd blow you up into eternity

Cheering and clapping followed, before an undercurrent of chatter gradually took over. "Reckon we've all got France written on our foreheads, lads."

"Well they ain't bringing us back here, that's a cert."

"Aye, my bro has been at that do. Says they've had it worse than us lot."

"This'll be the fourth Christmas – has to end soon, surely."

"Who knows?"

Ross started passing round what looked like tins of tea or treacle, except they were filled with alcohol. This was a regular inclusion in the Australian parcels from home. The men all tried to keep straight faces and not attract close attention from the nurses. Games began with a fair amount of gambling. Skittles, throwing stones at empty tins and simple games made up on the spot, like hopping while carrying a mug of water, or leaping over a hedge without damaging it or themselves.

Edward declined the grog after the first unsuspected mouthful, but still joined in as they all larked around like school kids. Then Ross announced they would have a wheelchair race around the lake. No one was to run while pushing a chair, but speedy walking was permitted. There was room on the bank for four chairs side by side, and only the fit and able could take part. Three soldiers, still requiring of a wheelchair, were carefully helped on to benches and a fourth chair was rushed out from inside. The least heavy men were picked as passengers, and of course, Edward and Ross made a perfect team.

Everyone had their favourites. Even the nurses cheered, and for once Matron did not make an appearance. When Ross and Edward were clear winners, each was presented with a hastily woven crown of leaves. "We're Olympic winners!" Edward said, and they laughed some more until Ross said, "Aye and we'll win this sodding mess of a war. You and me; we're survivors and don't you forget it mucker!"

***

The hospital ship – a converted passenger liner – painted with enormous red crosses, was overloaded with sick and injured men. Entire decks were huge wards for the most severely wounded. Those who were well enough, like Edward, were not given a specific place to bunk down but had to make do with what they could find. A group of them huddled together on kit bags, with a blanket each, in a stairwell by the kitchens and laundry. The nights were cold, but when the galley door opened a breath of heat washed over them with an assortment of smells; not always appetising. Sometimes, they could scrounge an extra cup of soup or Oxo or some bread and dripping – but food was not plentiful.

It was important to keep out of the way of the medics who were struggling, in some cases, to keep men alive long enough to reach England. Hardly a day passed without at least one burial at sea. The dead were wrapped in a sheet, placed on a board and covered in a Union Jack. The captain or another officer attended with the chaplain, orderlies, and often the nurse who had looked after that particular patient. The chaplain gave a blessing and said a couple of prayers before the board was hoisted on top of the rails and the body slipped from beneath the flag into the water. The brief service was held without general announcement or the knowledge of most of the soldiers on board.

When the weather was fine, a sergeant put the soldiers, who were well, through some exercises, but then they were left to themselves to ramble around. This was mainly on the top deck where they might manage a game of hockey or quoits. Any of those recuperating, who were able, were helped up to the top deck also. Fresh air was essential, and they were wheeled up and down by the nurses, who wanted as much peace and quiet as possible for their patients and put a stop to the rowdier games. All those going home on leave, like Edward, were encouraged to chat or read to the sick or help them write letters.

After exercises, one ash-grey morning threatening rain, Edward chose to stay outside and continue walking from deck to deck. The thrust of the ship in the swell and tumble of the water suited his mood, and he smiled. Steady on his feet, in spite of the roll and sway, he thought of home drawing closer when the now familiar screen, towards the stern of the ship on deck 3, stopped him in his tracks. A rumour had spread earlier that morning that eight were due to go to Davy Jones' locker.

Closer to the screen, a stocky man in a wheel chair sat alone. There should have been someone with him. Edward moved ahead then across the deck and turned to approach the man face to face and avoid startling him. The chap showed no signs of noticing him. A blanket was tucked around his legs and a scabby scar laced across his bald head, in contrast to the pallor of the man's face. Those unmistakable bushy eyebrows framed a brooding face.

Edward took a step back. It couldn't be, he thought. The man looked too old. His eyes were fixed on something, but deadpan under a deep furrowed brow. He looked like a dead man sitting. "Sergeant Smithers? It's me Bullseye. Shall I stay a while with you?" Without altering his gaze, and hardly louder than a whisper, the man in the wheel chair replied, "Suit yourself."

"Are you here for the burial?" Edward ventured. Smithers stirred, "I should be with that lot. If I could get out of this fucking contraption, I'd be over there with 'em!"

"Jeez, Sarge, sorry to see you here, but you must be on the mend."

"You bastard! I'll never mend. Lost a sodding leg."

"That's a bad'un for sure, but you're alive, Sarge."

"What for? Army's all I've known. What other job can I do?" Tears dribbled down Smithers' face, gathered at his nose and dripped off his chin. He made no effort to wipe them.

Edward squatted on the floor next to him. "Your wife, sarge? And little Charlie?"

His sergeant attempted to straighten himself up in the chair and raised his voice. "She aint goin' to want me like this, and our kid'll think I'm useless. Can't play footy, can I?"

Edward glanced over at the screen surrounding the funerals, wondering if they had been heard, but no one approached. "Does she know you're coming home?"

"Nah! Going to some other hospital first, to get a false one." He flinched, growled and clutched his blanket. His brow had beads of sweat. "Praps it'll not give the pain as much as the one that's gone!" and he spat viciously.

"I reckon your missus 'll be right glad just to have you home, Sarge. I know my ma will."

"Mothers are different lad. You don't have a girl yet, do you? I might as well have hopped the twig completely."

Edward rose to a crouching position and placed a hand on each arm of the chair. He pushed his face right up to Smithers, so that their noses almost touched. "Begging your pardon, but you're talking a great pile of shit. If I was talking like this, you'd have me pegged out again on that bloody wheel or worse! Come on Sarge, it's not right!"

Smithers stared right back at him, and Edward was glad to see a spark of anger in his eyes. He made to move back, but his sergeant grabbed hold of his arm. "You're a good man Private Holmes. Always thought it. Happen you can waste a bit of time with me."

So, every day, Edward sought out Smithers. He helped him write a letter to his wife, telling her the bare facts about his injury and loss of limb, but expressing hope for the artificial leg that was to be made in England. It took three attempts because Edward insisted that Sergeant Smithers remained positive throughout. It would be posted as soon as they docked. There was plenty of time to play cards, and for Edward to read a battered old copy of Coral Island that Smithers had been given by one of the nurses. They both enjoyed the adventures of the three shipwrecked boys, and their loyalty to one another.

Sometimes they talked about the Palestine Campaign, and Edward's first and only battle. Smithers heard the whole story of Edward's and Gerry's attempts to shut down the enemy machine guns in their sector. Smithers told him that, by all accounts, the allied forces had lost that battle and the following one in April 1917. "We should have had 'em that first time, you know. Usual cock up at the top. Right hand didn't know what the left hand was doing. Orders were to break off the action as soon as it was dark, unless Gaza was taken."

"So, it was all for nothing?"

"Often is son, but by God we'd have done for them that day if we'd hung on another half hour."

Smithers also told Edward that the whole regiment was returning to England by the end of the year then going on to France. Only two men remained from his old section, Edward and Reg Parkinson. Several remnants of sections had combined. Edward tried to remember the faces of the friends that were lost; all the pals from William's year, who had joined on the same day. A wave of nausea made him regurgitate part of his breakfast. He spat over the rail and bile filled his mouth as he thought of the horrors that he had seen the day of the battle, and then of the bereaved parents he would encounter at home.

One morning, during rough weather, Edward went below to look for Smithers. Unsure of which staircase to take, he found himself on a corridor unlike those higher up. It had not been transformed to a large open ward, but still had separate cabins. The lighting was dimmed. Every door was open, but metal bars were fixed across the doorways. Each room held a single man. At first, Edward thought they must be prisoners. One man was pacing like a trapped animal and banging his head on the wall when he reached the other end of his cell. Another was drooling in a heap on the floor and twitching every few seconds. Yet another was tied up completely in a white garment, and rocking himself. A prickling of pins and needles ran up Edward's spine. He was about to turn and run, but his teeth were clacking together and his body began to shake.

"You've no business down here!" a voice called. Edward clenched his teeth and took a deep breath. He mumbled an explanation and was redirected. His muscles strained as he climbed to the next deck, and his legs became putty, so he had to rest on the top step a minute. He decided not to mention the experience to Smithers, but paced the top deck that night before a more fitful rest than usual.

Sick for that gal

A sunless dawn struggled up the sky as the ship approached Devonport. Sea and sky were different shades of grey. Edward, and his companions, jigged about in the grasping ice-cold air. Not one of them had a greatcoat for the winter in England. Chain-smoking, they swapped stories about what they would do first when they landed. A chap called Henry shouted, "First pub I come to, I'll be downing the proper ale till I can't stand up." Several men chuckled, agreeing that drink was a priority.

"I want to see my Sal first. Reckon she owes me a good time," called George Sykes. Dragging a crumpled photo from his tunic pocket, he planted kisses on it as he thrust his hips back and forth.

"You'll be giving her the clap, Georgie boy," prompted Andy Byrne, and there was more guffawing and thumping of shoulders.

George clenched his fist and swung round to Andy, "Never went with a whore!"

There were several jeers of disbelief, and some friendly jostling, when a louder voice cut in, "We're all due a bloody good bath before we go near any girl. Meself, I also want some grub in me belly and me own bed." The banter turned to favourite home-cooked meals, and a few admitted they were desperate to see their homes and parents again.

They docked at 7 o'clock on a Monday morning. There was no welcoming party, and it took hours to unload the sick and wounded. All able-bodied were roped in to fetch and carry stretchers, equipment and personal belongings.

Field ambulances, buses stripped out to make room for stretchers, and horse-drawn wagons took all the sick to their next destinations. Some were due at local hospitals, while others were going further to specialist units. Edward found Sergeant Smithers on the dockside with three other amputees; all due for Queen Mary's in Roehampton. "It's been a pleasure, Sarge. Get your new leg bloody working, won't you?"

"Will do, Holmes. And you stay out of trouble – every kind. And thank you – for everything."

"I'll not let you down, Sarge."

"I don't believe you will, Holmes."

Finally, those going home on leave were gathered together after midday and marched to the station. There was just time for Edward to send a telegram. *Docked -Home by midnight.* Many of them had to get to London stations first, with a couple of changes en route, before making connections to final destinations. Eight of them bundled into one compartment, passing round the Woodbines; relishing the warmth and cracking jokes. They talked a little too loudly, in their excitement to be going home, and a mother pulled her daughter closer to her when she opened the compartment door. Her face was as sullen as the glowering sky outside; her pale blue eyes, red-rimmed. She tutted then clenched her lips tight before pushing on down the corridor. The soldiers ceased their laughter for a few moments.

Soon the clackety-clack rhythm of the wheels and the heat sent Edward to sleep until he was nudged to change at a connecting station. A couple of other soldiers also extricated themselves from their slumped pals. Three trains to reach London and they crawled and stopped several times at nowhere, and too soon the obscure blanket of night snatched away all landscape. They pulled down the blinds for complete blackout, which reminded the soldiers that the war was at home as well. There was a stretch of silence before they spoke in muted voices, shared cigarettes and dozed.

A crisp wind cut into them as they left the cosiness of the compartment and made their way out of Waterloo station. No buses were running, and

Edward had to get to Euston. Three of them ran together, complete with kitbags till the wind stole their breaths as they crossed the river. They were not as fit as they hoped. A further wait at Euston gave them time for a cup of tea and a Chelsea bun. They sat on their luggage, in the dimly lit waiting room, savouring the first food they had eaten that day. "Almost as good as me ma's Eccles cakes." Edward munched as a group of soldiers, in hardly recognisable uniforms, lurched in. They looked and smelt as if they had bathed in farmyard muck. Even in the gloomy room, Edward could see that their hair was matted above ashen faces with eyes full of exhaustion and pain. Edward could not help but stare until one man sneered at him, "What you gawping at Nancy boy? Never seen a proper soldier?"

"Sorry, mate. Are yous back from France?"

"'Course! Where the fuck has you been in your clean duds?"

"Hospital. Egypt. Be in France soon."

"Lambs to the bloody slaughter! You'll not see the like in hell!" the grimy soldier called, as he turned to catch up with his group.

On the train, Edward dithered at the doorway of the silent compartment full of these soldiers who had returned from France. He couldn't think of anything to say, so he handed in his packet of cigarettes. They were passed around, with mumbled thanks, but not returned. The dishevelled men looked down at their feet or at the blackout covering the window. Edward shifted from foot to foot. They looked like a bunch of moth-eaten dogs after an illegal fight. One of them cleared his throat and spat on the floor, "Fuck off and leave us be."

***

Having changed at Birmingham and Crewe, it was almost midnight before Edward was standing on the platform at Stockport. His kit bag seemed heavier, his feet like wooden blocks. He hesitated. The temperature was so sharp that he felt brittle as he moved slowly towards the exit, but suddenly, the familiarity of his surroundings, even in the night sky, made him smile. For the first time, in over a year, he knew exactly where he was, even at this time of night, and no lamps lit. None of the flamboyant colours and sweet aromas of that hospital garden – though he could recall them quickly. Here was the usual roofscape of shadowy chimneys; some still smoking.

A second wave of energy pushed him on down Station Road, across Wellington Road South, along Wellington Road and up Lord Street. He was breathless and his cheeks hot when he opened the door to his mother's warm kitchen and called out. "Ma!" The fire was still lit, and an oil lamp burned on the window ledge looking into the yard.

She ran down the stairs. "Edward!" she called out, trying to hold back tears. She clasped him to her and would not let go. Edward was content to rest in the hug he had longed for.

"You're only skin and bone," she said eventually, standing back from him but not quite letting go. "You're half yourself! What happened?" and she practically pushed him into a seat at the table, and was pouring him a cup of tea as she sniffed and grabbed the corner of her apron to wipe her face. A thick piece of toast spread with plum jam was put in front of him, and before he had devoured it, his mother was fetching the bathtub from the yard, boiling more water and making more toast. She didn't stop talking, "I'll have to make pies to build you up and barley broth. Why did the army let you get so thin? Do you really have to go back?"

Edward grabbed hold of her skirt, "Ma, stop! Just for a minute. He pulled her onto his knee so that she giggled, and he hugged her once more. "Stop rushing about like a dervish."

"What's one of those?"

"A swirling dancer – out there."

"Egypt?"

"Yes, but don't ask me about it."

"What about your illness?" She stood up and looked down at him, staring into his eyes.

Edward's father and younger brother clattered downstairs and into the kitchen. Frederick pushed past Joseph, who was rubbing his eyes and yawning. Rosa stood to the side, and Frederick pulled Edward to his feet and shook his hand vigorously. He took him in a hug, clapping him on his back. "'Tis grand thee have returned safe, lad," he said. "We've been right scairt for thee."

"Aye Fred, and now he's no more than bone and rags," his mother said.

"No matter that lass; get some grub in him."

"Glad you're back Eddie. Ma's been saving her best food and preserves for you. We'll not be starving now!" said Joseph. They all smiled, and Rosa busied herself, making a fresh brew and putting thick slices of bread on the toasting forks. "We'll celebrate properly tomorrow."

"If it's OK. Just now I'm desperate for a bath and bed," said Edward.

"No bother son, we'll get off now. Joseph 'n I 'ave to be up at five anyroad. I'm at post office for time being, and our Jo's at gas works." They shuffled back upstairs as Rosa poured more hot water in the tub, laid out a towel and handed Edward a new bar of soap.

She busied herself with the pots as he undressed. He sank into the water then she quickly removed his pile of clothes and took fresh and ironed pyjamas from the rack above the range. "Sweet Jesus, Mary and Joseph, look at your ribs!" Edward immediately tried to sink further into the tub. "Pass me the soap; I'll do your back son." He squirmed at first and tried puffing out his chest but then gave in to her gentle touch and remembered what it was like to be a child again.

"My poor boy. How bad was it?"

"My illness was worse than the battle. I think France will be tougher. On the train, I saw men coming home from there. They looked beaten. Has William been home?"

"Yes, twice. Never seen such muck and Will stank worse than you! He wouldn't talk either."

"I know, ma. The men I saw, on the last train from the coast, were the same." He looked up at his mother and said, "I'm dreading it."

She took his face in her hands, "My job is to get you strong and well again." He smiled at her but couldn't hold back a deep sigh. "How's Gerry doing?"

"Oh, he's recovered really. He has some scars, and he speaks with difficulty."

"What do mean?"

"I think it's called a stammer; it's like he can't get his words straight out. You'll have to go see him."

"I will - in a while."

His section of the boy's shared bedroom was spotless. His bed had an extra blanket, as it was winter, and a new multi-coloured rag-rug next to it. His mother had pinned up some of the drawings he had sent home. Lined up on his chest of drawers was a book of ballads and two novels that his teacher, Mr Crabtree, had given him: A Tale of Two Cities and Oliver Twist. There was a collection of the carved animals Edward had made at school with a wad of plain paper and some pencils.

Every day there was good food; altered, patched and clean clothes; his shoes polished so that he began to feel self-conscious after making do and fending for himself. His mother had knitted him a thick green cardigan with large buttons and a collar and several pairs of matching socks. He wondered how much more special Christmas could possibly be.

Taking his old bike as a project; he removed the chain; cleaned and replaced it, repainted the mudguards; checked for punctures and pumped up the tyres; tightened the brake and bought a new bell. Most days he set off after breakfast with a cheese sandwich, a slice of pie and a bottle of homemade ginger beer. He headed first as far as Disley then gradually on to Chapel-en-le-Frith, Edale and Castleton, Hathersage and down to Eyam. He walked the ridges, made his way from Hathersage to Stanage Edge, climbed up to Peveril castle, Rushup Edge and Mam Tor.

At the weekends he took Joseph, but it was too cold to explore the caves round Castleton. He was keeping busy to avoid meeting the neighbours and friends who might have lost someone in the war. After a couple of weeks, though, he could not put off going to see Gerry any longer. Gerry's mother rushed at Edward and hugged him; thanking him repeatedly for saving her son's life. She took his hand and tried to push some pennies into his fist for beer. "No need for that. I'm as pleased as you are that he's alive. We'll be going down to the Buck and Dog. I can face the pub if he's with me."

Gerry's wound had left him deaf in his left ear, and he had developed a stammer. A prominent scar ran across his cheek to the missing tip of his ear but was not ugly. The rest of his injuries were under his hair. Gerry did not let his stammer hold him back. "T-t-took us b-b-back at mill." He giggled. "L-l-lots of la-lasses. A-a-am cour – cour-courting."

"Lucky you!" Edward put his arm around Gerry's shoulders. "I'm sorry about what happened. Should never have asked you to shoot that day, and I might have made you worse by getting you to the first aid post myself."

"B-b-bugger me, B-b-bulls- Bullseye. You, you ain't n-ne-ne never to bl-bl-blame your-yourself. I'm right glad I'm alive. I g-g-gets to-to st-stay h-h-home safe. I'm, I'm, I'm ja-jam-jammy." It took so long to say this that they both fell about laughing as they swung into the pub. Before Edward could speak, there were cheers from a few men too old to be called up. They clearly recognised Edward and Gerry and pints were soon waiting on the bar for them.

At first, Edward was embarrassed, having seen so little action. He soon realised, though, that any younger men coming into the bar, whether they were in uniform or not, were welcomed in the same way.

A group of girls took turns to play the piano and sing. *Pack up Your Troubles* and *It's a Long Way to Tipperary*. This was followed by a ripple of laughter around the bar when an older chap – not a soldier – began *Lloyd George's Beer*. Lloyd George was famous for draconian licencing laws and believed to have engineered watering down of beer in the breweries.

Lloyd George's Beer, Lloyd George's Beer,
At the brewery, there's nothing doing,
All the waterworks are brewing,

Lloyd George's beer, it isn't dear.
Oh, they say it's a terrible war, oh law
And there never was a war like this before,
But the worst thing that ever happened in this war
Is Lloyd George's beer.

Soon they were all in full swing again with, *Take me Back to Dear Old Blighty,* and had just reached the chorus of

'I should love to see my best girl/
Cuddling up again we soon should be,' when one of the young women nudged Edward.

"You've a good voice. I'm Elsie." She nodded to the piano. "Want to sing the next one with me?" He was taken aback by the request and declined firmly, but could not help noticing her sweet face and blonde curls. She walked to the piano but turned and looked directly at him so that he glanced over his shoulder to see if anyone else was behind him. His cheeks burned as he caught her eye again when she winked and smiled before starting *Keep the Home Fires Burning.* Everyone looked at her, and a gradual hush settled around the bar. She could certainly sing. After the clapping, Edward went to congratulate her and offered to buy her a glass of sherry, because he knew that would be his mother's choice. He was surprised when she said, "No, thank you, a bottle of stout, please."

Edward and Gerry walked her home with Gerry leaving the talking to them. But Edward was glad Gerry was there since apart from Molly in the hospital, which he did not think counted, Elsie was the first girl he had ever really talked to. He had to think hard about what to say, what to ask. His mouth felt dry. He did not stutter like his friend, but there were awkward gaps in the conversation, and he felt out of his depth.

She discovered how the boys knew each other, and that Edward was on extended leave and would then go for some retraining, but Gerry would not be returning to the front. Edward learnt that she worked at Christy's hat factory and attended the same church as his family. "I'll see you on Sunday then," she smiled, "I'm in the choir."

In church on Sunday, with his family, Edward wanted to turn around to search the organ gallery, where the choir sang, for Elsie. But everyone would have noticed and asked questions, and he was not ready for that. Beads of sweat prickled his forehead, and his collar felt tight at the thought of the micky-taking Joseph would give him, and the endless questions from his mother. He wondered if Elsie might be looking for him but had to resign himself to a glimpse of her at communion when the choir processed to receive the Eucharist before the congregation.

She was there, he was sure it was her, but she returned from the altar with her veil covering her face. After the service, the rain meant no one lingered to talk to neighbours or friends. He did not see her again until he returned to the pub with Gerry and his girlfriend, Hilda, the following Friday evening. They enjoyed more singing and piano playing, and the same jolly atmosphere, but Elsie did not look at Edward. It was only when Hilda teased, "You're sick for that gal aren't you; your eyes are following her everywhere," that he plucked up the courage to approach her.

"Took your time, didn't you?" Elsie said.

His mouth fell open, and his cheeks burned, and the words were slow to come. "I-I." He wanted to creep away but also to kiss her there and then. "Sorry. I wasn't sure."

"What's a girl got to do? Come on, I'll have another stout."

Elsie was working, but at the weekend there was a double bill of Charlie Chaplin films showing at the Plaza: The Fireman and One A.M. The two couples went together. Edward and Elsie held hands in the cinema, and after walking her home, he kissed her on the cheek and felt a foot taller as he ran home.

At a Silver Band concert, at Stockport Town Hall's magnificent ballroom on Christmas Eve, the four of them laughed as they tried the Turkey Trot and the Bunny Hug dances. Then, on Christmas morning, after the service, Edward and his family were introduced to Elsie's family. Her father asked, "When are you off, young man?"

"I've another two weeks, sir. Monday 7th I've to report."

"Aye, well let's not rush things with our Elsie, son. She'll still be here if you return."

Elsie grabbed her father's arm, "Dad!"

Edward felt a staccato beat beneath his ribs before a quickening of the pace. He looked at Elsie, and they both rolled their eyes, while his mother turned away from the group, and his father said, "'Course our Eddie 'll return. Knows 'ow t' look after 'isself, this 'un."

"No offence meant."

The two families went their separate ways. Edward linked arms with his mother, but they all walked home in silence.

On Sunday evening, 6th January 1918, Edward walked Elsie back to her house. Gerry and Hilda had been out with them but had said their goodbyes as they left the Swan and Angel. At Elsie's back gate, Edward took her in his arms, "Thanks for these last few weeks, Elsie, you've been smashing."

"Sorry I can't be at the station tomorrow." Edward took her face in his hands and kissed her gently on her forehead. "Better here," he said as he cupped her head in his hands and drew her face to his and kissed her fully on the lips. He wished that there had been more of these.

Frederick and Joseph were also working the next morning, so only Rosa could accompany Edward to the station. His kit bag was stuffed with extra socks, another new jumper, cake, tea, jam, tins of sardines and corned beef, matches and cigarettes. It was not his imagination that the bag was more substantial than when he arrived, but he was a little more robust. "Thanks for everything, Ma. You're the best in the world."

She stopped walking, "Son, how are you feeling now about France?"

"Better, ma. There'll be training again first. I'll get used to it." He held her tight, "No tears now, Ma. Keep saying those prayers and sending me cake, and I'll be well."

At the station, he urged her not to stand waving until the train was out of sight. "Get back home and keep busy. It's wash day anyway and bake one of your meat pies for tea." He gave her a final hug and walked away without looking back. On the train, however, he could not resist a glance through the window, and his mother stood beaming and waving, and he fixed his eyes on her until he could no longer distinguish her face.

Dreadful Deeds

Edward was assigned to a new infantry regiment and met a different company of men. He recognised Matthew Casey, who attended his church, but not the same school. The only person he knew well was Reg Parkinson, from his old section, who had been in William's class at school. Reg had been on a ten-day leave after several weeks in hospital in France, with trench fever. It was a relief to see a familiar face. Still, there was soon a close comradeship with both the new recruits and older soldiers. The older group were returning to the war after illness or reassignment. The new recruits seemed terribly young, and they were to receive a mere eight weeks training, compared with the four and half months Edward and Reg had gone through at the end of 1916.

Their new platoon commander was Lieutenant Cromer-Poole. Speaking with an upper-class accent, he was definitely a toff. But he mixed well and was not afraid of joining his men on exercises. He also found time to talk quietly to individual men. Those who were nervous or found it hard to obey orders or tripped over their own feet and were yelled at and given hideous punishments by Sergeant Floyd, were all given words of encouragement from the Lieutenant. Cromer-Poole was himself physically strong and continually emphasised that all the exercises the soldiers were put through, were building necessary strength and muscle. He was confident without being self-important or officious, and many of the new recruits admired him. He also spoke French, which they knew might be useful.

No one liked Sergeant Floyd, who was crueller than toothache on a wedding night. Edward thought that Floyd was worried about the lack of time to prepare for the next big push. As well as putting new lads through fierce drill and training daily, he had them up at all hours of the night marching with full kit. His small deep brown eyes pierced into every soldier in turn, seeking the tiniest deficiency. Then he barked out reprimands and doled out punishments for the slightest imperfection. He was as thin and stiff as a pace stick, which he did not have the rank to carry, but he enjoyed using a riding crop to flick at trainees. What was particularly irritating about Sergeant Floyd was that the only activity he joined them in was route marching.

Everything else he left to the veteran soldiers, who had been through it all before, to demonstrate. He watched and commented – usually negatively – on all physical exercises, rifle assembly and cleaning, marksmanship, trench building, bayonet practice and even boot polishing.

Edward and Reg agreed that he was the most brutal of all the sergeants they had come across. "Grow some balls. You miserable little shits, and stop crying for your mothers!" he would scream at the platoon. His very short spiky red hair and matching bristling moustache earned him the nickname Bog Brush. When bellowing orders, his square chin overhung further, and flecks of spittle rested for minutes on his face. It was hard for the soldiers, not to smirk.

He constantly attacked a lad called Raymond Roberts. "We want soldiers, not seamstresses," was a favourite refrain. One day, after humiliating him all morning, he ordered him to, "Fall out and meet me in the quad at zero one hundred hours sharp! A few more hours of marching might get your feet moving in the right bloody direction."

Roberts ran away before his appointment. Everyone else suffered the brunt of Sergeant Floyd's anger, which grew worse when no one could tell him who had last seen Roberts. The sergeant made it quite clear to the whole platoon that Roberts had brought disgrace to the regiment, and that a death sentence now hung over him. Extra drills and marches remained the daily penalty until it was time to leave for France. After the initial furore, his name was never mentioned again by Floyd. No one ever found out if he was caught, but Edward prayed for the lad's safe escape.

When the battalion of four companies – almost a thousand men – arrived in France, they were billeted in tents about eighteen miles behind the front line. Rumbling explosions, like quarry blasting in the distance, reverberated most days. Edward saw fear lurking in the eyes of most of the newly trained soldiers. He hoped his own face did not give away the cold shiver in his belly, and the reason for his urgency to piss when the rumbles seemed closer. Some days the booms definitely grew louder, and it seemed as if everyone was holding their breath. A hush fell around camp before the roars gradually faded. A few days later, without any warning, there would be a further upsurge, which foundered before reaching within several miles of their camp.

"Stop fannying around, you lot," shouted Sergeant Floyd, "not coming our way. They're in another quarter."

"It might give one the jitters," Cromer-Poole added, "When you've not heard it before."

"Well it's fucking working," added a new recruit called Jamie Reed, in Edward's section.

"You've heard nothing yet. Won't hear yourself think when you're in the thick of it."

It was evident to Edward that preparations were being made for something huge and imminent. There was a constant flow of lorries for days, and he helped to empty medical supplies; gas masks; stretchers; blankets; food and water and ammunition of every kind. Also, Lewis machine guns and railway guns arrived and even some of the latest tanks delivered by rail.

"Blimey, they look unbeatable." The same Jamie commented. He was smiling with excitement. Many of the soldiers stared at the tanks in amazement and walked around them. The crews promised all could have a closer look inside, when they had been inspected and checked off the inventory. The lads were like kids at Christmas.

"What do you reckon, Eddie? With beasts like these, they won't need much from us," Reg said.

"I'd like to think so."

All the companies stacked and stored the apparatus of war but made it manageable for quick removal. Mock engagements, trench digging, marching and exercises continued just as they had in training camp. They practised daily, putting on their gas masks in double quick time, and careful inspections were made to make sure they fit well enough. Warnings that every second counted and that hundreds had died, because they were too slow, added to general anxieties. Clear instructions were given to help each other and check for even the tiniest gap in the fitting.

During those preparatory days, the chaplain, Father Quinn, had a queue waiting for him to hear confessions. Half the men, however, had never been near a church in their lives. In case the worst happened, the soldiers were also urged to write a final letter home. This could be kept with the soldier or handed in to be posted if required. It did not have to be read by an officer but the advice given by their lieutenant was not to make it too morbid. They were encouraged to express pride in their sacrifice. Edward decided to keep his missive with him.

Dear Mam, Dad and Joseph,
If you are reading this then you know that I have fallen. The Boche has done terrible damage and caused too many to die, but we have all done our best to push them back. We have made a massive effort, but many will not return home. It is our duty. We do it freely.
My death will have been quick. Be assured, I won't have suffered. My sadness is for your loss. You know I love you all very dearly and will for ever. I am heartily sorry I went to war before I should, but please remember me with pride.
Your ever-loving son
Edward

Genuine illness was not punishable; fatigue was. The excessive exercises and preliminaries, however, were too much for some. Sergeant Floyd was pitiless. His new reproach was, "Lily-livered wankers!" Adding, "Do you want to shame yourselves, mumsy and daddy and your section, platoon, company, regiment and the whole god-damn British army?" His barking insults were tolerated by most of the men, and they tried hard not to incur his wrath. He kept them so busy there was not much time left to think about hard feelings. A more restrained bolstering was done by the chaplain or veterans or those who were just a little stronger at that point. Always, Lieutenant Cromer-Poole assured the men he'd be with them all the way.

Matthew Casey was a particular target of Floyd's brutality. He was frightened of this sergeant, and one night after a harsh lambasting, Matthew made a run for freedom. Edward knew his family. The lad had grown up on a farm in Marple, just beyond Stockport. He could easily manage a horse. He took a stocky pony rather than a grander mount, but it was its absence that was reported first. The young soldier had a few hours start, but his pursuers, on stronger steeds, tracked him down when he was walking the pony to rest it. His crime was compounded by having cast aside his jacket. He was wearing a blue pullover. He walked back into camp in handcuffs with his head bowed.

Retribution was unusually swift, due to the rumoured orders to advance in a few days. Names for a firing squad were drawn by lot from Edward's unit. His name was among them.

He searched out Father Quinn. "I can't do it. It's murder! Why did they pick me?" Edward cried. "I'll meet his parents back home and my ma and pa will be ashamed..."

"Stop right there! It's not about you! You'll have to pull yourself together, lad. I'm afraid your feelings are not important here, and it doesn't matter whether you think it's wrong."

Edward wiped his nose with the back of his hand, "Are you saying it's right? That's bullshit, Father! Are you saying I shouldn't have a guilty conscience? You of all people? I'm not doing it! The toffs can do it themselves!"

"The men have to know, Edward, that desertion can never be an option. It's a hard duty, but you must do it with honour."

"Fuck that! I expected you to understand." He paced up and down.

"He's a traitor, Edward. You might feel sorry for the lad, but there are plenty who would lynch him given a chance. We all have to do dreadful things in war. It has to be done for the good of all."

Edward looked into the priest's face and saw he was blinking back tears. "So, you do think it's wrong? But just 'cos you're an officer you have to side with them. Well you can bloody well give me absolution!"

"You'll have to decide for yourself whether it is right or wrong, Eddie, and live with it. I can't give you absolution before an event, but I'll pray you get the blank round."

"That won't make any sodding difference. I didn't join for this. Matthew's not my enemy, no matter what you say. It's Floyd's fault and well he knows it."

Edward had no sleep the night before the execution and smoked till his tongue was coarse and dry as a double baked biscuit. He padded back and forth, waiting in the dark shadows of the tents. He wondered where they would be holding Matt. There was quiet activity in the camp, and no one took much notice of a soldier who was not on duty, walking up and down. He wished he did not know the lad's name. The night's purple inkiness gradually receded across the sky, leaving a canopy of paler slate. There was a lull in the night's cooler breeze, and it seemed to Edward that the very air was holding its breath before his dreadful deed.

He thought that when the moment came, he would aim wide and then close his eyes, but the bullets would be tracked, and he'd be on a charge himself. It was hard to stop thinking about the fatal moment. The pulse in his neck was doing cartwheels. He wrung his hands together and pulled on the back of his neck to stretch away from the ache. As dawn approached, he heard the first chirrups before the ensemble of mixed bird song. The sky fused to grey, mingled with amber strands and brushes of pale yellow that grew stronger, as the sun climbed out of hiding.

At 05.30 a.m. the firing-squad were marched out to the perimeter of the camp where they waited for half an hour. Their Captain gave the orders, but Lieutenant Cromer-Poole was also there as the prisoner's friend.

"Left. Right. Left. Right. Left. Left. Left. Right. Squad halt! Right turn. Eyes front."

The rifles were on the ground in front of them. Edward felt his hands shaking and had to keep flexing his fingers. The officer waited as Private

Matthew Casey was led out with his arms tightly bound behind him and accompanied by Father Quinn and the medical officer. As they dragged him forward, the toes of his boots made two channels in the soil. Edward could not look at him directly but kept flicking quick glances. Matthew was weeping and crying out, "I'm sorry. I'm sorry. Please!" The medical officer had to tie him to the post and place the blindfold. Momentarily Lieutenant Cromer-Poole grasped Matthew's arm, whispered something, then stepped away. The medical officer pinned a piece of white cloth over the prisoner's heart. Father Quinn was praying aloud but in Latin. Even though Matt was a Catholic, Edward thought, what comfort would those words be?

The Captain shouted, "Take up arms!"

Edward steadied his aim,

"Aim!"

But at the word, "Fire!" he closed his eyes as he pulled the trigger. He knew his bullet would hit its target, but he could not watch. The firing squad dropped their rifles. The young soldier's head had fallen forward; his knees sagged. The bloody holes were scattered in or very near that treacherous little white cloth decorating his chest. Edward and two others threw up, but no comment was made by the attending officers. The captain dismissed the firing squad, and the eight soldiers were marched back to camp to carry on with their duties.

Sergeant Floyd was waiting. He passed out a measure of rum. "Don't think I'm going fucking soft.

Get that down your necks and report for exercises."
All Edward wanted to do was go to sleep.
"Remember lads, if men were not executed for
deserting, how many more would make a run for it?
We'll soon be going for the bloody Boche, let's all
concentrate on that."

The sergeant was right. Before midday,
reconnaissance planes were seen overhead, and fairly
rapidly news reports from scouting parties and
runners reached camp. The Germans had been
gaining ground and cruelly pushed back the allies for
several miles. The number of casualties was more
than a thousand in the preceding few days, but the
allies had retreated, not surrendered.

On the other hand, the latest news that afternoon
was that it looked as if the Germans had suddenly
slowed down. There had been limited action that
morning, and hints that the Germans had taken on
too much. It was believed, at long last, that the
Germans were in a weakened state. They were
apparently even short of food. Sections of the
German front line had taken significant damage.

Orders came down from the Lieutenant Colonel
that the battalion was to go forward immediately.
They were to work towards the southern end of the
German line, where their forces were reported to be
depleted. Some of the youngsters started grumbling,
"Shit, they ain't given us much warning!" moaned
Wilfred Farrow

"How can us get packed up just like that?" asked
Jamie Reed

"We's the new front line, eh?" remarked Arnold Duffy

"Come on lads, we knew the deal. After what I had to do this morning; we can do this," urged Edward.

"Aye, Ed's right. We've been practising for weeks," said Reg.

"Get your heads in gear," Sergeant Floyd yelled, "Moving out in two hours and all the new gear must be loaded on the trucks we've got."

The mounted troops set off first while each platoon of infantry made a human chain. Everything that had been unpacked a few weeks before was now stuffed into the available vehicles. Each truck left as soon as it was full, followed by the platoon that had filled it. There was no time to dismantle tents and no room for them anyway. Morale grew when further information filtered through that more tanks were definitely arriving, and moreover, American troops were on their way too. "They'll whip the arses of the Boche, won't they Sarge?" Percy Evans giggled.

"They'll certainly help, but we've all to do our bit!"

A fine drizzle persisted as they marched for a couple of hours. Apart from their drumming feet and the rumble of trucks overtaking them, it was surprisingly quiet. When they reached the rendezvous point, an older trench system in need of some repair, the promised tanks were rolling in. The men began to cheer. Sergeant Floyd jumped up on a pile of sandbags, "Shut the fuck up!" He continued with a glare that was enough to make a man freeze in his boots.

The first priority was to hastily secure the trench system with each platoon carrying out essential reinforcing and repairs on their assigned sections. Spades, mud, stones and bits of old duckboards and sandbags were their only tools. No hammering allowed. Swollen rats became a nuisance but were easier to dispatch in their heavier state with a whack from a spade or a thrust from a knife or bayonet blade. Along with the well-fed vermin, came the remains of bodies, bones and body parts that were not always removed for a second burial.

Jamie Reed had started to create a neat pile of bones on the remnants of a fallen soldier's jacket. Tears were dribbling down to his chin.

"We don't save them," Edward told him.

"There's no time and no fucking point in removing an unidentified arm or skull," Sergeant Floyd growled.

Jamie turned as white as a sheet when he was told to push them back into the trench wall, and pat them over with mud.

As each sector of the trench was sufficiently restored to last at least one night, the men moved away to eat their ration of Maconochie stew with a measure of rum. Edward was eager to take a closer look at the tanks. They were apparently slightly smaller than the older model, and, he was told, a bit faster, at eight miles per hour. Crews were proudly giving names to their tanks, and let some of the soldiers climb in and look around. The infantry would be following these when the attack began and deal with pockets of resistance from the Germans. There would be hand-to-hand fighting. Preparations continued into the evening and late into the night.

Edward climbed into Bodacious and was told, "These buggers might look invincible, but they can still break down," the driver said.

"You must feel safe in here though,"

"It's all relative mate. It gets bloody hot inside and the fumes can make you pass out. If we get stuck or tumble, we're sitting ducks."

As night crept upon them, the soldiers returned to the makeshift trench system before visibility was further reduced. The wet day had left a dense cloud cover with barely a star visible. The waxing gibbous moon was evident in the afternoon but out of sight that night. An hour later, a star shell burst through the darkness, and for a few seconds there was an iridescent sparkle in the droplets of rain. At least some of the enemy was nearer than expected. The light did not stretch right across the full front, but still a considerable section of what had become the current no man's land was illuminated. A complete hush fell under the brightness, and many of the soldiers threw themselves flat, while those in the shadows simply stopped what they were doing and remained frozen. Each man understood that the enemy now knew precisely where they were. They expected artillery fire, but gradually darkness insulated them again, and nothing happened.

Scouting parties were sent out into the night. Lieutenant Cromer-Poole led one of these groups.

Operational orders were issued, stating that they were to start moving before dawn, to try to regain some surprise. Every soldier was expected to keep going – no one was to stop until they had taken back the allied trenches. Trench systems named King's Common, London Pride, Manor Road and Market Garden were all in German hands. The soldiers were instructed to get what rest they could but be ready at a moment's notice at 4:30 a.m.

Everyone in Edward's section was too twitchy. "This is a bit shitty, ain't it?" said Private Wilfred Farrow.

"Better to die quick in battle than to die in wait," said Arnold Duffy rather grandly.

"What the fuck does that mean – that we're all gonna die?" called Jamie Reed

"I'm scared I can't do it," his mate Percy tried to whisper, but everyone heard.

"I don't want to die neither," Jamie said.

Edward started to sing,
Kaiser Bill went up the hill
To play a game of cricket
The ball went up his trouser leg
And hit his middle wicket.

Sergeant Floyd blustered in their dugout, red in the face. He did not need to speak. There was immediate quiet, but when he left, the lads tittered and Reg said, "Come on, lads, you can do this. We have to."

"We'll be following those tanks, remember," added Edward.

The tension eased, but no one slept.

At 4.30 a.m. a whispered message passed through the dugouts; "Zero hour in fifteen minutes." The unwelcome dawn had brought heavier rain, but the tanks were already on the move. The men mustered immediately. Some managed to drink a mug of tea and dunk a biscuit, but as they awaited the final command, the men hopped from foot to foot. They shivered; they scratched; they ran back to the latrines. There were white faces and glistening eyes and someone brought up his meagre breakfast right next to Sergeant Floyd, as they lined up in the muddy base of the trench. "Don't puke on my boots!"

"My guts feel like they're stewed, Sarge."

"That'll be gone before your next piss, lad. Deep breaths and swill your tot of rum in your mouth. Make it last a few seconds."

Several others followed suit, washing it over and under their tongues and almost smiling to one another. Lieutenant Cromer-Poole appeared and returned the smiles he noticed. "We're up for this, aren't we lads?" Many responded enthusiastically, "Yes, Sir!" and saluted just as his pistol shot signalled to move out.

Ahead of the tanks and the infantry, heavy artillery had begun to blast towards the German line. The bombardment crept forward in stages, just ahead of the tanks and infantry. The tanks were not travelling at top speed, but the men had to move quickly over uneven ground. It was hoped that the barrage and volume of smoke would disguise the approach of the noisy machines as long as possible because the plan was that they should not commence firing for the first ten minutes.

Fog and smoke were making it difficult for the infantry to see the tanks clearly. They followed the rumbling sound of their tracks under the heavy offensive; looking for the markings. There was no retaliatory fire for almost five minutes, when a freakish symphony of roars, clattering bangs, whumps, screams and whistles packed the air. Visibility was further reduced. Edward felt compelled to yell out, "Whaahh! Whaahh! Whaahh!" and the urgency to move faster and intuitively dodge and weave left and right was overwhelming, but he was uncertain he was moving in the right direction. He raised his rifle by instinct.

In spite of their size and structure, several tanks caught fire in front of the troops or were suddenly immobilised. Edward stopped in his tracks as two crews scrambled out, choking, and collapsing. One tank exploded in a blaze bigger than any bonfire he had ever seen. Edward felt as if he had put his face into an oven. The reek from everything that was burning made his eyes prickle and water, and his nostrils were scorched. He coughed and spat. Death racketed and shrieked all around him as he thrashed onwards and avoided other falling bodies. The surviving tanks were speeding up. Plenty of them seemed to be creating havoc ahead. Yet, soldiers around Edward were falling over like the ripple effect in dominoes.

The allied bombardment continued but did not stop the enemy. Eruptions of earth, stone and jagged pieces of hot metal were still slamming into the ground and bodies around Edward. Was it just a matter of luck, he thought, who fell and who remained upright? Eruptions of earth, stone and jagged pieces of hot metal were slamming into the ground and into the bodies of those around him. The allied gunfire continued but was having little effect on the Boche. The air was so thick with smoke and grit he could have eaten it. The din reverberated under his feet; rising through his soles and along his veins and arteries. It occupied his limbs, climbing and smashing inside his head. He shivered as if an electric current had whisked through him. The cacophony travelled beyond, into the air that was already reeling with noise. Was it the pandemonium that was propelling him forwards? He did not hear the individual bodies falling down or being ripped apart, nor the final cries and whimpers of the lost, but he saw their remains. His stomach flipped, acid burned in his throat and somewhere between his heart and his belly was an emptiness.

The allied bombardment was not halting the enemy's withering machine gun fire. His limbs moved of their own accord. He was running as if being chased by whips of lightning. He leapt, he ducked, he zig-zagged. He bounded over the shuddering ground and through the unclean laden air until he stumbled into a deep furrow that ran left and right about thirty yards each way. Visibility was slightly better in the hollow. He recognised his Lieutenant scrambling towards him. The expression on his face and graphic gesticulations urged those still upright to be ready for hand-to-hand combat.

There were about twenty-five British soldiers down in the ditch – several already injured - when a group of men in grey uniforms and helmets fell upon them. Shots were fired at close range from rifles and revolvers, but knuckle dusters were out too; blades of all sorts; and clubs and sticks. Khaki and grey twisted and struggled in the narrow channel. Edward had a fixed bayonet in his left hand, while in his right hand he swung a piece of wood studded with nails. He shifted his stance for better balance as another grey soldier jumped in, and the bayonet went right through the German's face.

Stunned by the bloody contorted face, Edward froze. Lieutenant Cromer-Poole immediately shoved him to one side, retrieved the rifle and bayonet and thrust them back at Edward. "Keep your wits, Holmes!" he yelled. The Lieutenant took a deep cut to his arm from another grey soldier, before two allied soldiers saw off the enemy. Only seconds had passed, but suddenly there was a muddle of dead khaki and grey soldiers. "Where the fuck did they come from?" Edward asked. His legs went from under him, and he sank to his knees and saw he had wet himself.

Another soldier stuck his head above the ridge and ducked down again. "Sir, Sir," he cried out. "I think our lot 'ave all run slightly off course. It's the bloody smoke. We've swung right. Less going on here. These shits must have been in that wood over yonder."

Cromer-Poole nodded grimly. They waited just long enough for someone to apply a dressing to the Lieutenant's arm, while others hastily separated the dead. The Lieutenant was all the while, giving instructions as best he could against the noise. Keeping in the ditch, they moved up the furrow and away from the woods. The Lieutenant was at the back and as the channel became less deep, he tapped the soldier in front of him. It was a signal that was repeated along the line. Then they all halted and looked back at him, waiting for the nod to go over the top. Before they had put a foot up the bank, a boom like a dozen kettledrums blasted the land in front them from a massive underground explosion. The earth erupted in millions of fragments before spitting back cruelly to bury the group in mounds of soil and stones.

***

Fourteen of them dug themselves out reasonably easily and shook themselves down, with nothing more than a few sprains, cuts and bruises. Among the survivors were, Edward and his friend Reg and the youngster Jamie Reed from Edward's section and others who were known to Edward from another section: Stanley Goodge, Arnold Duffy, Percy Evans,

Wilfred Farrow, Bert Rennison and Tommy Moore. The problem was their Lieutenant. He was alive but concussed and they couldn't get a murmur from him. His arm was bleeding again. "Let's make him comfortable," said Edward, "leave him to rest while we dig out some others."

More than an hour passed as they tried to remove soil, wreckage and stone and push it along the furrow. Four men were found; all were dead. "I think it's useless lads," Edward sighed and threw down his spade and that earlier ache under his ribs was there again, creasing him.

"We can't leave the poor sods." Jamie protested.

There could be someone, even if it's only one," Wilfred urged.

"We've been too long." Edward said, shaking his head. "They just couldn't breathe even if they weren't injured."

By this time the battle was rumbling miles ahead of them. Edward tried looking at the lieutenant's map, but it made no sense to any of them. "Maybe we should go back along the ditch, the way we came," he suggested. "We can keep low if we go that way and make for the woods."

"Are we bringing Cromer-Poole?" Tommy Moore asked.

"Absolutely. He's breathing fine. Just knocked out like a boxer," said Reg.

They manoeuvred the lieutenant and loosened his collar and wiped his face then held him up between Wilfred and Arnold with his arms around their necks. Progress was plodding, back the way they had come; stepping over the dead soldiers from earlier. It was deeper towards the end of the ditch and sloped almost to the trees, which were then easy to reach, and thankfully thick with shrubbery. The lad who had spotted the woods earlier was one of those lost under the detritus caused by the explosion.

It was not much more than a thicket. The group met no resistance, and when they cut through the trees, they found a narrow lane between two hedgerows. They rested in the bushes. Wilfred and Arnold were exhausted. "We'll take it in turns to do a fireman's lift," suggested Edward. "I'll go first." They proceeded slowly with no cover; five soldiers on one side of the lane and seven on the other, with Edward carrying the lieutenant.

Battle noise had not ceased but was an agreeable distance from them. About five hundred yards further on, a wave of nausea overwhelmed Edward as the events of the day repeated in his head. He let the Lieutenant down gently into Reg's hold.

Edward knew there might be pockets of the enemy hiding in the vicinity. "We need to keep really low, lads. Could be snipers."

"You're right, Eddie. Let's go even slower and watch very carefully," suggested Reg. "I'll have him next."

Pitifully slowly they stumbled on, passing the Lieutenant between them. He muttered and grunted a few times, but did not regain consciousness. About half a mile further on, they saw some barns over to their right, and smoke rising from a chimney beyond these. Their pace increased, but Edward slowed them down and told them to be very quiet. "I'll go and do a recce. Get the other side of this hedgerow, give C-P a rest, and keep flat and out of site until I return."

Both barns looked worse for wear, and some trees in an orchard were damaged by gunfire. He crept into the orchard, and noticed a chapel and to one side some freshly dug graves. Opposite the chapel was a rather grand looking building with the smoking chimney they had seen. The building had some broken window panes and bullet holes were evident in the brickwork and the dark oak door. To one side of this building, in a high stone wall, was an iron gate with one side hanging loose from its hinges, where a section of wall was missing. He climbed through the gap and on the other side of the gate read, the sign - Couvent de Marie-Eugenie de Jesus. He was standing on a road that led to a village, but little was left of it except some half walls of a church with its spire blown off, and the remnants of houses. The area looked more like a collection of jagged boulders from a quarry. The convent buildings were the most intact. He skirted back inside the grounds of the convent, bobbing and lacing between bundles of bricks or stone, and watched the main building for a few more minutes. A nun came around from the back of the house and started hanging washing in the orchard.

***

119

"I think the Boche has been and gone here," he told the others. "There's a convent, and I think we should ask for help there."

"Could be a trap."

"I don't think so. If the bastards were here, we'd know about it."

The group was welcomed by the remaining small community of nuns, who were determined to preserve the convent, and had taken in the villagers who were too old or infirm to leave. There had been fatalities in the village and amongst the sisters, who had been working outside on the day of the attack. Others nuns and some villagers had managed to hide in a tunnel, running between the convent to the village church. A small group of nuns had remained available in the house, to respond to the German soldiers' demands for food and drink.

Sister Claudine, the mother superior, soon had things organised. She brought Sister Euphrasia, the infirmarian, to attend to Lieutenant Cromer-Poole's wound and make him comfortable until he regained consciousness. She also checked all the other soldiers' gashes and sprains. The young soldiers giggled amongst themselves as Sister Euphrasia spoke no English and they had no French. She examined their ears, mouths, and looked into their eyes and held their gaze. She made several tut-tuts as she passed down the line. "Pas bon, pas bon," she said, shaking her head and frowning. A large bottle with a stopper was taken from a cupboard in the kitchen. It popped promisingly as the cork was removed and she insisted they each drink a tablespoon of some foul smelling dark brown liquid. As each soldier swallowed, they scowled.

"Un tonique!" she asserted. Finally, she held her nose and indicated to Edward and a few others that they needed to remove their clothing in order for them to be laundered. Their laughter ceased. She stood firm and pointed to a basket in the corner, then nodding her head vigorously she left the room. The solders all sat down at the long refectory table.

"I'm nay takin' ma troosers off, let alone ma kecks," Wilfred insisted. The others all nodded in agreement, but within minutes Sister Euphrasia returned with some lengthy ladies' pantaloons, followed by a couple of long aprons, cotton petticoats and two hessian sacks.

Edward whistled. "Whoa! They're not for us, are they?" He pointed to the voluminous knickers.

"At least they're big enough to hide your manhood," suggested Percy.

"I dunne care. You'll nay get me in ladies' gear!" growled Wilfred.

"Ger off, I'm having a sack," spat out Edward, but as he reached for one, a tug of war broke out.

Sister Euphrasia grinned broadly but clapped her hands as if demanding attention from small children. She shrugged her shoulders and frowned, "Yes, yes!" She held her nose and pulled a face of disgust. "Je reviendrai dans un instant." She glared at the soldiers without a flicker of humour in her face before scurrying away. They all stared at each other confused by her French.

"I think we have to do this, lads," said Reg. He and Edward pounced on the sacks before the others had a chance.

Oh! We'll never tell them

Lieutenant Cromer-Poole appeared in the kitchen just before a meal was served. "What the devil are you lot wearing?"

Sister Claudine explained about the necessary washing of some uniforms.

"You're being spoilt, lads," he grinned. "Make sure you show your appreciation."

Ham and mead were brought up from hiding places. Sister Claudine had plenty of secrets in the cellars that the Germans had not found. Edward devoured some warm crusty bread, with cheese, cured ham and sweet biscuits baked with honey. He enjoyed a measure of homemade mead, and asked if there was any more. A very pretty young nun, Sister Marguerite, who was serving them, looked to Sister Claudine. Edward was torn between keeping his eyes on the attractive face of the younger nun, and waiting to see the lieutenant's response.

"Seulement une petit mesure, merci," the Lieutenant replied in French. "Only a little, eh lads," he said to the men.

He then continued in French to explain to Sister Claudine that although they had no means of communicating with company headquarters, they should make every effort to return, as soon as possible, to their own lines. He would have to try to figure out where that might be. She worked with him to study his map and was able to explain where they had come from, and identified the turning that had led them south west of where he hoped to be. She gave him a cleaner and clearer map of the surrounding area. He wanted to leave immediately, but Sister Claudine insisted they would be better able to do this after rest and further planning. Besides which, it was already late evening, and the uniforms would not be dry until the following day.

Edward valued the proper bed he was given, in a vacant nun's cell, and fell into a deep sleep. But, images of the German soldier he had killed, circled in his mind like the flickering pictures from a Zoetrope. He woke up screaming and clutching his own face. Reg and the Lieutenant were holding his shoulders. "Whatever that was; it was just a dream, Edward," said the Lieutenant.

"Yep, mate. We're fine now," Reg added, "all safe." He put a mug of sweet tea in Edward's hand and sat with him as he sipped it. The Lieutenant left.

"It was that bloody German I killed in the ditch. Wish I hadn't done that."

"Come off it, ya bugger. It'd 'ave been you dead otherwise."

"I suppose."

"Bleeding kill, or be killed, remember!" He shook Edward gently. He must have spoken too loudly because a voice from the darkness called out, "Shut the fuck up!" Reg left him. Suddenly the comfy bed felt too soft and warm and Edward threw off the blankets and lay on the floor.

At first light Sister Claudine woke them and ushered them to hurry to the kitchen to collect the clean uniforms. She left them to remove their temporary garments, and replace their uniforms. They ate bread and cheese, while she disappeared to matins. Further provisions had already been prepared and a flagon of water. When she returned, she took a last look at the map with Lieutenant Cromer-Poole, who gave orders for the men to follow him silently. They were led down a corridor and out through the far end of the orchard to a narrow lane with high bushes on either side.

No one spoke as they trained their eyes all around and listened for several minutes. They tried to ignore the sweet birdsong and possible reasons why the leaves rustled. Keeping to the narrow country lanes that were marked out for them, they moved as quietly as possible, but without speed. They halted and ducked at any suspect movement nearby or unfamiliar sounds in the bushes.

In the more open areas, the landscape was often churned, but not furrowed for planting. There were deep uneven depressions, not from digging wells or ditches. Hedgerows were blackened and flattened. Busted trees, like random masses of firewood, confused the countryside. Fallen animals lay where they had died. Basic wooden crosses marked areas of hastily dug graves. Too many.

In one field, some bodies had not rested long before being regurgitated from their resting places by indiscriminate artillery fire. There was little evidence of decomposition. The youngest soldier, Jamie Reed, began to tremble and cry. "Save that for later, Reed," the Lieutenant said firmly but calmly. Edward was grateful that Sergeant Floyd was not with them. "Right now, we need to stay focussed on our safe return."

"But what's the point, Sir, if we only end up as manure for next year's crops?"

"Enough! Each of us needs to be to be strong for ourselves and each other."

Spring was fully dressed with blossoms giving way to bushy boughs as pretty as any late spring scene. Wild flowers decorated the verges and birds swapped songs unreservedly. Edward's spirits lifted and he remembered a few random words from a poem he had learnt at school. Something about the fair works of nature, and birds hopping, and twigs spreading, and what pleasure spring brought. Suddenly, the last two lines sprang into his thoughts;

Have I not reason to lament

What man has made of man?" He sighed deeply.

A snap of splintering wood on their left was followed by pht, pht, pht of bullets. Lieutenant Cromer-Poole called out, "In the hedge now! Ready to fire!" He held up one hand to indicate that they should wait for his signal. No one had noticed Private Jamie Reed in those few seconds. He looked as if he was sitting comfortably against the trunk of a tree, but blood dribbled at the corner of his mouth. The signal given, the remaining soldiers were shooting, aiming across the lane, but seeing no targets. There was no return fire, but they all kept shooting. Behind the tall bushes, on either side of the road, lay woodland. Lieutenant Cromer-Poole bent down to look at Jamie. A bullet hole was visible in his upper chest. By the time the lieutenant shouted to cease fire, Jamie was dead. He slumped on the ground with him.

They all stared at Jamie. There was still no firing from the other side of the road. Lieutenant Cromer-Poole instructed the men to move deeper into the woods. He pulled the dead boy himself into the cover of some undergrowth, but insisted that they must keep moving. They had to leave Jamie behind. There was no time to bury him. He told Edward and Reg to take all Jamie's ammunition, boots, socks, field dressings and any food. He made a mark on his map, and they covered him hastily with more branches and leaves.

Examining the map again, Lieutenant Cromer-Poole showed them where he believed they were, but could not reassure them as to the position of the enemy. He put them in teams of three, and himself with Percy Evans, now the youngest soldier. The Lieutenant ordered them to use any means to camouflage themselves as they walked, crouched or crawled onwards. Edward was with his pal, Reg Parkinson and Stanley Goodge, who had a badly sprained ankle. With his condition, they decided they were better crawling. Edward showed them how to blacken their faces with a clump of damp soil, and they grabbed leafy twigs to stick round their helmets and stuff into backpacks.

Although there had been some destruction it was a dense wood with a thick cover of tall ferns, clusters of abundant azaleas, witch-hazel and other wild flowers. Each group was to keep moving in an easterly direction following Lieutenant Cromer-Poole's lead, but slightly staggered and spread out across from him; rather than one behind the other. They adopted a long low-pitched whistle, starting with the lieutenant, at twenty-minute intervals, to indicate all was well with each group as they continued to move. Three short sharper notes, repeated twice, would indicate danger. In this case they should all drop flat to the ground and wait for further signals from the Lieutenant; either to fire, if the enemy was sighted, or to move on again. This game of cat and mouse was worse, Edward thought, than running straight at the enemy, but the ground gave him some comfort as they began to crawl.

Two phases of twenty minutes passed uneventfully. Then the thwack-thwack-thwack of rifle fire plugged into trees just behind the groups. Edward's group swivelled around and lay flat on the forest floor in one movement. He gave the warning whistle. He showed Reg and Stanley how to wriggle down into the detritus of the leaf-carpeted earth and spring flowers. Edward figured that each group would be trying to locate the shooters. A few more whangs. From the sounds of the shots, it was not their little group that was the target. He supposed that these shots must be from the same Germans who had fired at them on the lane, and killed Jamie. Anger displaced his fear.

He eyeballed his two comrades and indicated not to move a muscle and remain silent. In their stillness they could hear snapping twigs, crunching and rustling leaves about twenty yards over to their right. It could be wild life, but with his nose in the woody scent of the earth, Edward's eyes probed the trees and undergrowth. He spotted movement and fractured glimpses of grey, between the variegated leaves. In his sniper role, he might have taken a shot, but although they were very close, he was unsure how many Germans were there. He elbowed Stanley then used hand movements to indicate what he wanted to do. Stanley, in turn, nudged Reg. After the count of three, they were on their feet and running. They shouted and yelled as they opened fire in the direction of the enemy soldiers, and zig-zagged towards them. Around the sentinel trees, they drew the enemy fire, which was enough to mobilise the other three groups, and indicate the position of the enemy. In an instant there was a muddle of shots. Bullets were squandered. By the time the flashes had abated, four German soldiers were dead. Private Stanley Goodge had fallen too.

"We got them. The bastards!" Arnold Duffy leapt up. He was crying as he stumbled towards the bodies. He flexed his leg to kick one of them when he was dragged back by the Lieutenant and Reg. They held him firmly. "It's over, Arnie. We'll just drag them away to a bushier area and lay them side by side."

Edward was kneeling next to Stanley, straightening his friend's uniform and wiping his bloody face. "I forgot about his sprained ankle. He couldn't run so fast. This is my fault."

"None of us is to blame for this, Holmes," the lieutenant said and took hold of Edward's shoulder.

"Can we bury him, please?" Edward asked. The others looked towards Lieutenant Cromer-Poole.

"Go on, sir," Reg pleaded.

"Aye. We can do a good job 'tween us," Percy added.

Four men were placed at intervals, surrounding the other men, who started digging. The Lieutenant helped. They had rushed away from Jamie, but this time Reg suggested that they should say some words at the grave. They all looked at each other, blankly. It turned out that only Edward and the Lieutenant had ever attended a funeral, but neither could recall any special prayers. Then Edward remembered some of Psalm 23. *"The Lord is my shepherd; I shall not want. He maketh me to lie down in green pastures: he leadeth me beside the still waters,"* he began, and then found he could only repeat the same lines.

"Well, green woods, anyroad," one of the others interrupted.

"Respect, there," the Lieutenant demanded and joined in with Edward to the end of the first verse. Then he added, "Wherever you've gone, Private Stanley Goodge, rest in peace now."

"Yes, you're well out of this pal," said Edward.

"Your sacrifice will be chronicled and remembered," the Lieutenant finished.

The other soldiers nodded, and some added, "Amen."

The lieutenant ordered them to stay close together this time, and they reached the edge of the woods and a river without further incident. The sun had eventually burst through the leaden sky, and with a rising breeze, the land had begun to dry out. The embankment rose and fell along the course of the river. In some stretches it was quite low to the water, while in others a good four feet above. Violets, forget-me-nots and lily of the valley bobbed along the ridge.

Long past mid-day, they pushed themselves into the embankment where there were protruding roots of trees and natural hollows. The bread and cheese Sister Claudine had given them that morning was shared out. The flagon of water had been left behind somewhere. In the far distance, the familiar sounds of battle persisted, but right there, the remaining thirteen men sat silently watching the river and the sun's reflections rippling on its meandering surface. A few of them slithered down from the ridge and splashed their faces or cupped their hands to drink.

"We must keep moving east towards the sounds of the battle," Lieutenant Cromer-Poole insisted as he examined his compass and map. He decided against crossing the river, especially as some of the young soldiers could not swim. Believing that they were more likely to meet pockets of the enemy patrolling the river, he decided they would be better off back in the woods. He calculated that they would reach the far side of the woods in approximately an hour if he had worked out the scale correctly, and by then it would be almost dusk.

Advancing in silence again, one behind the other, they trod softly and stopped at every snap of a twig. Lieutenant Cromer-Poole took the lead and at ten-minute intervals, the second in the line moved to the back, for fresh eyes; making sure to keep looking behind and walking backwards some of the time.

Before the edge of the wood, the lieutenant stopped abruptly. They nearly fell into each other.

"What the ..."

But the lieutenant had already turned and using only a frozen stare and one hand movement he got them to drop to the ground. The men waited, hardly breathing. Voices carried then, and the smell of something cooking. A few threads of smoke wafted towards them. He eyeballed Edward to move forward. Holding up ten fingers, he pointed to his watch.

Edward crept ahead towards the smoke and the river. There were ten Germans in a small clearing. Some were preparing a meal. A couple of rabbits were roasting. The tantalizing smell made Edward's mouth water so much that he had to wipe saliva from the corner of his mouth. Those around the spit were chatting and had unbuttoned their collars. Three others were watching the perimeter of the gathering and had hold of rifles. Two more, sitting on the ground, were playing a card game.

Edward stole around the group and saw, as he approached the river, two more soldiers who were guarding a bridge. They were back to back, studying both directions of the river. They looked relaxed; it was hard to judge. Edward was envious that the enemy had time to stop to cook a meal. He wanted to scream and charge at them. His hand moved to the grenade he was carrying, but he paused and thought of his pals waiting for him. He might put them in further danger.

The Lieutenant chose not to attack, but instead to give the Germans a wide berth. There was not a great deal of ammunition left, and they had lost enough companions that day. While there was still enough light to ease them on their way, they should keep going through the wood, but following the river.

As the light changed, they moved out of the woods and scuttled through a large orchard. The trees were heavy with the tiny beginnings of fruit, and a carpet of petals danced in the light wind. Crouching in the far hedgerow, they saw they had reached another road. It was much more of a thoroughfare than the country paths they had followed earlier in the day, and there was a risk of passing vehicles, but it was the route they had to follow.

Walking into an evening breeze helped to keep them alert, and about an hour later they saw a rundown barn quite close to the road. Lieutenant Cromer-Poole said that if it was safe, they could rest for twenty minutes. In one corner, a scraggy pale brown cow sat in a stall.

"Are yous sure it's not a statue? S'not moving a muscle," said Percy.

"Bloody stinks for a fucking statue!" exclaimed Wilfred, pinching his nose and holding his other hand over his mouth.

They moved to the other end of the barn. There was no sign of a farmer. The rickety building was hardly weatherproof, but it offered sufficient cover to give them time to eat a couple of biscuits and sit or lie on some straw bales.

The next thing Edward knew, he felt someone tugging at him. He snarled and grabbed out; it was his friend Reg. "Sorry, mate, I must have been dreaming. I thought ..."

"I figured that. Where were you? Right strange mutterings you made."

"I could do with more sleep."

"Got to go. C-P's ready."

The full mask of night was slow to fall. Deep heavy dusk delayed pure darkness but blackened the trees and hedgerows making them compressed and foreboding. Edward, at the back of the line, was glad they were following a road. He did not have to concentrate so much and was drawn to the fading coral horizon, streaked with gold. Darker clouds lingering above the bands of colour resembled a giant bird of prey tracking a rabbit.

Progress was ponderous. Percy Evans; the other chap with an injured ankle was struggling, even at the reduced pace. He had to loosen his boot to accommodate the swelling. Two of the other men had just begun to support him; one at each side, when they heard a vehicle somewhere behind them. They squatted in the hedgerow and waited. Gradually the sounds suggested that there was more than one vehicle, travelling at a slow steady pace. Edward thought it must be a small convoy. The soldiers sank further into the bushes. Edward strained his eyes in readiness till they stung, but suddenly he whooped with relief when he realised that the three vehicles approaching were British ambulances.

"They're ours! Ours! British!" he cried and leapt into the road waving his arms at the first ambulance. All the hidden soldiers followed, forcing the first ambulance to halt and the other two to stop behind it. The lieutenant approached with his hands up, as the woman driver and someone sitting next to her, were pointing guns. He spoke to her briefly and pulled out documents. The guns disappeared. The ambulances were empty and heading for the front.

***

"We're good, lads. There are so many lost. Colonel MacNeice has to merge the remains of two ragged battalions. Everyone is exhausted and disheartened. A few more survivors were very welcome."

"Can we get some grub now?" Wilfred asked.

"Absolutely, and we've to fall back to the reserve trench for the time being and meet up with Sergeant Floyd."

Percy Evans groaned, "Not him again."

"Enough of that, Evans."

The lieutenant took Edward's hand and shook it. "I'm pleased to tell you Eddie, you are now Lance Corporal Holmes."

Edward's mouth fell open.

Reg was quick to slap him on the back, "Well done, mate!"

"Good job!" said Tommy Moore.

Finally, Edward managed, "Thank you, sir," and tried to smile. His thoughts were full of worries about what more would be expected from him.

That night the face of the bayonetted German catapulted into his sleep. He woke up shivering and got up to pee. Surely something was clutching at his back – like hands trying to get his attention. Lying down on the ground, he scratched his back on the floor of the dugout. A hollow voice in his head said, *"It's worse than I thought. Poor Matt. The German. Lads in the woods. It's all madness."*

He removed his tunic and lay down to repeat the action until he was satisfied that all he could feel were grazes on his back. He was done in. His limbs, heart and head were sore. Then there was that intermittent pain snarling at him. He was sure something was eating away at his innards. Perhaps it was his soul flown away. He had not thought about God in a long time. Perhaps he had a hole instead of a soul. He brushed down his uniform, made tea and sat outside the dugout smoking till dawn.

***

A week later, Edward was leading his section onto the battle field. He urged all his soldiers forwards. He was running ahead but sidestepping one way and the other. Quick, sharp movements and that sound erupted from him again, "Whaahh! Whaahh! Whaahh!" But he couldn't hear it under the relentless *takka-takka-tak* of machine guns. A fiend was in his boots, shifting his legs, swinging his arms. The earth was throbbing, bursting. Stones and soil whooshed upwards and descended like dirty fireworks. Noises like thunder that did not roll away, but kept recurring i even louder, bludgeoned his eardrums. Screeching, grinding, clanking all around. Bodies crumpled in front of the fiend and to the left and the right like cloth puppets without strings.

Pushing the enemy back daily, they sometimes set up a basic camp; used vacated trenches or deserted buildings. Usually, they were just in time for further action. Sometimes they could rest for a few days. Release from the front line gave a chance to wash and delouse, clean and repair uniforms and sometimes write home. Edward had nothing he wanted to tell his family that would not be censored, except that he was still alive. He sent a couple of Field Service postcards which listed several options. He crossed out everything except *I am quite well* and *I have received a letter from you.*

Days passed into weeks of always being on the move. Six days on the front line; a week in the reserves then moving up to the second line support trench, and finally returning to the front line. When the action began again, it was always at top speed in the ferocious drive to defeat the enemy; to replace the grey soldiers with khaki soldiers. Hundreds of Germans were captured, but just as many allied soldiers lost. Edward and his mates puzzled over the toing and froing of the action. The so-called big push amounted to no more than throwing pebbles at a tidal wave.

Some days little was demanded except a flurry of machine gunfire. At other times the business of war was so overwhelming that Edward found it difficult, in his rest periods, to distinguish what had been real or what he had imagined. Sleep or rest was snatched whenever the battle ceased.

One night, he remembered clearly that he had glimpsed a soldier whose helmet had been knocked clean off his head, but this figure had carried on running. The soldier had brandished his rifle and called out to encourage his men to keep going. As the soldier twisted and turned, Edward saw his mouth moving and watched his dramatic gestures. He recognised the unmistakable red hair of Sergeant Floyd and remembered that he too should be driving his section onwards. He turned momentarily and snatched a glance left and right and behind, copying his sergeant's signals. As he looked ahead again to rush forward, Sergeant Floyd was grounded, in a small ditch and clutching his belly, but half of his innards were plumped outside of him. There was a bloody mess oozing through his red hair as well. Edward knew he should not have stopped, but it was his Sergeant, and he was not yet dead. Edward screamed at those around him to carry on and dropped to the ground.

"Smoke!" gasped Sergeant Floyd.

Edward lit one, drew on it and placed it between his sergeant's lips, but Floyd had no strength to inhale. The cigarette dangled between his lips and caught in spittle as he coughed and winced. He was trying to speak, and Edward leant closer to hear him and heard him whisper, "Shoot me!"

Edward removed the cigarette and glared at him. Sergeant Floyd's eyes were boring into him, and he was nodding his head. Edward was shaking his. This could not be happening, but his sergeant maintained his gaze. Edward inhaled deeply then stumped out the cigarette in the mud. Crouching, his legs were rubbery and he landed on his backside. Fleetingly, there was a pocket of silence within the roaring monster of battle, and tears welled in his eyes. With effort, he gathered himself to a kneeling position and shuffled back a little to prepare his rifle. As he pulled the trigger and shot Floyd in his head, Edward screamed out, "Where the bloody hell are you, God?" He scrambled away, and his hollering was wrapped within the blinding noise of the combat.

Lieutenant Cromer-Poole was lost too. Reports were that he was first shot in the shoulder, but he continued to move forward before he finally copped a clout in the head. In the dugout a small group, who may not have known him like Edward's company did, were singing,

'When Very lights are shining
Sure, they're like the morning light
And when the guns begin to thunder
You can hear the angels' shite,'

Reg, Arnold, and Edward were slumped together and one or other of them told the singers to shut up. The three of them were sharing a mug of cocoa. They each sniffed and breathed in the steam before taking a gulp. Edward did not tell them his part in Sergeant Floyd's death, but that he saw him die like a hero and he was sure 'C-P' would be honoured too.

"Yeah, didn't take to Bog-brush, but C-P was summat else," said Arnold.

"Sergeant Floyd had to be bad, to make us good," said Edward.

"Thing about C-P; he wasn't ever a toff," said Reg. "Always with us."

They all murmured agreement, and Edward added, "He was never without a plan; what to do next. Always knew the right thing to do. He was the best man I've ever known." Passing the cocoa mug, he shuffled onto a bunk with a couple of slats missing and no palliasse.

As he was drifting off, he tried to go through the list of those soldiers he had known, who were now gone. Podge, Carl, Frank, Bazzer, Freddy, Bill, George, Tom, Geoffrey, Clive, Bobby, Jamie, Stanley, Matthew Casey and Sergeant Floyd and C.P. He stopped. There were more, but he had already forgotten some of the names. He started again, trying to recall each face, but they were muddled and eluded him. He was following them, passing through swathes of flapping uniforms hanging on washing lines. Was he in the convent orchard? No. These uniforms were bloody, shredded, stinking. So much blood. Where were his friends? He should search.

***

Several weeks into the latest big push, the remains of Edward's section had a rest period, a little further back from the active lines. The section was down by four men and had to wait for replacements. Those remaining sat cross-legged in their underwear, on the duckboards of an old trench. On a warm day, the dugout was too stuffy. Their uniforms had been taken to be washed, to rid them, temporarily, of lice. The blighters would begin to return within forty-eight hours. They were waiting to be called to have a bath. A large vat of hot water was being prepared, behind the cook's station, next to the laundry. They would take it in turns to use the same water. Lots had already been drawn, using cut-up matches. At least there were only eight men that day. Edward was number three.

As the water did not remain hot for long, it was essential to be quick, using the carbolic soap lavishly and thoroughly. Who knew when the next bath would be? A four-minute wash, and no pissing in the tub, were the strict rules.

Slipping into the warm water, Edward would have liked to sink beneath the surface, but it was already too grimy. He recalled the welcome bath he'd had at home, during his Christmas and New year leave. It seemed a lifetime ago. His mother had scrubbed his back with some sweet-smelling soap and passed him a warm towel when he'd finished. Here, the remnants of overused towels were threadbare and barely useful. At least they had clean underwear, though who this had initially belonged to was anybody's guess.

Cowed by the weeks of fighting, surviving, the horrors they had witnessed and losing their pals; no one was chatty. They returned one by one to sit where they were previously, leaning against the trench walls, either smoking, snoozing or staring at the floor. Without warning, a bloated rat, having fed on human waste, trotted between them. No one moved; no one screamed. Gone were the days when sections competed to see who could kill the most vermin.

Reg got up and went in their dugout, to return with a couple of packs of cards. They played without gambling or much comment. Going through the motions, they whiled away a few hours until late afternoon, when they lined up for their evening meal. This was soup, with an undisclosed name, but it contained plenty of peas and the odd lump of meat. It did not resemble Rosa's pea and ham soup. There was bread and a hard biscuit to finish, that needed to be dunked in a mug of stewed tea so that it did not break teeth. The rum came around as night fell.

***

A rasping death breath and the bayoneted face of the young German startled Edward, before merging with Sergeant Floyd's pleading eyes. What was wrenching his guts? Was he injured? The need to piss woke him? Finding himself bathed in sweat, Edward dragged open the buttons on his tunic then waited to see more clearly in the gloom. He made his way to the bucket, and the stink of shit made him retch. His heart was doing a crazy tap dance as he stumbled back onto his shakedown. Grunts, farts and moans from other disturbed sleepers prevented further slumber. He did not care. He searched for the rosary beads that his mother had sent months before. He intended to give each bead the name of a fallen friend and pray for them. But was there any point? Did God even see this buggered up war? He was about to fling the beads across the room but shoved them back in his pocket.

Matthew Casey; the impaled German; the eyes of Sergeant Floyd filled his thoughts yet again. Could the doctors have put Floyd back together? The Lieutenant would have known if that was possible. He took a notebook from his inside pocket and unfolded the photo of himself and some pals and a few girls from back home in 1914. Unable to distinguish the faces, he went outside for a smoke. In the light from his match, he realised that he and Reg, and Gerry, who had copped a Blighty, were the only ones left from the group in the park that day.

Another dun day rose slowly out of the purple night. Perhaps his torments could be limited to the dark hours he thought. He would make himself busier during the day. What he longed for, however, was to close his eyes, block up his ears, lie down and hide under his mother's bed, like he did when he and William and Joseph played hide-and-seek. Others were stirring as he returned, and he put on a clean pair of socks his mother had knitted for him.

***

Once again, they were advancing in woods, and most of the trees had been reduced to kindling. The land had been fought over more than once. The earth, softened from days of incessant rain, had sucked down equipment in a chaos of blasted trees, wrecked machinery and bodies not yet buried. A tank, with broken tracks, lay abandoned at a crazy angle, another was bellied. Wagons squatted with splintered spokes and dead horses lay with frenzies of flies. The choking air made the men leap over the obstacles and not look back.

They had to keep changing direction, and then a runner arrived to tell them they were exposed on their left flank. They could not see the threat, but the runner said they were to head for the open fields to their right and to pick up speed. "I can't see what the plan is for today," Edward told the runner, "except to keep going somewhere." As they moved into the open, enemy machine guns were upon them immediately.

Edward rushed onwards, yelling at his section to keep up. Once the inner fiend started yowling, he leapt and bounded, as if he knew what to avoid, before he dived into a crater. He sank a few inches into the muddy gathered water at the bottom. He had to drag his feet free of the gloopy earth, cling to the crumbling side, and catch his breath. He turned to glance up at the edge of the crater, hoping his men were following him.

There was Reg, floundering and convulsing, as he tumbled down. Blood spouted from his neck and groin. His face held a hideous expression. Reg was falling. Edward had to lurch to one side to avoid him landing on top of him. "Fucking bastards!" Edward screamed. He was spattered in his friend's blood. Then it pooled out of Reg, soaking Edward's uniform and the spongy ground. He cradled him, stroking his hair and wept as he waited for his friend's last shudder.

Scrambling out of the crater, he joined a group of allied soldiers relentlessly pushing back the German lines. *Kill or be killed*, he said to himself, several times. A grey soldier lay groaning on his back in the mud. He was clutching his left thigh and blood seeped through his trousers. But his right hand held a Luger pistol.

With one swing of his rifle, Edward knocked the pistol flying before the trigger could be pulled. He plunged the bayonet into the chest of the grey uniform; wrenched it out and thrust in again. Casting his weapon aside, Edward pounced onto the grey uniform, grabbed its shoulders and shook and slapped it until the bloody mass of Reg's gore on his tunic had doubled.

***

Lying awake that night, Edward's eyes stung, and his guts were queasy again. His whole body ached. The faces of his friends and the young German swam around in his head again and made him feel dizzy. He struggled to understand his feelings. Where was the young man who had started out so eagerly to make a difference in the wretched war?

When sleep finally came, it was fitful, and in the first groggy moments of waking, he believed he had struggled out from underneath a pile of dead bodies and wrenched out bayonets from each of them. He was not where he had lain down to sleep. Not in the dugout, but right by the latrines and the odour of faeces and quick-lime made him gag before he jumped up to look for the enemy. They knew that Germans might be lurking there, waiting to leap on sleepy British soldiers anxious to relieve themselves. After a couple of minutes, he realised he was not even carrying a weapon, and there was no immediate threat from any Germans.

He followed the smell of cooking. It turned out to be something resembling porridge. He took a few spoonsful, and a mug of tea then wandered back. A soldier came running full pelt at him,

"Have ya heard rumours?" he called and carried on moving, "Germans want to sue for peace."

"Get off! We're here till next year at least," answered Edward, trotting along with him.

But a few days later, on a frosty November morning, a newly appointed Sergeant Roberts demanded their attention. It was at 10 o'clock. "Message from HQ. Top Brass has signed an armistice. No fighting after 11:00 hours today."

His face was a mixture of frowns and smiles, "We hold fast here," he said, "no one's going to cop it in the next hour. The killing's over."

"Are them lot just going to drop their weapons?" asked a soldier.

The sergeant shrugged, "We're going home!"

"What? Just like that?"

"What does it mean?"

"How can that be true?"

"Does we 'ave to take them all 'ome as prisoners?"

"Shut it! All of yous. Give the sarge a chance." Edward yelled.

""Don't put your weapons down yet, but we'll wait for further instructions. It's finished."

How could it be so simple, Edward thought? Who had actually won if there had been no final battle? Powerless with tiredness and the devil of all headaches, he slumped to the ground. Many others had done the same, and every minute of the next hour ambled forward. Some men were already catching up on missed sleep. Others were openly writing in notebooks that had been forbidden or playing cards; delousing their jackets; darning socks or polishing their battle bowlers. One or two were actually cleaning their rifles.

Roberts had hardly finished speaking when Lieutenant Farquharson, who had replaced Cromer-Poole, arrived. "As the sergeant has said, hostilities cease at eleven hundred hours today. Troops will stand fast on the outpost line already established. All military precautions will be observed, and there will be no communication with the enemy. A flare will go up at the appointed hour. Further instructions will follow."

Edward must have fallen asleep for suddenly the noise of a group making a countdown stirred him. For a second, he was just Edward, then he remembered that ruddy German soldier, and he was ashamed, and all his lost friends. As the flare went up, a few voices cheered and some soldiers hugged, but there was little commotion. Edward only stood up when the rum was passed around, swallowing it in one gulp so that he coughed. Others had done the same, and it made them laugh between the spluttering, and they clapped each other's backs then fell silent.

No further orders were given, and as they moved towards the dinner wagon a soldier began to sing: "They wouldn't believe me,"

'And when they ask us,
And they're certainly going to ask us
The reason why we didn't win the Croix de Guerre
Oh! we'll never tell them, no we'll never tell them
There was a front, but damned if we knew where.'

Je t'aime

Edward did not get home for Christmas in 1918. Demobilisation depended on terms of service. Those with less than two years in 1918, and not staying in the army, were left till last. He waited for months in an Infantry Base Depot near Le Havre in France.

The war may have been over, but the men who were detained in France, however, could not leave the army. The rules were that they were serving soldiers for up to twenty-eight days after they returned to their homes. All the daily routine of drills, weapon skills, standards of uniform and behaviour, physical exercises and marching continued. It was hard to conform to something Edward believed was pointless. He longed to be gone from France and resented acutely that he was missing Christmas with the family. Now that the chaos and horror were over, Edward did not want to be continuously reminded that about soldiering. He needed bury everything that had happened. He had to all into the past, like a secret lost in the ether of time.

Some days the sky pressed down on him, and it was an effort to drag his legs forward. On other occasions, a scream was trapped inside him, crawling in that space he now called his lost soul. It resembled a stitch one might develop after running too hard. Had he escaped death by running too hard when his friends had fallen all around him? Tears often welled for his lost companions and had to be quickly smudged away, but then he had the wretched nightmares about not being able to save them. Uncertainty about the future wedged itself in his throat and could take his breath away.

It was a bunch of new faces all over again, and none could replace those who were the vanished. The novelty was plenty of sport; it was distracting for periods of the day. Edward discovered that he enjoyed boxing. Football and gambling were also popular. Some soldiers wrote poetry or drew; even knitted. Others wrote longer letters home, now that censorship was not so thoroughly applied. The soldiers also competed with one another to collect the best war souvenirs. They took it in turns to join a raiding party; returning to a nearby front line to search. The German Pickelhaube helmet was the most prized, but weapons left behind, shell fragments and nose caps were also collected and oddments of

151

German uniforms. There was no shortage of wood for whittling, and Edward made a model Medium Mark A tank and a Sopwith Camel fighter plane for Harold. Soon, other soldiers offered to pay him to create mementoes for them.

Despite varying degrees of damage, the nearby villages soon resumed their previous activities. Farmers returned to their land; boulangeries sold bread again, and bars were eager to accommodate the new business while the British remained in France. Most evenings, a truck was filled with soldiers being dropped off at one or other hostelry. The driver endeavoured to return the same number unscathed. Sometimes there was music, and it felt like a party, especially when local girls appeared, and wanted to make friends with the British boys.

Edward liked the effect of alcohol. He felt less morbid about his experiences. The camaraderie improved his mood, and alcohol became something to look forward to. He sampled Cognac, Calvados and Pernod. The latter was his favourite. Some of the wine tasted more like vinegar, but it was the cheapest, and after a few glasses, he discovered that it did not matter. But if he drank one too many, Edward became agitated and unsteady. Instead of being amiable and good-natured, he was argumentative. At worst, he was loud and aggressive. Once or twice, as his new mates said, he went 'proper crazy' as if he was in the middle of a battle.

"You've gotta watch it, mate. You'll do someone damage."

"Aye. Those fists of yours could be lethal."

It took two men to walk him outside, and let the cold air have a sobering effect, or to hold him down while a third threw water over him.

"Sorry, guys," he said, after the several rescues. "The booze does something to my brain." He was genuinely embarrassed. "I promise I'll put a limit on it. But, hey, keep me in check, will you?"

It was the headaches that followed the excess of drink that finally drove some sense into him. He was more or less incapable if he had a migraine and a drunken headache. He struggled to lift his head up, and zipping lights flashed in his eyes. He was unusually hopeless at the daily procedures and on a charge when he let the team down by opting out of a boxing tournament. He would typically have won, and it caused a lot of resentment. He knew he was an idiot, but the alcohol flattened his memories. Without the booze, he could soon sink into melancholy that swelled like a gathering storm. After a couple of months, he decided to take a limited amount of money to the bars, and he would never borrow from anyone.

***

The jolly proprietor at Le Cavern looked after the gramophone and played smooth jazz and light classical songs. Pretty barmaids, with smiling eyes and soft clothing, ensured that glasses were not empty for too long. One evening, warmed by a couple of brandies, Edward was trying to make conversation with one of the young women. Her bouncy black curls falling around her flawless pale cheeks and luscious red lips caught the attention of many. Her English was limited, but Edward smiled as she tilted her head and looked at him quizzically. Then she waltzed away with a little swing to her hips but quickly returned. An impish grin filled her face, and her eyes twinkled with mischief.

Some of those sitting with Edward whistled.

"You're on a promise there," one laughed.

She came right up to Edward and placed her forefinger under his chin and looked directly in his eyes. "Je suis Florence." She pointed to herself and repeated her name before planting a kiss on his cheek. His mates cheered as Edward tried to imitate her actions. When he moved to peck her cheek; she made sure he caught her lips. She pushed herself forward, and he felt her breasts against him and smelt the sweet whisper of roses as they kissed intensely.

She pulled him away from the bar, and holding hands, they ran outside giggling. There were steps to climb at the side of the building. Edward missed his footing and laughed some more. A soft light shone through a curtained window, and as they entered the room, candles were already flickering on a small table in the centre. Coloured material, draped from the ceiling to the floor, covered the window. Against one wall, a ruffled bed, but Florence stopped him. "L'argent. Mon -ee," she said and held out her hand.

He was puzzled for a few moments, but as she continued to hold out her hand, he understood. He dug in his pocket and dropped a handful of coins in her palm. He began to unbutton his jacket, but his fingers felt as if they were wooden blocks and the buttons seemed too big to escape their holes. She counted her money before starting to help him.

Florence pulled off her blouse and slip easily. Her pert breasts and nipples, like small raspberries, mesmerised him. He wanted to touch them straight away, but she pulled him towards her, and as their skin met a warm tingle began in his groin and ran up his spine. Her hands explored his back, and she gently stroked the scar on his shoulder and kissed it before moving to unbutton his trousers. A swish of her skirt revealed her total nakedness. The intense pleasure was suddenly all too much for Edward.

Florence shrugged, smiled and moved away to dress. Mortified, Edward did not go back to the bar but waited outside for the return transport. He hopped on at the back. There were more cheers from those who knew where he had been. A shower of questions followed; Edward forced a smile.

Florence's beautiful body filled his thoughts, and Le Cavern quickly became his favourite bar. He tempered his drinking further, to save his money for more encounters with her. He believed he was in love and learnt to say, "Je t'aime." He repeated it to her, in between kisses, and was not deterred by her chuckle and reply, "Nice boy." Her accent beguiled him, and her laughter was encouraging so that one evening he made her understand that he wanted to stay in France and marry her.

"Stupide garçon!" Florence shouted.

He got down on one knee, and begged her; his eyes boring into hers.

"Non, non, non! We 'ave the fun. No love you. Jamais!"

She kept away from him in the bar. The proprietor, now not so jolly, kept his eye on Edward. After seeing Florence enticing other soldiers, Edward chose an alternative bar and tried to forget her.

It was the beginning of March 1919 when Edward finally reached Portsmouth. A mixture of excitement and anxiety made him feel sick. He longed for the safety of his kitchen table and his mother's cooking. He could almost smell her best meat and potato pie with thick gravy. He pictured the fire in the range and the washing hanging over their heads. He thought of Joseph's football chatter, and William bragging about soon owning a car. He imagined his dad interrupting and reminding them to thank their mother for the excellent food.

But there was a further delay at a Dispersal Camp in England. There were numerous forms to fill in, and ration books handed out. All weapons and equipment had to be returned and individually examined. Money was deducted from final pay if there were any damages. Uniform could be kept, but not worn for more than twenty-eight days. If preferred an allowance was provided for civilian clothes. Men were allowed to travel home in their greatcoat but had to carry the Z50 army form to return the coat to a railway station when they would receive a pound in return. Small groups of no more than forty were selected to go home together so that arrivals at towns and cities were staggered due to high unemployment and rationing. Medicals were given, and finally, the Z11 Protection Certificate and Certificate of Identity were issued. The waiting was interminable, but on the other hand, Edward now worried about how he'd fit in back home, and about facing the parents of his dead friends.

At Edward's medical, the doctor commented, "You're a lucky lad," after listening to Edward's breathing and looking in his mouth and ears.

"Really?" Edward asked.

"That blackwater fever you had, is a killer. You survived." The doctor

shuffled through some papers on his desk. "What medication are you taking now?"

"Aspirin for headaches. I get migraines often. An iron tablet and one to purify my blood."

"I see." He paused. "Sit down a minute."

"What's wrong?"

"This little tablet is not for your blood. It's for your mental condition."

Edward jerked upright. "What the heck do you mean?

"Very high fevers over several weeks, causing periods of unconsciousness, can affect what goes on in your head."

"You mean, I'm loony?" His voice rose.

"No, no. Calm down. I'm not suggesting anything like that. I'm not a brain specialist, but how well do you sleep; do you have bad dreams; visions? Maybe do things you can't always explain?"

Edward slumped again in his chair.

"You know about that?"

"I've seen a lot of cases similar to yours during these last few months. You mentioned migraines."

"Yes. I thought I got the migraines because of all the loud noise we had at the front. But I still get headaches now and flashes of light, like tiny sparks in my eye. Then it's like seeing through a cracked mirror."

"That does sound like migraines. Maybe, they have nothing to do with the war; maybe they do. We don't really know why people suffer this type of headache. I'm not sure that they are related to the night time terrors."

Edward sighed and looked at the floor for a moment. "I do often wake with a migraine after I've had a nightmare. Sometimes, I try to stay awake at night - 'cos I'm bothered about what I'll do while I sleep. Of course, I always fall asleep eventually. When I wake, I can usually tell if I've had a nightmare, but I can't remember much of what happened. I sleepwalk. I'm knackered the next day."

"This is what I've heard before. Do you relive the action you saw?"

"I think so. The lads straighten me out; tell me I say stuff as if I'm in the middle of a fight with the Boche."

"Well, Edward, physically, you are a fit and strong young man. You have no significant injuries; got all your limbs despite everything you've been through. I believe you need some good home food; lots of undisturbed sleep in your own bed; and given time, you will get over this."

"I don't want my family to see me having these episodes. How will they cope with me?"

"Best to be honest. Tell your folks what can happen, but that you need plenty of rest for a few weeks, and then you'll be as right as rain."

"I don't think I'll find it easy to explain."

"What else can you do? Keep taking all the pills. They are supposed to help you sleep. I'll give you a letter for your own doctor to explain what they are. I'm giving you a grade B."

***

The train seemed to gallop towards home. Edward jiggered about when sitting, and was up and down to the corridor and toilet, smoking non-stop. Leaving the compartment once more, an older soldier, by the door said, "What's the panic? You're going home; not over the top, son."

Edward's eyes flared. There was a snarl in his throat, and he was about to raise his fist.

"Hey, hey," the chap appealed as stood up, and took hold of one of Edward's arms and guided him out onto the corridor. "What's up?" he took out a cigarette and offered it to Edward.

"Sorry. It's just." Edward shook his head, "How will it work? Going back? We're all a bit crazy, aren't we?"

"That's true, and I suppose you don't want to answer a pile of questions? Yeah?"

Edward nodded his head.

"Best make that clear as soon as you arrive. Get stuck into some work. It'll take time, but you have to find your way through. Or what was the point?" He nudged Edward towards the window and pulled it down. "Lean out and scream your head off. You'll feel better."

Edward hesitated.

"Go on. No one will hear."

The clackety-clack, clackety-clack of the wheels was suddenly louder. *We're going home. We're going home.* They seemed to say. A rush of cold air and a great slap of wind in his face made his eyes water. He yelled long and hard against the force. Bringing his head back in when they entered a tunnel, he made his way to the toilet. In the mirror, he saw a smudge of soot on his cheek and could not help smiling. He returned to the window and screamed all over again.

When he returned to the compartment, he grinned at the older soldier. "Thanks. Great idea."

"Find a place to do that at home. Yeah?"

***

Stockport station was just as he expected, but less crowded than it had been during the war. More than a year had passed since Edward had last been home. He did not want a fuss, so he hadn't told the family

160

the exact time of his arrival. No one gave him a second glance as he walked to the turnstile. He was glad of this, dreading meeting anyone he knew. He felt wobbly, like a kid called to the headmaster's office, and that gaping emptiness lurked in his belly.

"Home at last, eh?" the ticket collector said, trying to take Edward's docket.

Edward gulped, still holding on to his Protection Certificate, so the collector had to ask again to see it. "Um. Yes, thank you," and he walked down the long station approach hardly glancing up, to avoid the eyes of any passers-by.

At the main road, he waited for a couple of trams to trundle past. He stared at the buildings ahead - the miscellaneous roofs of terraced houses; the church with its steeple; the library on the corner; the smoking stretched-out chimney columns. It was a blustery spring evening; a moon a sliver off full, and Stockport's leaden hues enveloped him. He pulled at the collar of his greatcoat and crossed the road briskly.

In the ginnel at the back of the houses on Lord Street, some boys were kicking a football. He stopped for a moment thinking Joseph might be one of them. The ball bounced towards him, and he kicked it back.

"Thanks, mister!" one of them shouted, before dashing away with the others in pursuit. Edward chuckled, but something fluttered in his chest, like a bird coming to rest, as he threw open the back gate of number 62. His mother was at the kitchen sink, which overlooked the yard. They collided into a hug at the back door.

His dad, William and Joseph all crowded in until there was a bundle of bodies in the doorway.

"Let him through," his mother managed before dissolving into tears.

"What's taken thee so long?" his dad asked.

"Why're ya still in uniform?" Joseph wanted to know.

"Just the greatcoat. I hand that in on Monday."

"All right kid?" came from William. He shook Edward's hand and held on to his arm with his other hand. He looked Edward in the eye and nodded.

"Later, Will. Ok?" Edward said.

"Let's get sat down," his mother interrupted as she started dragging off his greatcoat. "We'll have a brew then I'll carry on making the meal."

The table was set in seconds, and a great pot of tea enveloped in a knitted tea-cosy was placed in the middle. "Did you kill as many Germans as Will?" his younger brother asked. Edward clenched his jaw as he glared at Joseph. A hush fell in the room. His mother's stirring of a pan, with a metal spoon, was suddenly louder.

"You don't need to know that shit, Joseph," Edward said between his teeth.

"Ed, Ed, not in front of mother." His dad clipped Joseph around his ear but put a hand on Edward's shoulder. His mother attacked the pan even more vigorously.

Edward felt sleepy in the kitchen's warmth, and after a refill of tea, he began to slump in his chair.

"Hey, Ed. 'Twas Tommy Evans farewell match with Hatters today at Edgeley Park."

"He made it through the war!" Edward forced himself to sit up and open his eyes. "That's brilliant. Did County win?"

"No," Joseph sighed, "but weren't his fault. Team will miss him."

"I'm sure, but lots of things will change after this war." He glanced around the table, but no one responded. Then he looked over to the range, where his mother had stopped stirring and had turned to look at him. The spoon was in her right hand; her left hand on her hip; her head tilted to one side. She held his eyes for a moment before giving him a gentle smile.

"I tell you what Joseph. Have a look in my kit bag." His brother soon found all the models that Edward had carved for him. "A bit late, but happy birthday."

"Great! But what about souvenirs? I got a German shell case; a field -dressing and a square of real grey uniform and a cigarette tin our Will got off a dead German."

"Sorry, Joseph. I didn't collect reminders – got plenty in my head." He blinked as a streak of memory, too fast to be clear, ragged at the edges, made him shiver.

"Aye, that's enough, Joe," his dad said and gave him a little push. "Go put that safe while mother's dishin' out."

His mother placed steaming thick vegetable soup with barley and chunks of homemade bread in front of everyone. Edward savoured the aroma for a while before tucking in. Afterwards, he ate three slices of bread covered with sweet blackcurrant jam. "The best, ma, thank you," he said. "All from the allotment, dad?"

"Aye, son. What abaat going down pub now? Welcome thee 'ome proper."

"Tomorrow, Dad, please. I've not slept in days."

"Anyroad, I'll go tell Tommy. He's oft' asked abaat thee."

"Cecelia and I are off to the pictures," William announced.

"A new girl, Will?" Edward asked.

"Yep." He grinned, and there was a twinkle in his eyes. "I think she might be the one."

"Really?" Edward said with some emphasis. "That is good news."

Joseph whooped a whistle and got another tap around his ear from his father. He jumped up from the table, "I'm going to show the planes to Walter. I'll be at number 54."

Alone with his mother, in the peace of the kitchen, Edward stretched and yawned. "It's great to be home, ma, but I need to sleep."

"There's something else, isn't there?" Standing with arms akimbo, she looked directly at him, and Edward had to turn away.

"You're troubled son, aren't you?"

What could he say? For a moment, he thought about what the doctor had told him, and the old soldier on the train, but the truth and the memories were crushing him. All he could manage was, "I'm not very well, ma. My head's all mixed up, and I get bad headaches."

"We'll get the doctor."

"It's not just headaches... There are nightmares. I see things in my dreams and think they're real. Sleepwalk. I might be crazy, ma."

She crouched down at the side of him. "Look at me, Eddie. You're home safe. We'll take care of you. Good food and plenty of rest will soon make a difference."

"That's what the doctor said." The beginnings of a smile twitched the corner of his mouth. "I'll try really hard, ma, but I don't want everyone to know."

"Of course not," but Dad and the boys need to know."

"They'll soon see. Ma, I don't want to go to the asylum!"

"Not while I've a living breath, Ed. Never!" She stood up and put her arms around him. "Let's get you a drop of Dad's brandy, and off to bed with you."

He took his shoes and jacket off, but then fell onto his perfect bed and slept until noises of someone stirring downstairs roused him. For a few seconds, he could not remember where he was, but the comfort of his bed reassured him. He sat up. There had been no senseless behaviour in the night, or he would have been woken and remembered that. His brothers, sharing the same room, were still asleep. He decided to go down and fill the bathtub, but his mother was ahead of him. It was already in place, and she was boiling pans of water. "Have a long soak. I want to get the roast on and pudding made before we go to church."

"Oh, ma, I won't be going to church," he said as he slipped into the water.

"Why's that then? Your Dad will be disappointed."

"He'll have to be."

"Son!"

"Ma, I think God was a casualty of war out there, or he gave up."

"Well, he watched over you, no mistake."

"Are you sure about that?"

"That's a terrible thing to say."

"Ma, I lost everyone. I had to do terrible things that I'm ashamed of. If there's a God, he did nothing to help! All those other mums - just in this road, who have no sons coming back to them."

"I understand."

"No, ma, you don't. You can't. I don't even want you to." He stopped scrubbing and splashing and gripped the sides of the tub. His mother turned away from him, and he knew she was crying. "I'm sorry. Please try to explain to Dad."

"We'll pray for you, son." She busied herself at the range then went to wake the others.

They did without breakfast on Sundays because of fasting for twelve hours before receiving the Eucharist. When he heard them trooping downstairs, Edward retreated to the outside lavatory, to avoid any confrontation with his father, for the time being. After they had all left, he hung the bathtub back in the yard then set the table for lunch. There was still his kit bag to empty and be sorted.

When the family returned from church, there was none of the usual chatter. His dad opened his mouth as if to say something, several times, but eventually went in the yard to smoke his pipe. William sat behind the Sunday newspaper, while Joseph circled the kitchen table holding one of the planes Edward had made. Still a kid at heart, he made noises he thought the flight would make, but muted, and whispered, "Attack! Attack!" until Rosa said, "Sit down now, Joseph," and she and Edward put dishes of steaming vegetables on the table as she called Frederick in to say grace before the meal, and carve the meat. Edward did make the sign of the cross with them, but looked down at his plate, barely mumbling the words. *Bless us Oh Lord and these thy gifts, which we are about to receive from thy bounty, through Christ Our Lord. Amen.* What he really wanted to say was, "Your hard work and dad's allotment put this on the table. It had nowt to do with God's bounty!"

Instead, he said, "Thanks, Ma. This is wonderful." The others nodded and made noises of agreement as plates of juicy beef – still quite pink – were placed in front of them. The gravy boat was passed around, followed by perfectly roasted potatoes and Yorkshire puddings.

Frederick had remained standing while he carved, but as soon as he sat down; he challenged Edward with a tumble of questions.

"What you planned, son? Shall us start decorating agin? I can quit post office. Will 't be Boar's Head tonight? Shall 't call for Gerry? 'S been asking after thee."

Edward recalled a similar situation, four years previously, when he had given in to his father's urging. He fidgeted and looked at his plate. When he looked up, he tried smiling. Instead, he shook his head gently, and finally said, "Give me a while, hey, Dad. It'll be great to do nowt for a few days."

"You've thee 'ole life ahead a thee now, son," his dad said, "Tek it, and mek it good!"

***

Edward declined to go out at all in those first few days. "I've money put by," he told his mother, "I can give you some while I think about the future." He explained to her that there would be an office at the railway station where she could return his greatcoat. "They'll give you one pound, and you can keep that."

"Why don't we go together?" She cajoled him, but Edward refused.

"I'm not ready to go out just yet."

For several days, he sat about in the warm kitchen in just his trousers and a vest, drinking cups of tea, smoking and browsing through the stack of old Evening Chronicles kept for lighting the fire. He went out in the yard only to use the lavatory and sometimes returned to his bed for periods during the day.

"Just going up for a think ma," he'd say.

During his sixth night at home, however, he woke in a sweat, yelling. He felt several hands holding him down. Voices were calling out, and a lamp was shining down on him. He struggled against the grip of these people and a person sitting on his legs. He screamed out, "I'll have you, you bastards!" A hand slapped him hard across his face.

"No! Take the lamp, William. Let me hold him," Edward heard a woman shriek.

His mother pulled him into her arms, holding him firmly. There was a muddy darkness in his head, but then he felt Rosa's soft uncoiled hair and smelled the familiar scent of Castile soap, and understood where he was.

He pushed her aside and scrambled out of bed, "Sorry! Sorry, I need the lav," and he hurried downstairs and out to the yard. He sat while his entire body shivered until even his bones felt cold. When he re-entered the kitchen, his parents were waiting. His mother gave him a cup of hot Bovril.

Fear grasped him around his neck so he could not swallow before tears filled his eyes. "I was hoping it would all stop when I got home," he said, and he sat down.

"You're safe now, son," said his mother, and she got up and put her arms around his shoulders.

"I know that, but I still have these nightmares and headaches." He could not look at his parents but began to tell them that he had to take tablets and some of what the doctor had said at his demob medical. But he did not add that he thought his head was all mashed up or that his mind felt like a monster lurking in the dark, ready to pounce on him. He clutched his head with both hands, willing the monsters to leave him alone.

"You'll be reet, Eddie," his Dad said. "Doctors is clever. Sure, you'll get over it all. Tha needs to get goin' and get a job. Tek thee mind off of it."

"Dad, stop it. I should have told you before. Sorry. I don't know what I want to do yet. I thought I was going out there to do some good. Now, I don't even know what it was all for. It's the things I saw. Things I had to do! I can't tell you about them and I shan't."

"Aye, aye, son. We know it were bad. I've read papers, and Will's told us some."

Edward got up from the table. "Oh, Will, Will. He's grand, yea! Back to his old job and a girl. All sorted."

"Tha turn is comin' son," his father said.

To Edward's surprise, there was a sense of relief once his family knew about his restless nights, but there were more nightmares. Most of the time, they dealt well with his disturbances. William and Joseph, sharing the same bedroom with him, became alert to noises he made in his sleep. They rose quickly to try to wake Edward then sat with him, and made efforts to calm him. Rosa always appeared with a cup of sweet tea, and sent his brothers back to bed, while she stayed until Edward had finished the drink. Frederick kept away, most of the time, and mentioned nothing the following day.

One night, however, William returned very late from the pub after seeing his girlfriend home. He had hardly climbed into bed when Edward began shouting out in his sleep. William gave him a smack and started to shake him, "Jesus! Get over this, mate. We've had enough."

"Get your sodding hands off me, you filthy Boche." Edward thumped and kicked his way out from under the bedclothes. They were both throwing heavy blows, and Joseph was shouting, "Stop it! Stop it!" until Rosa and Frederick burst in. Each of them had to grab hold of one of Edward's limbs.

The following morning Edward complained of a severe headache. The pouring of tea; stirring of cups; scraping of toast was too loud. "I don't want to talk about it – right." Anger and embarrassment bubbled inside him. He glared at William, in particular, and took breakfast upstairs.

On another bad night, he knocked the tea right out of his mother' hand and pushed her to the floor. Her wrist caught a jagged edge of the broken cup. William was there in an instant. "Christ almighty, Eddie! Get a grip!" Edward stared at the faces in front of him for a few seconds before turning over and falling straight back to sleep. The following morning, he did not know what they were all talking about.

"What's the bandage for, Ma?" he asked.

"It was what happened last night when I brought you a drink. Just an accident."

"I did that?"

"It's nothing to worry about, son."

Alarm that he had hurt his mother crashed into his chest, taking away his breath for a moment. "I'm so sorry, Ma. You know..."

"I know, Eddie. No more talk about it."

***

Eventually, there came an evening when Edward felt he should accept his dad's wish for him to accompany him to the pub. "Just don't draw attention to me, please, Dad. You don't need to talk about me to anyone there. I'm no kind of hero."

"Eddie, thee should be proud of what tha's done."

"No, dad. Thousands did what I did, and they're not fucked up like me."

"That don't tek away what you did. You was a brave kid."

"Thanks, Dad."

"You's just goin for a drink with yer ol dad, reet?"

Edward followed his father, through the heavy door, into The Bird in Hand. He scanned the room for all the older men. They would be the ones asking questions. Then he set his eyes down at the floor till they reached the bar. His dad had just ordered their Guinness when Sydney Clough was at Edward's elbow and made him jump. "Yous just got back, eh?"

"Couple of weeks ago." Edward turned away from him, hoping that was it.

"What action did you see then?" Sydney asked.

Edward juggled words in his head. His first thought was that people might think he had avoided action because he had survived. His stomach lurched. He could only stare at Mr Clough and then at his dad.

"A mite too soon yet, Syd," his dad said, "Give the lad a while." He picked up the two pints and urged Edward away to a corner. As soon as he sat down, Edward took a long swig.

They sat in silence for a few minutes as his dad filled his pipe. "Let's do dominoes," Frederick suggested, "on't ledge behind thee." The game was underway when they heard someone calling out. At first, they took no notice. Then Edward heard clearly,

"PASS – CHEN - DAELE, lad; was yous there?" Larry Grogan came swaying over to them. "Was yous at Passchendaele, lad?" he repeated.

Frederick laid down his pipe and put a hand on Edward's arm. "Steady tha goes son."

"I wasn't in that area, Mr Grogan. Sorry. There was action all over the place."

"Aye, Larry. France is a reet big place," his dad offered.

"I just wanted to ask if tha knows where 'tis, like? Our Tom fell there."

Edward had no idea, and felt bewildered but managed, "I – I'll find out for you, shall I? That help?"

"Aye. Want to figure where our Tom is buried, see."

"Of course. I'll get a map for you very soon."

"Thanks, Ed. Glad yous got back safe."

"Thank you," Edward said, and let out a deep breath as Larry trundled out of the pub.

"That weren't so rough, was it, son?" his dad smiled, and Edward returned it.

A Second Chance

"Been w-w-wonderin' when you'd get here! There was a r-rumour you were home." Gerry laughed and grasped Edward's hand before giving him a hug. "R-Right glad you made it. Look at you! Pub then?"

"Can we just stay here and chat today?"

"F-Fine, I'll get kettle on."

Edward said nothing till his friend sat down again. "How long did it take, Gerry, till you felt easy with people when you came home?"

His friend looked at him and took a couple of sips of his tea. "You fee-feeling all off beam now you're back?"

Edward put his head in his hands. "I'm so glad to be home, Gerry. My family's great. It's just everything is normal here, but I'm a mess. It's why I've not been out much. I was on death's books all the while I was a soldier, and yet not taken. That must seem so unfair to all those families that lost out. I don't know how to answer their questions. Some people make hurtful comments too."

"L-like what?"

"I walked to the library with Ma, to borrow a map, and when we passed the bus stop, I heard a woman say, 'Here's another one come home to take our jobs.' She must have known who I was, and a spark lit up inside me. Then a girl started giggling, and suddenly I was on fire! I had to run home before I thumped someone."

"Folk are worri-worried about jobs- they don't mean to be cr-cruel. I had comments at first. As if I'd g-got in-in-injured on pur- purpose to get Blighty."

"I'd have walloped them for you!" Edward exclaimed, but Gerry shook his head.

"It takes t-time, on both sides, but most are pr- pretty de-decent too. Do th- things keep coming back to h-haunt you?" Gerry suggested. "I was at least a y-year going over in my head w-what h-happened to us, on that day I was sh-shot. There's a bl-bloke at work still troub-troubled, and he's been back m- months since early last year."

"Does he say much?"

"No, he h-hardly talks at all. All we know is, he was a t-tun-tunneller. He's s-sometimes angry for no re-reason; f-frowns a lot, st-stamps around a bit, but we leave him b-be usually."

"I understand him not talking, Gerry. All our mates have gone, and it wasn't pretty. Those great buddies we trusted; joked with; marched with and shivered in the mud with." Edward paused, and there was a crack in his voice as he continued. "They were there one moment and cut through the next. We could do nothing to help one another; just join in the same massacre. I was with Reg at the end. It was bad...hell. I had to leave his body. I can't tell any of these families what it was really like."

"You got me out, Eddie. I'm sure it's b-best, as you say, n-not to give the h-horrors to the fam-families, and they d-don't mean you any ha-harm."

"But I feel guilty because I'm the one who came home."

"P-put it 'tother way, Eddie," Gerry suggested. "S-sup-suppose you'd been l-lost, and a lad were t-talking to your folks. You know what to say."

Edward sighed. "You're right, Gerry. I'm being an idiot. I'll try harder to face these sad parents."

***

Edward felt safe with Gerry. They cycled out to a pub in Cheadle Hulme on Friday nights, where they were less likely to be troubled with local gossip and questions. He learned that Gerry was engaged and soon to be married to Gladys.

"What about you, Eddie? Will you st-start seeing Elsie again?"

"I've been a rat, Gerry. I didn't send letters, and she stopped writing."

"She's a g-great girl. Sure, she'll un-understand."

"No, it's worse. I fell for a French girl called Florence."

"What h-happened? Did she f-fall for you?"

"I thought so, at first," Edward said slowly. "I was a mug, but mad for her. It was just sex," he added in a whisper. "She was a hooker and laughed when I proposed."

"Did she sp-speak English?"

"'Course not," and then he laughed at himself and Gerry joined in heartily.

"Well, if y-you're int- interested, Elsie sings at the White Lion now, in Underbank."

***

Still thinking about becoming a carpenter, Edward went up to Millington's again to see if there was a vacancy, but they had stopped apprenticeships for the foreseeable future. He sat on a wall outside and gave a fleeting thought to Pear Mill, where they made cotton. He did not want to work with crowds of people, and he imagined the machinery would be very loud – so that was out of the question. The colliery also. All that banging and it would remind him of the blackened land of the war and the tunnellers and being buried alive. It made him shudder. He wheeled around and returned home by a longer route. Perhaps painting and decorating was his destiny, he thought.

"It's a job, love. You already know you can do it, and something else may turn up later," his mother suggested as she poured him a cup of tea and placed one of her famous scones in front of him. A factory whistle hooted out lunch break as he fell asleep in the warmth of the kitchen, and was still there, with his head on the table, when his father returned from the early shift at the Post Office.

"Not again, Rosa. Why do thee let the lad do this?" He thumped him on his back. "Yous can't carry on like this, lad."

Edward leapt to his feet. He took up a stance, as if aiming a rifle, and rushed to the back door. "No more, no more, you bastards!" Edward shouted, and pressed himself first against the wall then inched the back door open. Charging into the yard, he yelled, "Forward!" before crouching fleetingly by the coal hole, kicking the toilet door open then bursting into the kitchen again.

A hammer blow hit him, full pelt in his stomach. He doubled over and collapsed on the floor and became aware of shouting and sobbing. Looking up, he saw his parents' faces full of fear.

"Sorry, son. I had to ram thee wi' back of yon chair. You coulda hurt your mother."

"I'm sorry, I'm sorry. I didn't know. Did I hurt you?"

"Not this time, Eddie," and she held him in her arms, but he was inconsolable.

The following day, when all the others had gone to work, she sat down next to Edward and took his hand. "I think it's going to have to be working with Dad, son," his mother advised. "I daren't think what could happen if others saw you like you were yesterday."

"I'm sorry for frightening you, Ma. I don't know where that came from."

***

One Sunday afternoon, Edward and William were sitting on the front steps, enjoying some warmer weather and sharing a cigarette. "Was gonna ask you to be my best man, Ed."

"What? You're getting wed?"

"Yes, but we think it might be too much for you."

"What d'you mean? Being the best man? What do I have to do?"

"Sort of managing everything and be calm and nice to people."

"I can be nice like anyone else. You know that. Besides, don't we just have to turn up looking clean and smart?"

"Sorry, Ed." William stood up and stamped out the cigarette. "I've spoken to Ma and Pa, and they think it best if I ask my mate, Archie. These turns you have."

"Oh, fuck off! So, I'm not good enough, eh? Wouldn't want to shame yous all."

"Bloody hell, Ed, we're alive. We've come through. You have to forget it!"

"Well, I'm only half alive," Ed shouted back, getting up to eyeball his brother. "It's like there's someone else inside me; some part of the real me is lost."

"You need to get a grip." He pushed past Edward. "We've all come back with fucking demons," and he stormed off down the street.

"Don't worry, Will, I won't embarrass you at your precious wedding. I won't bloody be there!" he shouted after him.

***

Frederick had been hired to spruce up the top floor and some old offices at Christy's Hat Factory. Edward knew his dad was thrilled to be decorating again. Frederick thrived on seeing freshly decorated walls, smooth paint finishes and perfectly matched sheets of wallpaper. Edward loathed the smell, the repetition, and being confined most of the time indoors. More than these issues, he hated that his dad was paying his wages. It was like being just out of school again. But he knew his dad's heart was big, and his mum was thrilled to see them working together, and all of them felt he was safe. The family needed him to be earning, now that William would soon be leaving home.

Edward spread the distemper with the optimistic colour name of Light Buff. Up and down; up and down; dip; repeat. Every now and then, if his dad was not looking or he had gone for a smoke, he splattered the wall by flicking the brush, then rushed to wash most of the wall. Windows interrupted each section of wall, and splodges of paint had to be wiped from these too. Distemper dries very quickly and cannot be painted over when dry because the first coat just comes away. So, he had to slap on the new layer as fast as possible, to make sure his father did not catch him out. Feeling particularly bold, he might place the bucket at the far end of the room, and send his brush flying through the air in a delicious arc before it sank with the inevitable splosh and splash. Of course, occasionally he missed. Sometimes he tested himself on the step ladder to see how far he could stretch out with his brush, before he had to move the ladder. One day he and the ladder came crashing to the floor. Luckily, neither he nor the ladder were broken. Slops and globules of paint, however, adorned the skirting board, the wall, a window, and were sprayed across the dust sheet on the floor.

Edward wished decorating did not give him so much time to think. The more he told himself to forget about the previous two years, the more his thoughts turned to specific episodes, and he sank within the memories. He tried thinking of absolutely nothing, but that only made him agitated; it was impossible to blank his mind. The most helpful solution was singing songs and reciting poems, even nursery rhymes. He tried to learn some new verses from The Golden Treasury, which was a book his teacher had let him take when he left school. He knew nothing about poetry except what he'd learned by rote in school, but he avoided poems about war, turning instead to descriptions of nature from Wordsworth and Thomas Hardy. At the library, he also found and loved, *How They Brought the Good News from Ghent to Aix*. It was full of energy, and Edward liked to imagine himself riding the trusty steed, Roland, though he had never been on a horse.

Despite Edward's splashes and falls, Mr Christy was pleased with their work and asked them to tackle the stairwells. "Something – not too bright – not too dark," was all he said.   Frederick suggested Distemper Yellow Ochre, which was darker than Light Buff and more of a tan colour. It reminded Edward of the sands of Egypt, but at least it was a proper colour.

When the hooter went for the workers' lunchtime, on the day Edward had begun the stairs, he stopped painting and moved the dust sheets to one side. He heard the approach of rushing footsteps along the corridor approaching the stairs. Thuds, thumps and clacking of ladies' heeled shoes, like a miniature landslide descending. He started singing, *I'm Forever Blowin' Bubbles* as he tidied away the paint and put his brushes in water.   He had reached the line, *'I'm dreaming dreams, I'm scheming schemes'* when he heard,

"Is that you, Edward?"

Bent down, swilling his brush in the water, he froze on the spot. A woman's voice. He turned and stood up to face Elsie. Two or three other girls had stopped with her and peered at him as he blushed.

"Who is it?" one of them asked.

"An old friend, I think," Elsie said.   Her eyes looked anxious.   Edward's chest felt like a woodpecker was pounding it, while his knees felt like blancmange.

"Can't stop today, Edward, we're rehearsing a show, and we only have twenty minutes."

He stared at her without blinking.

"Meet me tomorrow at the canteen, yes?" she urged.

He nodded dumbly and watched her hurry on downstairs, then turn at the bottom to glance back at him.

The next day, he was in the canteen five minutes before the hooter sounded. He bought a cup of tea and sat near the servery with his back to it. She would recognise him easily in his overalls. He wanted to be the first to speak, to start to make apologies for not writing. The words ran around and round in his head, but he was surprised when she plonked her tin of sandwiches down and said,

"What schemes then?"

Puzzled, he stared at her.

"Yesterday," she added, "you were singing that song."

"Just a song, Elsie. Listen, I'm so sorry I never wrote. There was nothing nice..." She stopped him and reached across the table to touch his arm.

"I admit I was upset. My dad was furious. I promised to never speak about you or to you again."

"So, why this?"

"Father Russell has talked a lot about the horrors and sufferings you soldiers went through." She opened the tin, took out an egg and cress sandwich and bit into it. "Praying for the dead is the norm, but now he asks us to pray for those who've returned," she said through her mouthful.

Edward nearly laughed at her muffled voice, but she was getting up.

"Just getting a cuppa," and she joined the queue. When she returned, she said, "Then Gerry came to see me."

"What did he have to say?"

"That you'd had the worst time and felt bad that you'd not written."

Edward smiled, "So you forgive me?"

"I'm working on it." She winked at him and bolted her lunch. Edward had no appetite. As she got up to go, she said, "Come and see me at the pub on Friday night, and we'll talk more."

Gerry and Gladys accompanied him to The Cross Keys. Edward felt as nervous as the first time he had dared to ask her out. Tripping over his own feet as they went to find seats, Edward slopped beer down his pullover, while trying to save the bottle of Theakston Old Peculiar that Elsie liked. He wanted it to be ready for when she joined them. Gladys helped to dab his pullover dry with her handkerchief, "Relax, Edward, she wants to see you."

"I don't deserve her."

"Shut up and enjoy the evening. OK?"

He just had time to put a smile on his face before Elsie appeared.

"We'll get a table nearer the piano, so we can see Elsie when she sings," said Gladys.

Elsie waited until they had moved away. "I see you have a good memory," she said, raising her eyebrows at the stout.

He smiled, "There's plenty I don't want to remember."

"As long as you remember the important things," she said before taking a sip.

The landlord came over to ask her what time she wanted to do her set of songs, and they agreed on eight o'clock.

"Gerry told me you are not very well," she said to Edward, "since you came home."

"Hmm. Remember how ill I'd been when I was out in Egypt before I went to France?"

"Yes, blackwater fever wasn't it?"

"With complications," he added.

"Gerry thought you might not want to tell me about it."

"It's not the illness so much, but something else that began there." He stopped; feeling his mouth was suddenly dry. Elsie was looking at him with wide eyes, obviously expecting more.

"It's hard to talk about it," he said quietly.

"Please try," she said.

He wanted to open out to her. "Well, I still have to take tablets I was given in Egypt. I get awful headaches from time to time...but..."

"Edward, if we're going to start seeing each other, you need to trust me."

"Oh! So, we are going to start seeing each other again?"

"Don't change the subject."

He drank his beer slowly but kept looking at Elsie. Her fingers stretched lightly over his hand.

"I have nightmares Elsie. The war comes back to haunt me, and I can get quite physical!"

"Do you sleepwalk?"

"Sometimes. I hate it. I can wake up quite a distance from my bed and think I'm still fighting the Germans. My folks wake me up, and I don't remember then what it was all about. It's crazy. I'm ashamed."

"Ashamed? You're not doing it deliberately. I bet many blokes will be having nightmares after the battles."

"It wasn't just the battles. There were other terrible things I had to do." She was silent for a minute, and he could not hold her gaze.

"The way I see it, Ed, this awful time will pass eventually, and you owe it to all your lost pals to live a good life to the full, and I'd like to be part of that."

Now she held his hand firmly with both of hers. "Come over and sit with your friends while I sing. Then we'll have another drink."

***

William announced the date for his wedding to Cecilia. His bride to be wanted warm weather and scented roses, so they had chosen August 5th. Cecilia's parents paid for formal invitations, and William handed theirs to Edward, Joseph and his parents. They were on cream card edged with gold with copperplate script and announced that Mr and Mrs Morton requested the pleasure of their company at the event. Rosa rushed to hug her eldest son. Edward supposed she was overcome with pride for her eldest boy.

Joseph stared blankly at the card, "Blimey, what does this say?" he asked.

"We've all been asked to William's wedding, you chump," said Edward, who wondered why they needed fancy summonses, as both families knew all the guests. Why not just tell them the arrangements? He wanted to suggest. His first instinct was to throw his own on the fire – it was too showy - but his mother's evident joy stopped him. His father, with a broad grin on his face, was shaking William's hand. "Well done, son. 'Appen 'tis time to grow up now," but Edward started to prance around the room, like a silly child, shouting, "William's having a posh wedding!"

He knew it was immature, but could not think of anything else to say or do, and when he reached the door to the stairs for the second time, he disappeared. He jumped the treads two at a time. Sitting on his bed, he tried to crush the invitation but only creased it in his hands, so he stuffed it in a book. He did not begrudge his brother's happiness, but this felt like a further insult, to be asked so formally to go to the wedding when he was not good enough to be the best man.

His mother insisted that both families should share all further expenses. She was looking forward to an 'outstanding occasion,' she said. Cecilia's parents were naturally delighted. Rosa's eyes sparkled with every conversation the families had about the wedding, and there were plenty. Cecilia, her mother and Rosa took over the kitchen, to plan and discuss, at every opportunity.

How were they going to seat thirty-seven people in the church hall? There were enough tables, but some of the chairs were a little wobbly. They would have to check them all ahead of the day. White table cloths and decent cutlery were essential, which meant borrowing them. They were sure the church would let them have the large metal teapots which always appeared after the May Day procession and Whit Walks. The men would want some ale as well and should there be sherry for the ladies? Perhaps some homemade lemonade?

"Are you buying a new outfit, Maud? As the mother of the bride, I'd say you deserve one," said Rosa. The three women chuckled.

"Of course," Maud replied. "I'd like to wear lilac. We're going to Manchester next week, to Kendal Milne.

"Oh, that's posh!"

"My sister and Cecilia's cousins are in charge of Cecilia's dress. Beth's a brilliant dressmaker, but I can't ask her to make mine as well."

If Edward was at home, he sat on the stairs, sometimes with Joseph, and they eavesdropped and struggled to suppress their giggles at the women's excitement. The discussion about a visit to the high-class department store was somehow particularly funny to the hidden brothers. Their laughter became so loud that there was no choice but to enter the kitchen. They pretended they had been larking about upstairs while Edward tried to teach Joseph some magic tricks with a pack of cards. They were then dragged into a discussion about the music for the wedding. Would there be a hymn to walk down the aisle or a piece of music played on the organ? Would the organist be available? What about other hymns during the nuptial mass?

"And what about music at the wedding reception?" Cecilia asked. "Will and I would like to dance after the meal, and I think some of the Silver Band have agreed to come and play for an hour."

"Grand!" said Edward, "We know quite a few of the players."

"What about some gentler more traditional music for us older folk?" asked Rosa, "maybe during the meal?"

"We'll have to borrow a gramophone and some records," suggested Edward. "Perhaps Mrs Lannesbury might lend hers."

"Mum, we haven't told them about Great Aunt Dorothy," said Cecilia in a quieter voice.

"What about her?" Joseph asked bluntly.

"Well," Mrs Morton started slowly, "she has a booming voice."

"And she always makes rude comments," added Cecilia, "she says she speaks her mind."

"I've asked my sister and her husband to take her in hand," said Mrs Morton frowning at her daughter, "don't worry."

"But she smells of over-boiled cabbage," added Cecilia, and as her mother tutted loudly and gave her another stern look, Edward and Joseph did not dare to look at each other for fear of laughing again.

"I have to invite her, but I promise she won't spoil the day," Mrs Morton said emphatically.

Finally, there was the food to talk about, and they agreed to share the responsibility for it between several members of both families. Rosa was pleased to offer to make the cake and ice it. "Why not use Dad's handcart?" Edward suggested. "We can cover it with a clean sheet, to transport the food. Everything just needs to be delivered here, the evening before the wedding."

One Saturday morning when Frederick was in the parlour reading the newspaper; William was at work and Joseph out playing football; Mrs Morton called again. Edward decided to stay out of it and sat on the stairs once more. His mother was getting her famous scones in the oven when he heard Cecilia's mother say, "We think it would be lovely if Edward and Joseph showed all the guests to their seats in church,"

"Oh, yes," said his mother.

Edward, however, thought it would surely be perfectly obvious where everyone was to sit. He was churning the stupidity of the idea around in his head when Maud added, "I mean, Edward will be all right to do that won't he? William says he doesn't usually have bad turns during the day."

Edward froze. After waiting for a response from his mother that never came, he jumped up and burst into the kitchen. "William had no right discussing my business with you," he shouted, and his voice rose even higher, "and if you're all so worried that I might spoil things, then..." he caught sight of his mother's worried expression and paused for breath, "perhaps I don't need to be there."

Mrs Morton had risen to her feet, attempting to apologise. Edward brushed past her and out of the back door, leaving it open. He kicked the washtub in the yard, threw the dolly stick and slammed the gate. It was a wet, blustery morning, and he had no coat, but he ran down the ginnel and continued until he reached Gerry's house.

"This bloody la-di-dah wedding!" he exclaimed from underneath the towel Gerry had given him to dry his hair. "I could do for my brother!" He retold what he'd overheard.

"Y-you didn't h-hit the woman, did you?"

"Course not, but I might thump Will."

"Eddie, w-what is it that makes you s-so heated?"

Edward was initially confused that his friend needed to ask this question. Another cinder of irritation smouldered inside him, but he could see that Gerry was genuinely concerned.

"I'm mad about what's happened to my head; to me; who I am now, and I think my family has had enough of me." He wrung his hands together and looked down at the table.

"Just st-stop this rubbish! I don't know a l-lad what's m-more loved and care-cared for than you, Ed."

"So why are they so troubled about me showing them up at the wedding?"

"W-Worried for your s-sake, not theirs, and they don't know h-how to help."

"So, it's pity they have for me?"

"Shut up and l-listen! W-Wills-William's wedding day is sp-special, and he's a r-right to have it all go well. It's what I want, and wa-wait till it's your turn."

"Who'll have a barmy bugger like me?"

"Give over, Ed! 'Tis yous sorry for y-yourself. You were ne-never a ninny in't war. You've to face this. T-talk to your folks more. If you try to h-hide it, the th-thicker it'll get."

Edward sat still and silent for several minutes. "It was bad enough the family seeing me all messed up in the head, but now I'm embarrassed other people know. Humiliated. My thread of hope was that being home would make it all go away. But I am plagued with memories of the action, and all those lost pals.

"D-did you do anything t-to be ash-ashamed of in the war?"

Edward held Gerry's gaze for a few moments. "I'm ashamed of almost everything, Gerry," he said, and he held his head in his hands before looking directly again at his friend. "I've never told anyone, Gerry, but I was part of a firing squad."

Gerry let out a long whistle of breath. "They were or-orders, m-mate." Edward nodded. "P-Point is, you're not guil-guilty of any-anything," Gerry continued. "I h-have these sc-scars for all to see, b-but you're sc-scarred too, inside, mate. You think everyone c-can see them and they are h-horrified, but it's only one other family and me.

"Thanks, Gerry, you always put me right. I let things get to me that don't mean that much. I shouldn't have shouted at the woman."

When Edward arrived home, the house was in darkness, apart from an oil lamp glowing through the kitchen window. Edward entered quietly and found his mother asleep over the table. He nudged her gently.

"I didn't think, Ma. Mrs Morton must despise me now."

She smiled and reached in her apron pocket and produced an envelope that looked familiar to him. "Far from it, son. She understood. She wanted to apologise to you, and Cecilia and William want to invite Elsie."

The night before the wedding, William, Edward and their father, gathered at the Three Tuns Inn with some of William's pals. Edward had made a firm decision to measure his drinks carefully and stay calm. He listened and laughed at the usual banter about William's last night of freedom until closing time. Then he sincerely wished his brother luck and said, "No hard feelings, Will. I know I can be a bother."

"And some!" William replied, but he shook his brother's hand enthusiastically and slapped him on the back.

***

Wagner's *Bridal Chorus* announced Cecilia's entrance. This was followed by all the verses of *Heav'nly Father Send Thy Blessing*. There was plenty of time for the congregation to admire the bride's dress, which was ivory silk and slim-fitting with a lace hem. She wore a full-length veil. A short piece covered her hair and face. The rest was gathered at the nape of her neck. It flowed out at the back to form a short train at the floor. There were scattered gasps of admiration at the delicately embroidered flowers, over a foot in depth, which decorated the full curve of the hem, as it brushed along the polished parquet aisle. Creamy roses mixed with vivid pink ones and fronds of greenery formed her bouquet.

Edward had to admit that she looked splendid, and William was smart in his crisp new suit, white shirt and maroon cravat. When Edward caught sight of Elsie, however, his biggest smile was for her. She wore a lace blush-pink dress with a square neck and three-quarter sleeves. It was loose-fitting and fell to mid-calf with a slight swirl at the hem as she walked. Her shoes were cream, and around her head was a band of cream lace with two pink roses attached.

The nuptial mass stretched onwards with a sermon, more hymns, and the playing of Beethoven's *Ode to Joy* during the signing of the register. Finally, the bride and groom processed back down the aisle to Mendelssohn's *Wedding March* and out into a perfect summer's day with golden light, arched with a splendidly clear blue sky.

There was some dallying outside the church while several people took photographs. By the time the congregation reached the church hall, it was approaching midday. The Catholics had fasted for twelve hours before receiving the eucharist, without even a cup of tea. They fell upon the pies and sandwiches, baked ham and roast beef, potato salads, eggs in aspic, devilled eggs, cheese platters, bread, pickles and mixed nuts. Florentines, butterfly cakes, pineapple pudding and Rosa's special two-tiered fruit cake, were exclaimed upon. The special cake was faultlessly iced in white with perfect miniature roses on the top. It took pride of place on a raised stand, in the middle of the food table.

Although the guests began with welcome cups of tea, very soon sherry or gin was poured into those cups. Frederick and Edward dragged a barrel of beer out from behind an innocent-looking screen and placed it on chocks on a table. Edward held it steady, while Frederick displaced the bung at the bottom of the barrel by hammering in a tap. A cheer went up and again when he beat in the bung on the top, to release air pressure. Jugs, glasses and pewter tankards were quickly produced.

During the meal, Viennese waltzes had played quietly on the borrowed gramophone, but afterwards, tunes from Jack Hylton's orchestra encouraged the younger ones to start dancing. Edward was happy to join in the fun as Elsie taught him some new steps. Most of the older men gathered around the barrel and further crates of beer. The older women collected together farther away from the gramophone. Some began the clearing up. By the time the friends from the Silver Band arrived, everyone, including Edward, had enjoyed plenty to drink, in between trying out the Camel Walk, the Jitterbug, the Shimmy and the Foxtrot.

The band struck up *My Old Man said Follow the Van*. Elsie began singing, and everyone joined in. A few more friends of the bride and groom arrived, and there were more songs and dances. William asked Elsie to sing *Always* for Cecilia. A hush fell over the room as everyone stopped to listen. By the last chorus, some were brushing away tears: *Not for just an hour, Not just for a day, Not just for a year, But always.*

It was as the band started playing *When the Saints Go Marching In* that Edward began to feel dizzy. He was sweating, and the room was hazy with cigarette smoke. He left the hall immediately and found his way to the presbytery garden.

Elsie, who had been watching, followed. Edward was unaware of her. She stopped in her tracks when she saw him on all fours inching forwards across the lawn towards bushes. Every few feet, he paused for a second, looked left and right and muttered something she could not hear. Under a rhododendron bush, Edward stopped. He shivered right through his body before being sick. Crawling further into the bushes, Edward turned and rested against the garden wall. Elsie assumed he was drunk. She was about to leave when he stood up and stretched out his arms as if holding a rifle. "I can't do this, sir," he called out, "It ain't right." He slumped to the ground again, muttering some more, and clasped his arms around his knees. Edward rocked backwards and forwards, seemingly unaware that he was banging his head against the wall.

"'Ello, Lass."

She jumped, and nearly called out, but saw it was Edward's father.

"Sorry love. Is our Ed with thee?"

Without looking in Edward's direction, she said, "He's not very well, but I'll stay with him till he's better."

Frederick looked puzzled and cast his eyes over the garden. "I can do that," and he started walking towards her, "'Appen you could get back 't party. It's too much grog I suspeck."

"It's all right, Mr Holmes. It's not the drink. I think he's had one of his nightmares. We have talked about them."

"Oh, lass. He might strike out, without meanin' 'arm. Wouldnay want thee 'urt."

"I'll leave him a while and go slowly," she insisted. "he's told me how you deal with it. I'd like to be here for him. I want him to know I'm not horrified."

"You're a kind lass, but I'll stay, 't be on't safe side. Don't 'appen much in't day. Be all the excitement." He sat down on a bench and patted the seat for Elsie to join him.

"He's over there in the bushes," she said. "He was banging his head." They sat together for a few minutes. "It's been a lovely wedding, Mr Holmes."

"Aye. 't has worked out grand."

"I think I'll just stroll towards him," she said, and she set off.

"I'll fetch water," Frederick suggested and hurried away.

As she approached, she spoke quietly. "It's just me, Edward. Elsie, here." She crouched down, so she was nearer his level. "Nothing for you to worry about. Can you hear me? I think you can come out now."

"Oh, bugger!" he shouted. "Go away! You can't see me like this."

"It's OK, Ed. I don't want you to worry, honestly. Your pa's gone for some water, but no one else needs to know about this. We'll get some fresh air together."

She continued to coax him, till he eased himself up and stepped back onto the lawn. His father was there in seconds, handed him the water and put an arm around Edward's shoulders. "All reet? All done?" he asked.

"Thanks, dad," he said. He rinsed his mouth out and spat in the bushes then finished a tankard of water. "I don't know what that was all about or what I did. Was it bad? Please don't tell mum or William."

"Nowt t' worry about, son. None other noticed. You've a grand lass here though. Get off through cemetery, and get a cuppa at Betty Bumbles by t'other gate."

***

They meandered down the long tree-lined drive, enjoying a breeze, and the skittish shadows cast from the sunlight through the leaves. By a flower bed brimming with purple salvias, crimson dahlias, tall yellow and orange daisies and soft pink buddleia, they stopped as Edward pointed out a pale blue butterfly with orange-tipped wings. Elsie moved towards it, "Can we catch it? It's so beautiful."

"I'd rather not. Butterflies have such a short life. We should let others enjoy it too." He paused and drew her towards him and kissed her forehead, then took a step back. "I'm so sorry you had to see what happened, Elsie. I'm so embarrassed."

"Well, I'm glad I was there. We've talked about these nightmares, and now I've seen one and know what to expect. It was soon over. And the bonus is we have the afternoon to ourselves." She pulled his arm through hers, and they carried on to the tea rooms.

There was a wake going on upstairs at the tea rooms, and no one else was downstairs. They snuggled together on a window seat holding hands, until the young waitress, dressed in a pastel green and grey uniform with a long white pinafore, brought them a pot of tea. It was served in a china teapot decorated with tiny pink rosebuds, with matching cups and saucers. "Very posh!" said Elsie.

"Nothing but the best for you, my lovely," he replied.

He turned towards Elsie and held her face gently as he looked in her eyes.

"Thank you," he said.

She leant into him and kissed him. The tea was untouched. They took a tram back to Lord Street and made love for the first time.

Towards a New Life

"I'm pregnant, Ed," Elsie said in a whisper.

"You're what?" He stared at her, feeling his eyes prickle. "Oh, my god, that's wonderful!"

"It's dreadful. My parents hate me." She snuffled into her hanky and began to cry.

"That's not possible. Can't be that bad."

"Daddy called me a whore!" She wept into Edward's shoulder, and he held her close.

"That would be the shock, Elsie," Edward offered, but felt like he could thump the man. "He'll come around when he realises that he's becoming a grandfather."

"I don't think so. Daddy said rotten things about you too."

"I can believe that, but Elsie, I'm so sorry love. We'll sort it. We'll get married. Things will work out." He was not at all sure how they would, but he had already thought about asking Elsie to marry him before he knew about the baby. "Perhaps your parents will think differently when they know I want to marry you."

"Sorry, Ed, I don't think there's much hope. They didn't want me to get back with you in the first place."

"Elsie Cooper," - he got down on one knee – "will you do me the honour of marrying me?"

She sank to the floor with him, "Of course, I will."

***

"Tha may 'ave been a chump son, but 'tis not so unusual. 'Tis life. Tha shan't be first nor last," said his father.

"You're not just doing the decent thing are you, son?" his mother asked.

"No! I swear I was going to propose, when I'd saved some more."

"That's good Eddie. I'm happy for you," but she frowned. "We can't have the fancy do we had for William."

"I don't expect it, Ma, but we should get married before - you know."

"I agree with you, son, and I am sure Dad will join with me when I say that we are happy to have you both here. We'll put a bed in the parlour for Joseph, and you and Elsie can have the room upstairs. It'll be big enough for a cradle as well."

***

On a cold November morning, Edward, Elsie, his parents and Joseph took the tram down to St Peter's Square. They crossed the main road full of carriages, cars, trams and hurrying people, who all seemed to be going in the opposite direction. The Register Office was inside a large red-brick building. Its façade was flat, broken up with rows of symmetrical windows at each level. It could have been a small factory. The lift boy directed them to the second floor. William and Cecilia were waiting there with one of Elsie's sisters, who carried a bunch of anemones to give the bride. Mr and Mrs Cooper stayed away.

The registrar ushered them into a room with subdued lighting and a small fire burning in the grate. There was some greenery on the mantlepiece and two candlesticks, each sporting a lit candle, both of which were half burnt away. A dozen chairs had been arranged, but there were only six guests, until a friend from the Silver Band arrived and another from the hat factory. Edward noticed Elsie smile for the first time that day. There was no dazzling dress for Elie. She wore the frock she'd had on for William's wedding - thankfully it still fitted well. It would not have mattered though because they all still had on their winter coats.

The words that remained in Edward's head from the short formal ceremony were: 'lawful', 'solemn' and 'contract.' There was neither music nor singing, and no procession down an aisle watched by the smiling faces of extended family and friends. When the official said, "It gives me great pleasure to declare that you are now legally married," Elsie sighed, and Edward hugged her and whispered,

"I love you, Elsie Holmes," and held her hand tightly.

When they got outside, it was raining, and they all ran to the Corner House to have tea and cake.

***

Elsie experienced the effects of Edward's nightmares a number of times, before the baby was born. Edward's restlessness could wake her and she would call his name gently and remind him where he was. It usually manged to wake him. Occasionally, she felt threatened, and had to slip out of bed. Rosa was always there to help her soothe him if she heard a disturbance. Daytime episodes were few because they avoided noisy crowded places, where possible, and moved away quickly from sounds such as factory claxons, shrill whistles, the hoot of a train. Elsie was becoming an expert at distracting Edward when she suspected an attack. Sometimes thunder was enough to bring on an attack or a smell like a bonfire. One time at the cinema, the reel of film snapped and was spinning and flickering. Edward thought he saw shell bursts. He went a bit crazy and the police were almost summoned, but Elsie got him out and down a quiet side street.

***

The baby was born the following May. It was a boy and they had decided to name him after her father, James, with Frederick as his second name.

Everyone was delighted when Elsie's parents agreed to come to the christening, and soon the Coopers were doting on their grandson and showing their love for Elsie as if they had never fallen out with her. They may not have loved Edward, but they got on so well with his parents that they all spent James' first Christmas together - Christmas Day at the Coopers' and Boxing Day at Lord Street.

Edward continued to work with his father. He made the best of it; accepting the responsibility of his new family. They worked well together, and Frederick made allowances when Edward had a bad night or one of his migraines. Some houses had been built in Hazel Grove, and Frederick won the contract to decorate thirty-five. There was plenty to occupy the two of them for several months. Tommy, Frederick's old friend and partner, had died in December 1918 from heart disease.

Elsie took up her singing again on Saturday evenings, and the landlord gave her a pound for two twenty-minute sessions. Usually, there were so many requests that her second slot went well beyond a half-hour, which is why he paid so well. Rosa and Frederick took turns with Edward to go and support Elsie and walk her back home.

The arrangement pleased Edward. There was always a thrill in seeing how much people appreciated Elsie's voice, but he also loved the time he could spend on his own with James. Edward became adept at changing nappies, giving cuddles and heating the unsweetened evaporated milk. He sang lullabies that Elsie had taught him, and read James the tales from Old Mother West Wind and Sky Island. It was the most relaxing time of his week.

***

As babies do, James often cried during the night. When he was about ten months old, Edward was woken by piercing screams, which he did not recognise as his son's. Elsie stirred quickly to attend to the child, but Edward grabbed her roughly and had his hands around her throat. The rumpus brought Rosa quickly, but she had to call Frederick to help. It looked like Elsie was in grave danger and it took both of them to calm Edward and make him let go of his wife. All Edward could say was, "Sorry, I was dreaming again." He was ashamed and scared of his own actions. How could he not know his own wife? He took his pillow and slept in fits and starts on the floor for the rest of the night.

At breakfast there were obvious marks on Elsie's neck. He apologised profusely and Elsie showed nothing but concern. She knew it was not deliberate. Edward was not a violent man, and she loved him, but perhaps their sleeping arrangements needed rethinking. "Perhaps separate beds would help," his mother suggested, but after discussions, it was agreed that Elsie and James should move downstairs to the parlour to sleep. Joseph could return to his old bedroom to share with Edward. Joseph, Edward thought, used to look up to his big brother. Now, he was the first port of call, when Edward had a disturbed night.

Edward missed the comfort of Elsie in his bed. The sweet early morning murmurings and gurgles, as James awoke, were no longer his privilege. A snuggle with Elsie downstairs, had to do, before he climbed miserably to his childhood room. He prayed that it would not always be like this, but could not see anything changing in the future if his nightmares continued.

He went back to his doctor, who had continued to prescribe the remedies issued when Edward left the army. Doctor Lewis stopped the prescription for the potassium bromide that Edward had been taking for several years, and started him on a barbiturate called Medinal. This usually gave him a deeper sleep, but the nightmares did not disappear. Furthermore, he found it difficult to wake quickly, and it was often mid-morning before he felt clear headed. His dad never troubled him about his early morning lethargy. Having to avoid alcohol was another setback for Edward. Sometimes he skipped his medicine for a couple of days, to have a night at the pub to listen to Elsie sing. Rosa and Frederick would always look after James.

***

A whole month passed before Elsie confided in her parents about her ordeal. She explained the circumstances, and Edward's problems very clearly. They sat grim-faced, in silence, until she had finished. "You leave that animal, and come back to us right now," her father demanded. "We warned you to keep clear of him!"

"He's not a bad person, Daddy, he's unwell."

"That may be," her mother's tears flowed freely, "but he could kill you or baby James."

"That's never going to happen. There's always someone to help. I love Edward, and I'm staying put."

"What about your responsibility to James?" her mother pleaded.

"We're married, mum; for better or worse. We've sorted everything, and he's got new medicine."

Later that day, Mr and Mrs Cooper rapped on the kitchen door and marched straight in bringing the storm of their anger. "You two have deceived us!" Elsie's father yelled at Frederick. "The girl is bewitched by him, and he'll be the death of her."

"Steady. Steady," Frederick's voice was calm. "My son's a grand 'n brave lad what's sufferin' due t' war. He's done nowt wrong."

Rosa busied herself with the kettle and tea cups. Elsie appeared with Edward, who was carrying James. "What's going on here? Who was shouting?" Elsie asked, looking from one set of parents to the other.

"How can you let him near the child?" her mother shrieked, and bustled across the room as if to take James from Edward.

"Don't you dare touch James!" Elsie warned. "I thought you'd understand, but you're full of hatred," and she stood between her mother and Edward. "Ed's a wonderful father and husband. We all understand him here, and one day he will be better.

If he wasn't so sensitive and loving he wouldn't have these nightmares," and she took hold of his arm and stood by him, firmly pressed into his side and glared at her parents.

"I'm sorry you feel like this, Mr and Mrs Cooper, but your anger is the sort of thing that could set me off," Edward said.

"You're an ignorant man! We're only concerned for Elsie and the child's safety."

"They are perfectly safe here, Maud," Rosa said, putting the teapot down heavily so that the tea slopped out of the spout. "We've made sure of it."

"Aye that's reet. 'Tis under control. Now go afore this gets worse. You've plenty of other kids to worry for at home," and Frederick moved to the back door and held it open. When they had gone, he bolted the door and leant against it. "Let's be 'aving that brew now lass."

***

Edward and Elsie were both miserable about their separation. The new medication made him sleep better, but he was often late for work, and felt he was letting everybody down. Edward could see no end to his being a burden to his wife and family. Would there ever be a time when he could be sure he would not hurt Elsie or James?

Once Saturday at the market, he bumped into Elsie's father who looked startled to see him. "Where's Elsie and James?" Mr Cooper asked. He glowered at Edward.

"They're at the park. Ma and pa bought us a lovely pram, and they're trying it out."

"Forget all that now." Mr Cooper, with ruddy cheeks, came right up close to Edward's face. When are you going to do the right thing?"

"What do you mean?"

"If you had anything about you, you'd leave our Elsie and James and get far away, where she won't find you."

Stunned by his words, all Edward could do was stare back at Mr Cooper's angry face. His father-in-law's eyes were full of fear. "What? Go where?" Edward managed. "I can't leave my wife and child."

"For god's sake, man. Have you seen the adverts for Australia? Only ten pounds! We'll not tell her where you've gone. Get on one of them blooming boats, and let our lass have a happy life with someone else." He suddenly pushed Edward hard in the chest, and Edward swinging back automatically, caught Mr Cooper firmly on the chin, and sent him reeling.

Edward immediately went towards him to apologise, but Mr Cooper pushed him aside and began to hurry away. "We'll tell folk you died; get gone!" he called back.

Edward watched Mr Cooper until he disappeared in the crowds. Then he sat down on the steps at the bottom of Underbank. Should he actually leave his wife and son? Could he? Weren't they managing? Maybe they should be more than managing. Elsie deserved to be truly happy, not simply happy enough. James needed a proper dad. Was he utterly selfish staying with Elsie? Hadn't the whole family been through enough with him? He wanted to talk to them, about his uncertainties, but they were the very ones he could not speak to. People stepped past him; one or two enquired if he was all right. "Just having a think about things," he said and continued to sit puzzling and conjuring possibilities. When he thought he had the answer, he decided to talk to Gerry.

***

"I d-didn't know it was this b-bad, Ed." Gerry's voice sounded shocked.

"Is it bad enough for me to go, then?"

"N -no. I'm r-really sorry you're still s-suffering is all." He handed Edward a bottle of beer. "C-can you t-tell what br-brings on the n-nightmares?"

"If only, Gerry. Yeah, too much drink, a headache, a smell, a noise. Mostly when I'm asleep. I see what happened in the war all over again, and the fallen men, and I have to act. I end up out of bed often. Later I don't remember much."

"N-no better at all since you came home?"

Edward shook his head, "When I think I am getting better, I have another bad one". He gulped some beer. "Whatever way I look at it, Gerry, I think Cooper is right."

"B-but you're m-m-married. The boy?"

"I know," and his voice faltered and he laid his head on his arms on the table and wept.

"Oh, Ed! This is C-Cooper's fault. You need more time."

"I don't know what to do," he sniffed. "Cooper's threatened the police. You know I hit him?"

"Bl-bloody hell, Ed... Can't you just st-stay out of his w-way?"

"That's impossible. Promise me, Gerry, that if I disappear, you won't give any hint of where I might have gone."

"If you th-think that's for the b-best."

"I think it would be best for Elsie – I don't know."

***

There was a second Christmas – not a shared event, like James' first, shortly after he was born. A jolly Christmas day was spent at Lord Street. James had new toys and knitted clothes. Edward sat on the floor with James and helped him with the building blocks he had made for him and the animals from a Noah's Ark he had constructed. His mother's Christmas dinner was its usual success. On Boxing Day, though, Elsie's parents had insisted that she come to them with James but without Edward.

Frederick and Joseph went out to the pub in the afternoon, but Edward declined, complaining of one of his headaches. Rosa was content with some back copies of Home Chat that a neighbour had passed on to her. There were new knitting patterns she wanted to look at. Edward said he would have a nap to shake off the migraine. He took a cup of tea and two aspirins to his bedroom in the parlour. There was no migraine, but his head whirred with more questions than answers. The situation with Elsie's parents was never going to change. He wouldn't be surprised if they tried to persuade her to stay with them. The Coopers didn't even want to spend time with Edward's parents, when they had become good friends before they discovered Edward's problem. And, it was his problem. Maybe they were right to be so concerned for Elsie's safety, and James. If he did go away, then where?

Uncertainty and fear for the future swam around inside him. His guts felt like there were two fish there, permanently at battle. How could he live without Elsie and James?

Edward, convinced he was a liability, battled with his magnetic love for his family and his selfish desire to remain with them; to just let things be; to pretend everything would be fine. It was impossible though, to shake off the humiliation that he and Elsie slept in separate bedrooms. He dreaded James' comprehension of reality as he grew older and that he should be frightened of his own freaky father. Who could blame him? Horrifying images of Edward hurting, really hurting Elsie or James shattered any hope he might still hold. A prowling shadow tormented his thoughts and clutched at his heart.

***

Dearest Elsie,

You know sweetheart how much I love you and always will. You are so patient, kind and always see the best in people. I didn't deserve your love, but you gave it anyway.

I think I probably stole you from someone who would have been much better for you.

Our trip to Blackpool in August, before your parents found out about me, was marvellous, wasn't it? They couldn't wait to see the back of us, so they could look after James for a few days. He came home with a pile of new togs too. Between our parents, he's never going to be short of something to wear.

What a grand time we had at the carnival in Blackpool. I know you enjoyed the floats, the music and the costumes. The crowds were a bit much for me, but we did manage to see everything. Good job you chose our digs out in Bispham. You thought of everything, as usual. We had the best fish and chips anywhere, walking along the prom. Makes my mouth water right now. We loved the calm sea lapping at the shore, the fresh air - so different from Stockport – the blue sky, the mad seagulls and the sunny days.

The zoo at Blackpool Tower was also amazing. I loved those big creatures. That ballroom and the jazz band? Even better than our town hall. Wouldn't you love to sing there? I hope you do one day. Wonderful memories.

Thank you, darling, from the bottom of my heart, for all you have done for me just by loving me and agreeing to marry me and giving us our beautiful son. Thank you for persuading me to see Dr Lewis again. Those new sleeping capsules have helped, but it is still all random. The bad times are forever. Remember, I hurt ma once, and dad has pulled me away from doing other violence, and now I've hurt you badly. It could have been even worse. I daren't think. How can we know if that won't happen again, even with our crazy sleeping arrangement? You must worry about me all the time. You know, because of my condition, I might not have married you, and now I think I have taken advantage of your generous heart.

I've decided to go away, Elsie. You won't find me in this country so don't let anyone waste time looking for me. My heart is broken, but you and James have to be safe and have a normal life. I can't go on being a burden. Maybe on my own, after time, this thing will stop tormenting me. You need to put me behind you. I've left a little money under my pillow.

I haven't told anyone else. I can't face my family, and knowing Ma she would probably lock me up to stop me, but I have to go. Please don't wait for me. You are a beautiful girl and will find a chap worthy of you. By the time you read this I will be gone, taking my deep and lasting love for you and James with me. Love him for the both of us, and try to be happy in time.

Goodbye my darling girl,
Edward.

***

There were posters everywhere, and adverts in newspapers encouraging emigration to Australia. *Men for the land. Women for the home. Employment guaranteed.* Assisted passages were on offer because Australia wanted to expand after the war. It was merely a case of going to an employment exchange and making enquiries. Few questions were asked – similar to enlisting during the war. Edward looked strong and healthy and the British government needed to reduce the dole queues. His willingness to

216

go was all that mattered. The basic price was ten pounds. For an extra two guineas, he secured a four-berth cabin on deck D. On decks E and F, there were eight berth cabins and some dormitories for up to twenty people.

Edward waited to board the Ormonde, at Tilbury docks, on January 5th 1925. First and second-class passengers went aboard first. Edward's line consisted principally of single men, who carried their personal items in small cases, brown paper parcels, or like Edward, in old kit bags. It was a cold day, but Edward was perspiring. He felt a little dizzy with the noise and bustle of the crowd, and he was conscious of his galloping heartbeat. In his jacket pocket, he had a letter from his doctor about his medication; Ross' address, and some photographs he had taken from the parlour. He wanted to look at these, but worried he might be jostled in the crowds and drop them.

Upbeat music was playing. Colourful bunting and streamers attached to deck rails fluttered in the breeze. There were some sad faces and folks clinging to each other in tears, but also a buzz of excitement. The chatter felt light and bubbly. The happy faces reminded him of the images on some of the posters he had seen. He watched some first-class passengers wearing furs and fancy hats, shiny shoes and expensive-looking coats as if they might be attending a wedding. They were supported by porters bringing vast amounts of matching luggage, while men in bow ties stood about smoking cigars. Some of the ladies posed on the gangway, like fashion models that you might see in the newspapers, to have photographs taken.

Edward became twitchy; his feet were itching to run away from the milling line of people and right out of the docks. He turned to leave.

"Watch it mate!" The man behind him looked aggressive.

"Sorry, just seeing how long the line is."

He gritted his teeth. Despite the low temperature, a clammy sweat crawled around his neck, and he had to wipe his hands on his trousers. The ache for home, Elsie and James, was palpable – as if his innards were being strangled, and taking away his breath. It was that feeling of loss again, that he had in the war. He closed his eyes and held on to his breast pocket until he was nudged forward as his line began the ascent.

The Ormonde had been a troopship during the war and hemmed in by the waiting crowds, Edward was reminded of his own embarkation to the Middle East. He knew one of the ports of call would be Port Said, to take on more oil. He had never imagined returning there, but in any case, as a third-class passenger, he would not have the option to leave the ship. Though, he would definitely be out on deck to look at the other stops on route.

Suddenly, the hubbub from bystanders and passengers increased with squeals, shrieks and cheers. He knew the crowd on the quayside would remain calling and waving, with passengers shouting as they leaned out over the rails. The emigrants and onlookers would stay until the Ormonde was pulled out into deeper water by the tugs. With no one to wave him off, Edward wanted only to reach his cabin, and claim a bottom bunk in a quiet corner away from it all.

***

A lot of pushing and shoving began. Along the narrow passageways, Edward kept his head down and forced his way through. He arrived a few seconds before the other three, allocated to D416, tumbled into the cabin. The tallest man, who was well built, with tight wavy fair hair and ruddy cheeks, introduced himself.

"I'm Sam and this is my kid brother, Ben. We're going to Perth to start a farm." His excitement was apparent as he shook hands.

"Going to Perth too. Meeting up with an old friend. I'm Edward."

The fourth passenger looked no more than eighteen. "Er. Adam. I'm going to Melbourne. Got an aunty there." He did not offer his hand.

"I have to get a bottom bunk 'cos I have nightmares and might even sleepwalk." Edward had promised himself to come clean immediately.

"Bloody hell!" Adam frowned. "Can't you bunk somewhere else?"

"This is all I could afford," he said calmly. "Actually, I'm not usually aware of what I'm doing, so if you think I'm a bit crazy in the night, it's best to throw water over me and sit on me," he added in more of a rush.

"We don't have to nurse maid ya?" asked Ben, looking very miserable. "For five whole weeks?"

"Hang on, hang on," interrupted Sam and looked straight at Edward. "Were you in the war?"

"Yes."

"That was years ago!" said Ben.

"Shut it! You were lucky to be too young, Ben." For a moment, he looked as though he might thump his younger brother.

"I was at Messines and Ypres in '17," Sam told Edward. "Went on for fuckin' months – madness – all for a bit of soddin' land, and no good to anyone after."

"Middle East first then France in '18." Edward offered, and Sam shook his hand again.

"Right," Sam continued, still holding Edward's hand, "bottom bunk for you, and I'll have the other. You two squabble over the top ones."

The room was little more than a box with narrow wooden bunks. The mattresses were about an inch thick, but sheets were supplied and a grey blanket. The space between was just wide enough to provide a small washbasin.

***

It was not an unpleasant voyage. In the third class, there was a basic lounge with tables screwed down and benches around the walls. A corner section was big enough to play either table tennis or shuffleboard. There was a smoking room, a small bar and tiny shop selling postcards, stamps, cigarettes and necessary items like soap and toothpaste. On D deck, in the evenings, someone was always ready to play the piano, and a sing-song would soon follow. Once a week there was a concert, film- show or magician to entertain. Third class passengers were permitted on C deck to get fresh air and were allowed in its lounge to attend the Sunday service with second and first-class travellers.

Edward went once, for curiosity's sake, but was astonished that the third-class passengers were ushered to sit down at the back of the room, as soon as they entered. The other passengers swept past them with their noses in the air, dressed in finery and dripping with jewels. At the end of the service, the third-class members of the congregation were asked to leave first.

Generally, days were spent playing card games, dominoes, draughts or shuffleboard and table tennis. Endless fun could be had passing a shuttlecock without it touching the deck. Arm wrestling contests sometimes developed into bare knuckle boxing. Edward avoided these, but Sam always won his bouts. Occasionally, fights broke out when too much drink was involved with gambling. The lack of women did not help. Five men to each woman. Adam, however, had struck up with a girl who was also travelling to Melbourne. They rarely saw him after that, and often he did not return to the cabin at night.

Some betting was involved in all the games but usually for pennies, cigarettes or food at meal times. Folk appeared anxious to hold on to the money they had brought with them. Edward had little appetite during the voyage, so he was not concerned about losing his rice pudding or a piece of cheese in a game of Cribbage or Poker.

Every clement day, Edward went up to C deck. He gazed at the vast sky and expanse of ocean. He loved the different colours of the water – sometimes bright turquoise and at other times, inky black. Toulon was beautiful with its mixture of wooded hillsides, gleaming deep blue sea and warm sunlit stone. There was little to see at Gibraltar, and the clustered building in Naples looked uninviting. These were good days, but he never stopped thinking about Elsie, James and his family. The ache in his stomach was permanent. Sometimes he sat alone, pretending to read a book, but studied the photos of Ethel and James and another of the family group at William's wedding.

In the thirty-five days it took to reach Freemantle, Edward had two disturbed nights. He was shouting, *"Bastards! Bastards!"* and his roommates managed to wake him up. On the second occasion, he fell out of his bunk and crouched beneath the basin, looking left and right. The brothers called his name then took a firm hold of him and walked him out to the lounge. They gripped him on either side as he wriggled and protested.

"We've got to save them," Edward called, "we can't wait here. Come on, lads. Don't be scared."

"It's OK, Edward. It's all done," Sam repeated. "We're all quite safe. Nothing happening here."

An episode in the dining room, however, was more serious. A group had begun banging their tin trays on the table in protest about yet another serving of burnt porridge. Edward held his head in his hands for a few minutes, but as he looked up, his face was twitching, and he eyes blinking rapidly. Then he leapt to his feet with a cry. He ran at the noisy group and began beating the first person he met. A couple of men at that table started laying into Edward, and it took all of Sam and Ben's strength to drag him out of the melee.

"What's 'is problem, the freak?"

"Fuckin' mad man. I'll bleeding show 'im."

"Stop! Stop! Sam called, and fortunately, there was some respect for him, due to his prowess in boxing. "Sorry, chaps, sorry. He'd too much to drink last night," Sam said as they dragged him away. "He'll be dead sorry he caused bother," he said finally.

"He'll be dead, period if he tries that again."

Edward wrestled with the brothers, like a trapped animal, but Sam was more robust than him, and Ben held on for dear life. They pushed him up to C deck for fresh air. When Edward recovered, he could not remember what had happened but had the wretched headache again. He thanked the brothers and wanted to apologise to the man he had thumped, but Sam advised against it. For the next few days, the brothers flanked him closely when they went for meals and made sure they sat well away from the man he had attacked.

Edward's sea legs were steady, and during a couple of rough spells it was his turn to help the brothers. Ben suffered so severely that he was ready to throw himself into the sea.

"Make it stop or just let me die."

Edward cleaned up after both of them, rinsed their clothes, brought water, and persuaded them to eat some dry bread.

The final few nights before they docked, he found it difficult to sleep. While at sea, he was neither in one place nor the other, but once the ship arrived; his old life would be over. He crept up to C deck several times, in the dark. Leaning against the rails, he took out the photograph of Elsie and James, though he could hardly distinguish them in the poor light. He still believed he had made the right choice. Both sets of parents would be on hand to take care of Elsie and James. But he worried about her being sad, and the boy crying for him. He cried himself, at the thought that as James grew up, he would have no recollection of his father. He would never again hear James talk. He'd never watch him kick a football, and hoped Joseph would show him how to play. There would be no whittling him new toys. He should never have married Elsie, but she was pregnant. Perhaps it would have been easier for her if he'd abandoned her then. But she had definitely been the one for him. Was that selfish? Thank God he had not injured her more seriously. Perhaps it was foolish to hang on to their photo. He wanted her to find happiness; to forget him. He contemplated chucking it to the wind.

But no, he clutched it more tightly to his chest and whispered a prayer for them.

***

His new life would now be at Ross' ranch. He would learn to shear sheep and manage the land. Edward had a letter from Ross to prove to the authorities that he had a job. There were also instructions on how to get there. Sam and Ben were going to the Farmers and Settlers Association. They would be taken out to some land that needed clearing and given ten shillings a day. If they cleared the area in in the time allocated to them, it would be handed over to them to farm.

The Ormonde entered the Gage Roads channel for Fremantle Harbour in the early hours of the morning. The ship anchored there until dawn, when a safe passage could be made to the quay. Crowds were already gathered on the decks for a first glimpse of their promised land. Although it was the middle of the night, in February, the air was dry and hot. The darkness kept the excitement to a low buzz at first, but as the cloak of night lifted, so the level of chatter rose. An extraordinary chorus of loud gabbling chitchat, infused with more piercing shrieks of joy, filled the air as the ship moved slowly to its allocated dock. Disembarkation took hours, and steerage class were the last to put their feet on Australian soil in brilliant sunshine.

Although Ross' ranch, Wallabungo Station, was eighty miles north, the officials knew of it. They read Ross' letter,

225

"How come you know Ross?" they asked.

Edward told them about how he and Ross had spent time together in a hospital during the war, and that satisfied them. They shook hands with him and pointed him in the direction of the tram that would take him to the railway station.

"When I get to Martin Street, I've to go to the pub and introduce myself," he told the three officials, who looked genuinely pleased for him.

"Ah, that'd be right. The Dunedoo," one of them said with a hearty grin on his face.

"Good luck to you, Tommy."

"You'll not look back."

"Have a wonderful life."

On the train all the windows were open, but relief from the heat came only in intermittent wafts of breeze. Edward remembered Ross' descriptions of his country, and that he called the land the bush or the outback. Very soon there were no buildings, just the vast landscape with strange dry red soil, a spectacular assortment of brightly coloured wildflowers, bushes, enormous ferns, clumps of trees and broader stretches of woodland. He smiled when he saw his first Western Grey kangaroos and stood up to the window to find more. For miles and miles, the land was empty of any humans. At a creek, he noticed a collection of exotic looking birds and some looked like the parrots he had seen in Egypt.

"Why is a station called Martin Street, in the middle of nowhere?" he asked a fellow passenger.

"Well, your first property owner out here was Henry Martin." He grinned at Edward. "Near everything is called after the family around these parts."

He located the Dunedoo quickly but decided to explore the town first. He was astonished at the wide straight streets and the grid line system of the roads. It looked neat and symmetrical and so different from the winding streets of England where houses were tightly packed together, often in rows of terraces. Here the buildings were usually single storey, wooden dwellings, built separately at wide distances from one another. The roads were dusty but the air was pure, unlike Stockport, with its smoke and fog. He discovered that the pleasant sweet smell that filled the air was from a Sandalwood plantation and sawmill on the outskirts of the town.

In the bar, they knew Ross Jackson.

"Biggest sheep station for miles."

"Ripper bloke! Spends well in town, and fair dinkum with shearers."

"Johnno, from the store, has instructions to get you up there."

"Reckon Ross 'll be stoked to see you."

Wollabungo

Johnno, at Martin's General Merchandise Store, assured Edward that it was only another hour's journey to Wollabungo Station, now that they had motors. He wore faded blue dungarees and his white hair, still thick and crinkly, capped a leathery face. His hazel eyes were welcoming and edged with laughter lines.

They were travelling up to the ranch in a flatbed truck with fold-down sides. It was stacked with assorted boxes, tubs, sacks and parcels, several rolls of thick fencing wire, and a brand-new axe. Johnno flung Edward's kit bag in with everything else.

"Climb up then," he nodded in the direction of the cab.

As Edward opened the door, he was met with warm wet licks from a large black and white collie. Edward patted him.

"Meet Jock. Had him from Ross these seven years." Johnno fussed the dog, and Jock's tail walloped up and down on the seat. "Not much at herding, but he's been the best pal."

He continued to chatter throughout the journey. His father had started the general store in a small wooden shack, at the foundation of the town, in the gold rush. Born in Martin Street, he knew everyone for miles around. He spoke of two of his sons killed at Gallipoli, and he told Edward that Ross had lost his parents to the Spanish flu, shortly after the end of the war. Ross now ran the ranch with his younger brother and sister.

"He's always glad of an extra body."

"I'm ready to try anything."

"Good on ya, mate."

With Jock snuggled between them, the truck trundled and rattled on, in the baking sunshine, Edward was sweating heavily and kept wiping his brow. Johnno pulled up in the welcome shade of some trees and passed Edward a flagon of water.

"Have a drink. Then slosh some right over yourself."

Edward stepped down from the cabin and relished the refreshing water as it soaked his hair and shirt and dripped down his back. The intense heat would have him dry in minutes. Taking a breath, the air seared his nostrils and his throat. He drank more water, and poured the flagon over his head again. Johnno laughed.

"Will take a while. Need a good hat and always carry water."

Ten minutes later they were driving under the wide wooden arch that carried the name of Ross' ranch in bold blue letters – Wollabungo. In smaller print on the right-hand side - Jackson property. They progressed up a drive edged on either side with tall trees. Their dramatic red flowers made Edward gasp. He had seen similar trees on the way, but here the trees were bunched together. The contrast of the blossoms, with the green leaves and baked earth, was spectacular.

"Red flowering gum trees," Johnno said, "always the last to flower towards the end of summer."

The drive suddenly opened out to reveal a wooden single-storey building, painted in cream. On either side of a double grand-looking oak door, Edward counted four shuttered windows. Just below the level of the tin roof, a bullnose roof, covering a veranda, stretched along the front of the house. Tables and chairs were placed at intervals with tall potted plants between. Johnno drove twice around a circular bed of mixed flowers, lying in front of the house, and tooted his horn as he went. He stopped at the foot of the steps to the grand-looking door.

Edward heard dogs barking as he climbed down from the cab. At the top of the steps he turned and looked beyond the bed of flowers to an immense span of bleached grass stretching to the boundary. A line of poplar trees marked the fence line, which continued beyond the width of the grassy area – the lawn. A large pond lay to the left, and deck chairs waited under a canopy of the red gum branches. Edward could make out a croquet set, and marked to one side was a giant chessboard with painted white squares and burnt grass squares. The pieces lay in a muddle.

The front door opened behind him, and as he turned, Ross clasped him in a bear hug, "Strewth! Bloody hell, Eddie. You made it!"

"Watch it," Edward shouted, "I need my breath."

Ross was twirling him around so fast that they stumbled and laughed like small boys. Johnno chuckled too as he was unpacking the flatbed.

"Holy-dooly, Johnno, come on in and help us celebrate. I never thought to see this old cobber again."

"Yup. Don't mind if I do. I'll have a small Bundy."

"Rum's a good notion! You'll enjoy it Eddie. Not like the shit we had back then."

"Could I eat something first?" Edward asked.

"Ah, Nora'll fix up some grub. Come on in."

The front door opened onto a wide corridor. Woven rugs in reds and greens lay along the polished wooden floor. Another passage ran left and right about halfway along. Ross took them beyond the intersection to a door on the right, which led to a huge room with a stone fireplace. There were comfortable sofas and chairs with occasional small tables and a card table, bookcases, a writing desk, a grand piano, and in one corner a homemade bar with rows of wines and spirits in a cabinet. Edward loved the floral wallpaper with greens, orange and coral colours entwined in an exotic pattern. A dado rail ran around the walls, painted in a green shade that matched a colour in the wallpaper. At a higher level, works of art hung from the picture rail, but over the fireplace, and dominating the room, was a striking portrait of a man and woman in smart riding clothes. Thick peach coloured curtains hung at the long windows, which opened like doors onto another veranda that overlooked several paddocks, one behind the other, at the side of the house. Edward could see horses.

"This is our family room, Ed. My sister, Sophie is the arty one, and chose all the decoration after ma and pa passed. Wallpaper sent from England."

"I love it. Really smart."

Ross was ringing a small hand bell, and even before he replaced it on a table, a plump woman with grey hair, tied in a neat chignon, bustled into the room.

"Ah, Nora. Two extras for grub tonight, but the lad needs something to be going on with. Eddie this is the wonderful Nora, who looks after every one of us. This is Eddie all the way from England."

"Pleased to meet you," Edward said, shaking a floury hand that Nora wiped hastily on her stained apron.

She smiled at him, "You met this one in the war, didn't you?" she said nodding towards Ross.

"That'd be right."

"Well, bless you, son. You're very welcome here," and she held on to his hand for a moment longer than was necessary, and looked into his eyes and smiled, before leaving the room.

"Nora's been with the family since before I was born. Couldn't manage without her. Her husband, Danny, looks after our horses, and their son, Greg, is one of my stockmen."

Ross poured generous measures of rum into cut glass tumblers, but Edward waited until he had eaten a thick cheese sandwich, brought within minutes by a girl wearing a spotless apron. She looked about fifteen.

"Thanks, Mary," Ross said.

"Yes, thank you," Edward echoed, "That's great."

She blushed, bobbed a tiny curtsey and scurried away.

"Mary helps Nora with cooking. Only been here a couple of months. Sweet kid, but dead shy."

"You have servants." The intonation of a question was definitely there, and Johnno snorted,

"There's a lot of folk here, Eddie." Johnno continued.

"The house and grounds need as much looking after as the sheep," said Ross. "I don't treat any of them as servants. They are all essential, and do a valuable day's work to keep Wollabungo going."

"Aye, 'tis a bonzer job to be taken on here," said Johnno.

"Let's get the gear in the truck put away before we eat," said Ross, "Then I'll show you where you'll kip."

Johnno dumped Edward's kit bag on the steps, and the three of them squashed into the cab, followed by Jock. The dog sat on Edward's knee and licked his face. As they moved off, Jock put his front paws on the open window frame and stuck his head out. Johnno drove down the left-hand hand side of the house and beyond, to all the buildings at the back. They passed barns, smaller sheds and a large raised water tank, next to a well that was surmounted with a windmill water pump. Johnno stopped at one barn and jumped down to pull off a couple of crates. He disappeared inside for a few minutes. Beyond what Edward thought must be stables, the truck halted again, and Ross helped move the rolls of wire from the truck to an open sided shed, where there was plenty of other equipment. They turned back towards the house but had a further stop at a massive pile of logs – some still sizeable tree trunks. Here, they left the axe with a young man who was stripped to the waist, sorting the wood into different piles. His bronze torso glistening with sweat, and his blond hair was tied back with a bit of string. A tattooed snake in green and red wound its way from his wrist up the length of his right arm. It continued across his shoulder, before its tongue finished at the back of his ear. Edward knew this would be quite out of place in Stockport.

"Bloody good show, Ross," the man said, "just what we needed," and they shook hands.

Finally, Johnno pulled up outside a fenced and gated area at the back of the vast square-shaped house. Through the gaps in the fence, Edward could see what looked like an enormous allotment. When they entered the enclosure, carrying the remaining parcels, Edward realised it was a very organised vegetable garden with a small orchard. The veranda he had seen at the front of the house was duplicated here. They followed a path that skirted this until they came to the back door, which was wide open and latched back. Just beyond the kitchen, in a yard with a vine growing on a trellis, was another well with a hand pump. Further on again, an area where washing flapped on several lines. He noticed another woman, folding sheets.

"Leave it all out there, please," Nora called from the kitchen. "We've already got the table set."

They piled the packages neatly on the table and chairs nearest the back door then entered the kitchen. It was four times the size of the kitchen at Lord Street, with a long wooden table, down the centre, set for at least a dozen people. There were two sinks, and cupboards from floor to ceiling with glass in the upper half of the doors, displaying sets of crockery. The range and stone fireplace took up the whole of one wall.

"Ready in twenty," Nora said, looking at a fancy clock in a decorative wooden and glass case above the mantelpiece. A brass bell, like a school bell, sat below it. "Mary will ring in fifteen."

Ross showed Edward to his room, at the front of the house. Unlike his poky ill-lit bedroom back home, this had two long windows almost from floor to ceiling. From the front, he could see down the drive some way and to the bottom fence of the garden. From the side aperture, one could step onto the veranda overlooking the paddocks. Crisp white sheets, on the large bed, peeped out at the edge of two plump pillows, and over the top of an embroidered royal blue bedspread. One wall was painted a paler shade of blue with beige and copper leaves in vertical rows. Edward took in the wardrobe with drawers at its base; a washstand, complete with matching jug, bowl and several towels. A full-length freestanding mirror filled one corner.

"You've a grand place here, Ross," said Edward feeling out of touch with this new environment. He was about to drop his old kitbag on the bed, but decided the floor would be more suitable. Even compared with the impressive house in Bramhall, which he had helped his dad to decorate all those years ago, Ross' home, was beyond anything he had imagined.

"Great grandad and Grandpops did well in the goldrush," Ross told him. They built this together over forty years, with dad's help eventually, and started with just 100 sheep. But hey, have a quick scrub-up. I'll knock on when the bell rings."

As Edward entered the kitchen, he saw the table covered in steaming dishes of roast potatoes and several vegetables. Bowls of unmistakable lamb stew made his mouth water. Plates of bread, cut thick, were placed at intervals down the table. At home, Edward thought, they would have call them doorsteps. Jugs of water, homemade lemonade, and a collection of bottled beers stood at each end of the table. The lemonade made him think of his mother, followed by Elsie and James. He had a sudden wish that he could have brought them to this place, and his guts felt wobbly. In that moment of reflection, he lost his appetite.

The kitchen soon filled with more people - Ross' brother, Oliver, not so robust as Ross, but taller, stood up and shook Edward's hand. "Heard a lot about you, fella," he said.

"Not all bad, I hope," replied Edward, feeling a little uneasy.

"Not at all – you're very welcome," Oliver said and slapped him on the back. Their sister, Sophie, smiled and nodded to him. She had long golden hair, tied with red and green ribbons wound together. Nora sat down with her husband, Dan, and their son, Liam. There were two more stockmen, Jarrah and Bardo, who were Aboriginals. Mary, and Charlotte (from the washing line), Jayden (the snake man) and Logan, a stable hand, all greeted him.

The room was filled with chatter about a barn roof repair, fencing posts, a new pasture for some pregnant ewes, and a foal about to be born. The date for the next shearing needed a decision and plans were suggested for the accommodation for the shearers. Edward was wide-eyed and pondered how he would fit in to this busy community. He ate slowly at first, still churning thoughts about his family now so far away. The food, however, was delicious, and not having eaten much for most of the journey from England, he took a second helping of the stew. Although lemonade was his choice of drink, he soon felt sleepy and asked to be excused.

"Not before a night cap of Bundaberg rum, you don't," declared Ross, and there was a general cheer as clean glasses were passed around.

As he carried a second glass off to his room, Edward had to admit that the smooth brown liquid was like honey compared with their war rations.

***

A tapping on his bedroom door woke him to intense sunlight. He knew it must be way past early morning, and for a split second, he wondered where he was. He was just about to speak when Nora entered, carrying his large pitcher from the washstand.

"How's it going, kid?" She poured some hot water into the basin, "We're fixing lunch right now."

"Is it that late?" he said, sitting upright. Then, remembering his nakedness, he pulled the sheet up again.

"Nothing to fret over. It'll be there when you're ready; just bread, cheese and cold meat." She began to pick up his discarded clothes from the night before.

"You don't need to do that," Edward protested.

"These'll need a wash after your journey. Don't worry. Some of Oliver's old clothes are in the wardrobe. He's grown out of them, but they're still decent. He's more your build than Ross, but we need to put some weight on you!" She chuckled as she bustled out.

He knew he needed a wash, and it had been a long time since he'd enjoyed some hot water. The sweet-smelling soap and thick towels were just the job. The wardrobe revealed a few short-sleeved shirts with double pockets. He chose a pale green one followed by a pair of brown leather trousers, and a plaited belt that was easy to make as tight as he needed. There were socks, underpants and boots that reached above his ankles. They were a little too big, but he tied them tightly as well. Finally, a wide-brimmed leather hat that made him smile as he remembered Johnno's words from the day before. Trying it on, in front of the mirror, he felt self-conscious and decided not to wear it to lunch. He tidied his bed, and feeling cleaner and more relaxed than he had done in months, he made his way towards the conversation coming from the kitchen.

"Here he is," beamed Ross. "Grab some tucker. I want to show you around the place. Know how to ride a horse?"

"Never tried, but I'll give it a go," he said.

"We've a beaut lined up. Gentle ol' girl," added Dan. "Never been a stock horse, and plenty of kids learnt on her. She's saddled ready."

"Right," Edward managed; a little taken aback at the speed of everything.

"Ross, leave it till tomorrow," Sophie interrupted. "Let me give Eddie some instructions if he's never even mounted a horse before."

Edward was thankful he had collected his hat. The heat enveloped him as soon as he went outside, even though the height of summer had passed. The stables were brick-built around two sides of an irregular quadrangle. On the shortest side, lay Nora and Danny's thatched home. Edward stopped and stared, thinking of England once more. The open side of the quad led out to paddocks. Each of the twenty stable doors was painted blue and held a name plaque and a horseshoe. Jarrah was mucking out, and Bardo swilling down the yard. Liam, busy grooming a huge chestnut horse under a shadier overhang, waved to Edward. The horse was gleaming with perspiration and snorted several times as he was sponged down. Its tail switched away flies. Edward was hoping his mount would be somewhat smaller. Then Sophie and Dan appeared from a stall leading a dappled grey mare. It was a relief to see it was not as high as the chestnut. She had a distinctive white stripe down her face.

Her name was Shadow, and as Edward walked across to them, the horse nuzzled into the side of

Sophie's head. "Stand still in front of her," Sophie said, "and stroke her muzzle and neck."

Edward loved the softness of the lowest part of her muzzle between her nostrils. "Hello Shadow," he said, and she raised her head. "I'm going to learn to ride on you."

"Oh, heaps good," Dan chuckled, "I was gonna tell you to talk to her."

"First, we're just gonna walk with her around the paddock," said Sophie. "You can hold her reins, but I'll be on the other side. Keep chattin' to her," she added.

Shadow walked steadily, and Edward spoke softly, calling her a lovely girl and telling her he hoped he wouldn't disappoint her. At the end of the circuit, he stroked her neck again and leant into it, feeling the coarser texture of her mane.

"OK, let's get you up," said Sophie. "Stand on her right side and hold her reins, then put your left foot into the stirrup - I'll shorten them once you're on. Hold onto the saddle; swing yourself up and over, then place your right foot in the other stirrup."

Edward did not quite make the stretch with his first attempt.

"No bother," she said. "Reins in your left and grab the saddle with your right. As you swing over let go the saddle." She went through all the directions slowly. Edward had to sit square; hold the reins in a particular way; keep a straight back without being tense; use his calf muscles for cueing Shadow, and place his feet in the stirrups, not jam them. Horse and rider walked slowly several times around the paddock, with Sophie at their side repeating the instructions as they went. The lilt of Sophie's calm voice was encouraging.

"I have to control my body and Shadow's at the same time," he said.

"'S hard yakka at first, but you're doing good," Sophie said and beamed up at him. He returned the smile and felt more determined to succeed.

"We'll have a break, so you feel your legs again, then we'll see if you can get the hang of trotting. Ross is keen to take you around the place. It's ripper to see it from a horse rather than the Ute."

"I think I'll need to do more than a trot," he said.

"Fair dinkum. You're not frightened of the horse, are you?"

"No. Shadow's lovely."

"Then we'll have you on a canter in no time."

They tethered Shadow and went for lemonade and cherry cake in the kitchen.

"How ya going?" Danny asked, following them in.

"Loving it. The horses. And everything else," he said, looking around.

He felt himself blush so he turned away and pretended to cough.

Dan followed them out to watch as, this time, Edward mounted Shadow in one go.

"Sweet as!" he called and left them to it. With Edward back on Shadow, Sophie explained that to trot, he only needed to squeeze his calf muscles a little tighter into Shadow's sides. She had to remind him to keep his hands close in, holding the reins. "You'll bounce around a bit, but you'll soon get the rhythm. Don't be tempted to press harder than you need or she'll go too fast."

***

The following day, Ross was eager to set off on a tour with Edward.

"We won't go as far as the grazing pastures. Just to a billabong that should still have enough water to bathe and cool down."

They adopted a walking pace at first, and it was not difficult to talk. "Did you get home quick, when it all finished?" Edward asked.

"Yep. Shipped out straight off. Those galahs didn't know their arses from their elbows."

"Galahs?"

"The idiots - so called in charge – during the bloody battles. I think there was stupidity on all sides."

"Some great blokes though, Ross. Too many lost."

"Yep. Let's not get maudlin." He started talking about the ranch and how it had taken his folks years to clear the land for grazing. "They had to find and channel water then build the wells. The Abos were great with that. They know nature better than anybody."

How far does your place stretch?"

"As far as you can see and all the way around," said Ross.

It was hard to focus on riding correctly. Edward wanted to gaze at the limitless blue sky and the ever-extending country with its strange trees and flowers. A mixture of colours - from pink to red and purple, and white to yellow and orange, then combinations of all of them. Everywhere he turned, he was distracted by something new. But each time he stopped concentrating; he lost his riding rhythm and nearly fell off. Ross laughed, waiting for Edward to regain control.

"You're going to get bum sore and aching muscles you didn't know you had."

"There is so much to take in. I mean, look at that outcrop of rocks! They're shades of red and brown and all the different pockets of wildflowers sprouting in crevices. Those tuffty bushes – are they grey or green?"

Ross smiled, "Reckon I don't look very hard anymore."

"It's extraordinary. I'll have to do some drawing."

It was no wonder Ross had not been so impressed with the hospital garden in Egypt, Edward thought. They stopped chatting while Edward practised trotting again, and apart from their hoofbeats, the silence was pure and comforting. The soft breeze created by their movement caressed his face.

The Billabong, shaded by a few trees and some craggy rocks, did have sufficient water. They undressed, ready to plunge in the water when Ross stopped and held a finger to his lips. He ran in his bare feet to his horse and brought back a rifle.

"Quiet!" he whispered. "I think we got company. Feral dogs. Come for the water, and they're a sodding nightmare for the sheep. They put the ewes off lambing. We shoot on sight."

They ducked in the rocks and waited.

"Can I have a go?" Edward asked. I think I'll still be a decent shot."

"Good on ya. Be my guest," Ross said, and he handed over the rifle.

A pack of five dogs moved cautiously out of the bushes on the other side of the water. Edward decided to take the dog at the back of the group, and as the others began to scatter, he shot two more. The final two fled in different directions.

"Bonzer shooting, mate. You'll come in useful, Eddie. Now we need to move the bodies away from the water before all the scavengers arrive or we won't be able to bathe." They dragged the dead dogs about twenty feet into the bushes before heading back to the other side

The water was soothing in the heat and the sticky blood from the animals soon washed away. Afterwards, they rested in the shade of the trees, and Ross brought a few beers from his saddlebag.

"What's the story then, Ed? What's brought you out here now, besides catching up with me?

Edward took a few sips of beer. There was no point in hiding the truth. "Remember the time you found me under the bed in the hospital?"

Ross looked puzzled but nodded.

Edward paused again, then sat up and looked at Ross. "That shit never stopped. Did you get to France after Egypt?"

"Sure did. Fuckin' lousy hell hole. You?"

"Me too. Everyone I knew got shot down or blown up. My nightmares got worse there. I have tablets to help me sleep, but they don't always work."

"What are you telling me?" He turned to face him. "What happens?"

"I sleepwalk."

"And?"

"Well, I can be a bit rough."

Ross looked at him and raised an eyebrow.

"Even with people, I care about. I can hurt them, without knowing it at the time."

"Shit man, that's a tough deal for everyone."

"I know." He paused. "I've attacked one of my brothers, my ma and then my wife."

"You did what?" Ross grabbed hold of his arm. "And you got married?"

"Yes."

"Where is she?"

Edward shook his head, and his eyes stung as tears began to prickle his eyelids. "We've got a child too. A little boy, James."

"So, where the fuck are they?"

"I couldn't trust myself any longer, Ross. I left to keep them safe; let them have a good life."

"Bloody hell!"

"I hoped I'd get better at home, but Stockport is a sprawling mass of houses, side-by-side, and you can't escape the haunted eyes of the bereaved parents on the streets; in the market; at the pub. It's smoky and noisy. So many things set me off. I should have left ages ago, before I married. Elsie is such an angel, though, she helped me, understood me, but I still hurt her."

For a while, Ross sat silent, drinking. "You're here for good?"

"I think so, but if I'm a nuisance to you, I will move on again. I promise."

"Well, we'll get you fixed up with a doctor here. Johnno'll know someone who knows the right man. Maybe the change of scene, the fresh air, will make a difference. You're a brave man to do what you've done. I'm prepared to give it some time, but I'll have to tell everyone."

Squalls

Ten days later, Dan announced at breakfast that the mare was ready to foal.

"Is she restless?" asked Sophie.

"Defo," said Dan, "up and down these last two hours, and sweaty. Just waiting for her waters to go."

"Want to watch, Eddie?" Sophie asked across the table.

"That'd be great," he said, "but Ross might have other plans for today".

"No worries, man. It's bonzer if you've not seen it before. We'll get you doing proper work real soon," and he smiled. "You can't lounge around the stables forever."

"That's not fair, Ross," Sophie said, "won't be much use till he's a strong rider, and he does his share around the yard."

"Just teasing, Soph. Eddie'll have a go at everything."

Feeling uncomfortable, Edward was about to interrupt when Liam muttered something under his breath. Edward thought he caught the word, 'drongo,' but Sophie was pushing out her chair rather noisily, ready to leave. Edward left with her, but when they looked in Maggie's stall, she was lying down peacefully.

"Let's do a few rounds in the paddock. Danny'll call us," Sophie suggested.

Edward was continuing with riding lessons from Sophie, and spent part of each day at the stables. He liked all the horses, got to know their temperaments, and soon learnt how to groom, tack up and muck out. Everyone shared the tasks. Most of the horses were Aussie Stock Horses or Walers, with a couple of Percherons and two chestnut Arabs. It was one of the Walers, Magic Night – nicknamed Maggie – that was due to produce a foal. Edward loved trying to sketch the horses but found it more difficult than birds.

Sophie was not instructing from the sidelines any more but joining Edward and Shadow on her horse, Archer, as Edward practised trotting and cantering. She had also started Edward jumping, from a trot, over the lowest of poles. The first few times it was one pole set about four inches off the ground. Then Danny helped her create a short course in the paddock, and she raised the height of the poles a few inches each day. Edward was ready to canter to a jump that morning, while they waited for Maggie's foal.

They had shortened his stirrups, and he remembered to lean forward and get his weight central on Shadow's back, but he set off before Sophie said to go. After the first two successful jumps, he speeded up, and the rhythm was not quite right. Shadow kicked the pole then stopped abruptly, and Edward fell off.

He was on his feet immediately. "Sorry, my fault," he said to Sophie, and he patted Shadow, and started to remount. Liam was sitting on the railings, laughing.

"Like I said, bit of a drongo, eh," he called.

Sophie shouted, "Everyone falls, Liam. You know that."

"Suppose. Anyway, Maggie is about ready if you can tear yourself away."

"What's his problem?" Edward asked as they watched Liam walk away.

"Hmm. We've a bit of a thing going."

"He's your boyfriend?"

"Yes."

"Well, I'm married, Sophie. I'm not going to cause any trouble."

She stopped in her tracks. "Oh! Well, where is she?"

"Story for another day, Sophie."

She stared at him. "Fair dinkum," she said, but she sounded puzzled and went ahead to the stables.

Maggie was pacing and pawing the ground but stopped as her waters gushed out.

"Good girl," Dan called.

"Does that mean the foal is coming?" asked Edward. The mare lay down, and Edward thought she looked tired.

"She'll be right now," Dan added. He knelt down next to her and stroked her neck, then her belly and shifted her tail, which he had plaited earlier, out of the way. "Don't spook her, but come around here, Eddie."

A white opaque bubble appeared at Maggie's rear end, and he could see the shape of a hoof inside it and seconds later another. Then he was sure he saw its head, but it receded, and Edward gasped.

"It's grand, that'll happen a few more times before she finishes her contractions," Dan told him.

Edward watched her belly ripple, and suddenly the foal flopped onto the floor tearing the membrane.

"You bute!" Dan called as Sophie began to clap, and Edward followed suit.

The dark brown perfect colt wobbled onto his feet and crashed to the floor again, and Maggie started to clean it down. After another five minutes, the colt was trying to stand once more, and finally his four legs held him up, and he began to search for a teat.

Edward could not stop smiling. "I think we need a beer, Dan!"

***

The following day, Bardo was taking a horse and cart to Johnno's store for provisions. Ross asked Edward if he wanted to follow on Shadow and help pack at the other end. "It'll get you used to a longer ride, but still gentle enough."

Edward was happy with the distraction. The day was pleasingly warm but fresh with a few clouds, and Bardo went at a steady pace. It was easy to keep up and take in the landscape. A few of the trees were beginning to change colour.

Johnno greeted them at the store, and when they had filled the cart, he suggested The Grand Hotel for lunch. It was a smart wooden two-storey building, painted cream with green shutters and a red roof. The name reminded Edward that he had once been inside the Grand Hotel in Llandudno, with his family. They had been staying at a boarding house on Mostyn Street but were drawn to the enormous elegant building sitting at the edge of the Great Orme and overlooking the pier. His dad had treated them all to a Sunday lunch there, when Edward was about twelve. He remembered how they had all spoken in whispers, and his dad kept telling them to sit up straight and mind their manners. Women, dressed in black, with pure white aprons, frilled at the edges, served them. The building they were now in, was more like a large pub, with rooms above, and no one was speaking in a hushed voice. They had a meat pie with tasty gravy for lunch and a couple of beers. Laughter, smoke and the babble of conversation filled the bar.

Back in the kitchen that evening, the men agreed that the weather was on the change. Another stockman, Connor, had come down to tell Ross that fences needed repairing in the northern pasture.

"We'll get going on that first thing tomorrow," Ross said. "Eddie you can join us. I'll need Jarrah and Bardo, but Liam I want you to make sure there's plenty of water in the tank in the homestead pasture, and start checking the ewes' feet. We'll do a sheep dip when I get back."

The next morning, they rode out with double saddle bags stuffed with provisions, thick gloves, and some smaller tools. The main essentials: posts, saws, hammers, the wire and cutters were already in storage up in the pasture. Ross carried a rifle and gave one to Edward.

"More dogs?" Edward asked.

"Probably, and roos. They're most likely the cause of the broken fence."

By the time they reached the north pasture, it was mid-day. Edward was stiff and sore but did not complain. The store was a large three-sided deep wooden structure with a tin roof. Shelves down one side were full of equipment, and several tea chests were stacked in a corner with a small cart in front of these. Jarrah hitched-up his horse to it. They stopped briefly after filling the cart, to eat the sandwiches Nora had made. Then Jarrah set off, and the rest of them rode ahead to the damaged fence. Ross gave Edward further tips on cantering, and he was glad to practise in the wide-open space instead of a paddock.

They spent a couple of hours working together on the fence, wearing the thick leather gloves for the treacherous wire. Each section was crisscrossed with baling wire; then barbed wire wound on top. The posts were placed only a yard apart to make the fence as secure as possible, but Ross said, "Some boofhead roos will still give it a go."

No dogs appeared, but as the sky was clouding over and it was becoming humid, Jarrah spotted a group of kangaroos. He called them marlus, near a ridge slightly higher up from the pasture.

"They're huge," Edward said, noticing their dark greyish colouring with blacker patches on their elbows.

"That's a cert! The bigger buggers are near twice the size of the females. Grab your gun. We'll get a few."

"Can they jump the fence?"

"Yes, but most seem to know barbed wire hurts."

"We know that, don't we," Edward replied.

"No harking back, mate. This is now," and he patted Edward on his shoulder and smiled.

"The gunshots will make them run like the wind's up their jacksies, so we'll choose our targets first," Ross said. Edward removed the gloves and rubbed his sweaty palms on his shirt. They consulted briefly then checked their rifles. Edward stared straight at his mark, raised his arms and aimed. Ross must have been ready at the same time as two grey backs fell simultaneously. Then a frantic chase followed, to ground a few more. The beasts moved rapidly but, foolishly, they were moving towards them. Although Edward had seen kangaroos from the train, he was surprised at their size and long sturdy legs with large back feet. They could undoubtedly leap the fence if they wanted, he thought. He and Ross both winged a couple more and moved closer to put them out of their misery, as the rest leapt away. Jarrah and Bardo picked up one carcass between them. There would be a kangaroo feast later in the week.

When the gunshots had faded away, a hushed stillness fell over the land. The birds ceased their cawing, hooting and tweeting. The leaves were as still as a painted picture, and the warmer air coiled around their limbs making them sweat as they returned to the storage area.

"Storm brewing," Jarrah called. After this, the effort of riding in the pressing heat stopped all conversation. The massive sky turned a steel grey like a heavy vault ceiling. Suddenly, lightning cleft through the glowering sky, and the land was fissured with a splash of light. At that moment, in Edward's mind, the ground was fracturing. He shuddered. Three seconds later, a furious boom bowled over them.

Shadow cantered straight past the northern pasture barn, before she began to slow her pace...

Believing the enemy was closing in fast, Edward dismounted with the rifle. He sank to the ground as the rain began to hammer the red earth. With the gun slung on his back, Edward crawled into a cluster of bushes. Prepared to face the Boche; the rifle was ready. Someone was shouting over the rolling rumbles coming from above, and the thrumming, he believed, of shrapnel fragments falling all around. All that mattered was staying close for the first grey uniform. Edward squirmed down further into the ensanguined mud and heard his name called.

"Eddie! Eddie! It's me, Ross"

"Reg!" Edward yelled back. "I'm coming. Stay put!" Something moved ahead of him through the wall of rain and Edward fired.

"Eddie! Eddie! Stop now!"

"I'll get you, Reg," Edward wriggled out from under the bushes.

"Eddie! It's Ross. It's over. Drop the gun! It's over."

"I can't leave yet. It's Reg. I promised."

"Reg is OK, buddy. We can go now." Ross came right up and knelt by Edward. He took the rifle, released the magazine, and emptied the chamber. Then he put his arm around Edward. "Nothing to worry about now, choom," he said as he helped Edward to stand up.

"No! No. He's dead, isn't he?" Edward said and started weeping. Ross held him closer as if cradling a child.

Bardo was sent back to the barn with the cart and Shadow in tow. He took Ross's saddle, so that Ross and Edward could ride Hunter together. There were instructions for Jarrah to build a fire, put a large billycan of water to boil, and cook some beans and sausages. "Find blankets and some spare clothes in the tea chests," Ross said. "Get yourself dry. I'll bring Eddie."

As Edward settled, Ross said, "At least I know what you're dealing with now."

"I'm broken, Ross," said Edward as he shook his head from side to side.

"You'll be right, mate. You were just a kid when you set off to do your bit; I was older and probably dealt with it better."

"I'm far away from childhood now, Ross. I want to be normal."

"We'll get you to that doctor."

"Made a fool of myself," said Edward. "I'm sorry."

"None of that, Eddie."

"What will the others think?"

"They'll think what they're told. Let's get back to the shelter, and see if we've some grub to eat."

Ross jumped adroitly onto his chestnut Arab, and pulled Edward up behind him. "Hold onto me, and we'll take it slow."

For a few minutes, Edward was nervous without stirrups, and worried in case he should flex his legs accidentally, and encourage the horse to move faster. The rain was never-ending, but the thunder and lightning were declaring themselves further away. Their slow pace helped him relax against Ross. He let his legs dangle and was content.

"Can you tell me about Reg?" Ross asked. Calmed by Hot Sox's ambling gait, Edward felt able to describe the day when he lost his last friend in France.

The glowing fire was visible at the entrance to the barn before they reached it. They tethered Ross's horse inside, with the others, and fed him. By the time they had cleaned up and changed out of their sodden clothes, Jarrah and Bardo were dishing out the food. Ross produced beer, and said he was going to teach them all an old convict song. They laughed a lot as they attempted to catch the tune and follow the lyrics:

Cut yer name across me backbone,
Stretch me skin across yer drum,
Iron me upon Pinch island,
From now to kingdom come,
I'll eat yer Norfolk dumpling, like a juicy Spanish plum,
Even dance the Newgate hornpipe,
If you'll only give me rum.

He persuaded Jarrah and Bardo to provide a traditional Aboriginal song. Bardo made clapsticks, and he and Jarrah hummed together for a while before breaking into their own language. The rhythm was slow and the tone melancholic, and although Edward was enjoying it, he became very sleepy.

Blankets were dragged out, and they bunked down well away from the entrance. For a few moments, through the dying flames of the fire, Edward watched the repeated dance of fat droplets crashing into the earth and listened to what sounded like a thousand pebbles hitting the tin roof.

Sometime during the purple night, Edward was shaken awake by Ross.

"What's happening?" he asked, and yawned.

"You were calling out in your sleep," Ross said. "Just wanted to be sure, you're OK."

"I don't remember. Probably dreaming some crap. Sorry."

"Don't want you wandering off in the dark. I'll lie right next to you, so you'll trip over me if you move, and wake me up."

Edward fell asleep almost immediately and woke only when he heard a billycan drop. The daylight was pewter grey, and it was cold, but the rain had stopped its teeming and splattering. Jarrah was already up and had made another fire. They drank coffee; refilled the tea chests; made notes of what needed to be replaced, then set off for Wallabungo.

***

"There's no simple solution," Doctor Gaskell, in Perth, said. He was older and taller than Edward, clean-shaven with a scar across his left cheek. His hair was neatly cut with grey flecks at his temples. He looked directly at Edward. "You know, we used to call it shell shock, but a single label doesn't fit the many symptoms the lads came home with."

"I've not met anyone else who has nightmares like me," Edward said.

"I have, believe me," the doctor emphasised. "The trouble is no one talks about it, and that's because what I call war shock was treated as cowardice for a long time."

"I know. There was a lad charged with cowardice," Edward said. "I knew him from back home."

"And what happened to him?"

Edward returned his gaze for a minute. "Even if he was a coward, they shouldn't have made me..."

Doctor Gaskell dragged his chair closer, "You were part of the firing squad?"

Edward nodded. "It still makes me cringe with shame," he said quietly, "he was murdered because he was scared."

"That must have been hell. I'd have felt exactly the same, but you knew you'd have been next if you had refused."

"Maybe that would have been the right thing to do."

"Rubbish, man!" The doctor got up and brought Edward a glass of water. "War forces us to abandon the precepts we learn as children. You were thrown into the turmoil with little preparation and expected to perform the most terrible deeds. It was the same for all of us."

"You served, too?"

Doctor Gaskell nodded. "Hmm – not Gallipoli but France. I was based at the number two Aussie General at Wimereux, near Rouen. I saw what war did to men." He paused and returned to his desk to look at some papers. "You were just a kid, eh?"

"Yes. I joined with my older brother."

"So, you'd just turned eighteen when the bloody hoo-ha ended?"

"That's right, sir."

"No need for sir," he said and smiled at Edward.

"Thank you. I didn't get home for months," Edward added. "That wasn't good either. It was during that time I knew I'd got a problem with the nightmares. I thought they would go when the fighting stopped."

"Do you think you could tell me why that lad ran away?" the doctor asked, coming to sit nearer to Edward again.

Edward released a deep breath, and shut his eyes. "He was scared, like all of us. Our sarge was being really tough. Most of us knew he had to be, but the more he shouted, the more Matt got everything wrong." He hid his face with his hands for a moment. "He was a good lad," he continued. "I knew the family back home. That's partly why I tried to get out of it."

"Are you able to tell me what happened?"

Edward clasped his hands together. He tried to start a couple of times and began to gyrate his hands, as if he were washing them.

"It's all right. You don't have to tell me, but I think it helps."

Edward held one hand tightly in the other, sat upright, and his recollection came tumbling out. With an artist's eye for detail, he described Sergeant Floyd, and his colourful language, Father Quinn and

Mathew Casey, not forgetting the precise little square of white cloth that had so suddenly turned bright red.

"Thank you," the doctor said, and Edward was surprised and looked up. "Have you spoken about this before?" Doctor Gaskell asked.

"A little – to a good friend."

"Ross?"

"Not this; only generally."

"I'll bet you came to Australia to try to be rid of your demons and keep your family safe."

"That's right. My family is safe; I still have demons."

"I believe it's good to talk it all out, so keep visiting me. Talk to Ross; he was there too. Try to enjoy the peace and beauty of our amazing country. Soak everything in, and let the terrors out." He rang a small bell on his desk and a lady, wearing a pretty pale green dress with yellow flowers, came with a cup of sweet tea for Edward, before he left.

Doctor Gaskell returned to his desk and began to write as Edward sipped the tea. "Are you going back to Wollabungo today?" he asked.

"No, it's too far from here. Ross has us booked in somewhere. We'll get the train back to Martin Street tomorrow then pick up our horses."

"You've a good friend there."

Edward smiled. "The best."

***

Several days before the sheep shearing season began, everyone except Dan, Nora and some of the girls who worked at Wallabungo rode out to the sheds to prepare for the shearers. The chap who had been hired to cook all the meals came with them. Cookie had his own horse and cart full of pots, pans, tins and potatoes. Jarrah followed with another cart carrying beer, rum, a full round of cheese and boxes of extra cakes and biscuits prepared by Nora.

As they approached, stockmen were already driving sheep into paddocks. The main building was long with stalls for twelve shearers on the ground floor and basic accommodation above. There was a small cook house on one side of the well. Tables, under canopies, where everyone could sit and eat, were nearby. On the other side of the well was a wash house and two dunnies, set about thirty yards away. At the back of the main shed were holding pens, passageways and compartments for the sheep to be shuffled, sorted and guided to each individual shearer.

Each of the shearers would be arriving by bicycle, carrying their own shearing equipment and anything else they might need for the few days they would spend at Wollabungo. The group from the homestead cleaned, swept and arranged everything for their arrival. They dragged out palliasses from storage and aired them outside, each with a blanket, before placing them in the cubicles in the loft of the shearing shed. They checked the well and the fences to the larger paddocks and counted the sheep arriving.

The shearers reached the sheds, more or less en masse, the evening before shearing began; their hollering and good-humoured jawing was heard before they were seen. A cloud of dust enveloped them as they rattled in on sturdy bikes, built especially for rough riding, with strengthening stays to stiffen the frame. The men looked like red sand monsters and shook themselves down as they laughed and cheered and made straight for something to eat and drink.

Edward was to be a roustabout, (an apprentice who learns all the jobs on a sheep station) helping to collect, sort and press the wool for packing or clearing wool tufts from the floor. Ross instructed him to sit and observe the first session. There were four runs of two hours each, starting at seven-thirty with a smoke break at nine-thirty and lunch at twelve o'clock.

He admired the speed and accuracy of the shearers. Each aimed to clip up to a hundred sheep per day for four days. They were paid per animal, with a bonus for the person who had clipped the most. No one spoke, but the constant buzzing of the mechanical sheers and thrumming of the steam generator became spellbinding. The men worked like machines; each action repeated with precision on every sheep pushed towards them. They never looked up.

The belly wool was removed first. Each section of a sheep's coat had to be placed by the roustabout in a different container. They then threw the fleeces across a slatted table for the wool to be skirted; picking out all the fibres, seeds, burs, sweaty bits and droppings as fast as possible. The finished product would then be rolled and classed before going in the final bins. When these were full, the collection was flattened with a mechanical press as tightly as possible and stuffed into bale sacks for transport. Once shorn, a couple of jackaroos steered the sheep into larger paddocks at the back. The flock waited here before returning to the grassiest pastures. Ross oversaw everything and kept his own tally for each shearer.

Edward just had to keep up with the pace, but he soon got into the rhythm and found the whole experience satisfying if exhausting. He wondered what his family would think if they could see him in his new job. At the end of each day, the shearers, aching from being bent double all day, did exercises or lay flat on the ground then paced up and down, before they could even take a shower.

By six-thirty in the evening, all were washed, to some extent, and ready for a feast. They cheered when Cookie appeared with pots of stew and beans, bread and cheese and brownies. Afterwards, the booze came out and they smoked and swapped stories. Someone played a mouth organ while a couple of others began a song about the life of a sheep shearer. Most were dead to the world by nine-thirty. Ross and his brother, Oliver, slept on either side of Edward's cubicle, but thankfully he slept soundly for three nights without incident.

On the last day, the whole party travelled back to the homestead for wages and a farewell shindy.

Some wives and girlfriends were there to greet the shearers, and everyone piled into one of the large barns. Trestle tables were laid with food and drinks with benches to sit on and bales of straw around the walls. In one corner a small band was already playing jolly music. Sophie sat down, quickly followed by Liam, opposite Edward and Ross.

A fiddle, banjo, double bass and accordion played upbeat music; unfamiliar to Edward. The Aussies clapped or cheered to most of the tunes.

Ross elbowed Edward, "Ah, this is a great one!"

"Ever been to a Bush Dance, Edward?" Sophie asked.

"Can't say I have. Didn't know there would be dancing," but Edward was already tapping his foot."

"We'll have you joining in real soon," Sophie said, giving him a broad smile, which he returned.

Liam glared at him. "Yous not learn to dance in your country, eh?"

"Of course, but to more town and city sort of music."

"Our music not good enough?" Liam snapped.

"Don't be a drongo, Liam," Ross said, "cut the snide remarks."

"The music's grand. I'd love to learn some new dances," Edward said. He looked straight at Liam, who gave a brief nod, but there was a definite curl to his lip and contempt in his eyes.

"Skull a couple of beers, Liam," said Ross, "and don't spoil the evo."

There was an awkward silence for a few minutes. "The dances are easy to pick up and shuffle through," Ross said. "Bruce, on the squeezebox, 'll shout out moves for some of the rounds."

"OK."

"And avoid too much grog with the dancing," Ross whispered in Edward's ear. Edward nodded.

The tables were removed. The dancing began, with a lot of clapping and exclaiming from the party-goers. The rhythm was fast, with a significant beat. Most people were dancing in lines facing each other, but there was plenty of twirling, twisting and spinning. All were smiling or laughing, and Edward couldn't wait to join them. Once in the middle of it, the moves seemed less frantic. Contra dance was straightforward, with two lines facing each other down the length of the barn. Each person on the right moved down the line dancing with every person on the left. Sometimes the women added unexpected spins or an additional step. It was great fun. When the people on the right ran out of partners, they raced back to join the top of their line.

After an hour, the band stopped for a break. All the dancers retreated to the straw bales at the sides of the barn. Liam staggered across to where Edward was sitting. He plonked himself down next to Edward. "Yous had enough yet?" Liam asked, speaking slowly as if his mouth was too full.

"It's good fun," said Edward.

"Crikey! Not bedtime, then?" Liam's voice went up an octave.

"What do you mean?"

"We all know Ross is... is protecting yous. Not the true blue, are you?"

Edward got up to move away, but Liam grabbed his arm and pulled him down. "Tell us all your little worries. I'm all ears," Liam said, twisting towards him, and flecks of spit splashed Edward's cheek as Liam struggled to enunciate each word. "Get stuffed, Eddie boy! Yous weak, just a galah. Stay away from my Sophie." Sophie approached in time to see Liam's firm hold and hear him shouting

"Liam, let go!" she called. "He knows I'm your girlfriend."

"He doesn't know when it's time to go home, though. Does he?"

"That's enough," and she sat on Liam's knee and pulled his arm around her.

Edward moved quickly to the other side of the barn, just as the lad who had been playing the banjo started to sing: *A strapping young stockman lay dying, His saddle supporting his head, His two mates around him were crying, As he rose on his pillow and said...* and suddenly everyone joined in a chorus,

Wrap me up with my stockwhip and blanket, And bury me deep down below, Where the dingoes and crows can't molest me, In the shade where the coolibahs grow.

Edward no longer felt like more dancing. As the band struck up again, he left to go to bed. He decided as Liam was drunk, to act as if nothing had been said, but at breakfast the next morning, there was no sign of him. Sophie was very quiet and hardly looked up from her plate.

"A ripper time last evo," said Bardo.

"And a few sore heads today," added Ross, with a chuckle, "judging by the gaps at the table."

"Couldn't rouse our Liam at all," said Nora, "not like him. Did yous fall out, Sophie?"

She looked up, startled. "No, but Liam did drink too much," and she blushed, her eyes glistening.

"What's up, Soph?" asked Ross.

"Nothing," she said. She got up and left the kitchen, her breakfast untouched, apart from having taken only one bite from a piece of toast.

"We'll have an easy morning," said Ross, "wait for everyone to catch up. Need to start on the dipping, and some of the old ewes need culling."

Cookie had provided the shearers' last breakfast in the barn, where the shindy had been held. Everyone went out to wave them off. A group of shearers larked about. A bike had been hidden, and there was chasing and laughter. Some of the men were struggling to fit their possessions back into the containers they had brought with them. A cheer went up as they finally wheeled down the drive, and Edward felt a tug on his arm.

"Sorry about last night," Sophie said. "He can be decent. I don't know him like this."

"Don't worry, Sophie. We'll avoid each other."

"But I want to be friends with anyone I choose."

"Thanks, but I'm going to have a word with Ross and see if I can be out of the way for a while."

***

"They've grown up together," Ross said. "Supposed to be getting engaged on her birthday or Christmas."

"She's a sweet girl, Ross, but I'm not after another relationship."

"I know that."

"Still, it worries me that Liam has a spiteful mind, but maybe it's just for me."

"He's a kid. Never had any competition before, and suddenly another good-looking fella turns up."

"What about the other young men at the station?"

"They wouldn't dare!"

"Neither would I."

"Look, we'll get the dipping over. I'll put you and Liam in different paddocks, then you and I will go off for a week or so to look at all the other paddocks, as the stockmen return with the sheep."

***

The next few months were taken up with checking all the pregnant ewes and culling all those that were not pregnant. An outbreak of parasites on a large group of sheep meant summoning the vet. He blamed it on unclean shearing machinery brought in by one of the shearers. Some sheep had worms. Fences, wells, the quality of the grass for grazing, kangaroos and dingoes; all needed constant monitoring. By the end of August, the new lambs were arriving daily. Everyone who could be spared, plus a few itinerant workers, helped. The ewes had been divided into smaller groups to make the process more manageable, but it was a task that could leave little time for sleep during September.

Edward worked hard and usually slept soundly. His nightmares were less frequent, and had not led to any violence, which gave him hope. His family never left his mind, and sometimes the notion that they should have come with him was a torment. He regretted that they had not seen the incredible life to be had in Australia. The ache he had for them and his parents made him lose his appetite on occasions, like their birthdays. In late October, Nora celebrated her birthday on the same day as his mother and he could not join in the fun. He made excuses to forgo the birthday tea. In his room, he reminded himself that there was no point to ifs and buts. The decision was right at the time, and they would surely have moved on without him.

***

In his spare time, Edward drew and whittled. Gradually, he perfected his illustrations of the horses. The favourite was Shadow, but there was a soft spot for Ross' mount, Hot Socks, so named because of white patches between his hooves and fetlocks. Definitely a magnificent chestnut with sturdy shoulders and a broad chest, but Edward particularly loved his strong forehead, wide eyes with long lashes and the way the forelock fell. He found it easier to draw the horses when they were tired and still, towards the end of the working day. At this time, though, Liam was often home from the pastures and helped out at the stables. Edward continued to avoid him.

There was plenty of wood for whittling. Edward admired the reddish-brown colours of the sheoak tree, when he had it polished, and the dark chocolate acacia wood. Dan's workshop was stacked, and he was happy for Edward to work there. Finishing off a pair of candlesticks one afternoon, Liam burst in then stopped immediately.

"Where's dad? What are you doing here?" he said.

"Your dad lets me use the tools so that I can make things."

"Why?"

"Why does he let me, or why do I want to make things?"

"Smart arse aren't yous? "You fucking pom. You take advantage of everything."

"I'm making Christmas presents," Edward said, hoping this would put an end to the accusations.

"Who the hell for?"

"All of you, actually."

"Well don't bother making anything for me!" He moved over to the workbench and picked up a candlestick.

"How did ya wangle it all anyroad?"

"What do you mean?"

"All our workers have to prove themselves first. Yous just waltzed in and got taken on." He threw the candlestick back on the bench and began to walk around to Edward's side.

"I work as hard as anyone else," Edward said, putting down his tools.

Liam was standing up close to him, and wagging his finger in Edward's face. "Yous don't know ...," he began.

Just then, Dan entered. He stared at them for a moment. "Both of you come with me. It's Shadow. She's down and won't get up."

Shadow was prostrate, in the full heat of the sun, while the other horses were standing under the shade of the trees. She was sweating and snorting, and the pulse in her neck was clearly beating rapidly.

"That's not the hot weather," Dan said. He started to examine her legs, feeling gently up and down a couple of times. "There's a sodding fracture just below her knee."

"Bloody hell!" Liam said.

"What does it mean?" asked Edward.

"You drongo! We're gonna have to shoot her."

"Oh, my God! I'm sorry." Dan, looking at Edward. "I know you love this horse." He turned to Liam, "Go and fetch a gun."

"Can nothing be done?" asked Edward. Dan shook his head and began to stroke Shadow. Edward knelt to talk to her as he had done right at the start of his riding lessons. "You beautiful girl. You're a champion," he said.

Sophie came hurtling through the yard and into the paddock in front of Liam. As she reached the horse she fell to her knees and wept. Edward leaned towards her and put a hand on her arm. He was grabbed at his shoulders and lurched away so that he landed on his back. Liam threw the gun towards Dan, and was on top of Edward, astride him and pinning him down.

"You fool!" shouted Dan, "the gun could have gone off," but Liam was preoccupied with punching Edward in the face. It was difficult for Edward to defend himself because one of his arms was under his opponent's knee.

"Stop! Liam, stop!" yelled Sophie, trying to grab at him.

"Hands off my girlfriend!" snarled Liam, and with each word he landed another thump. Sophie had to jump to one side.

"Stop, Liam! He didn't do anything."

Amid the commotion, the crack of a gunshot echoed around the paddock. Liam leapt to his feet. Sophie screamed. Edward rolled over and curled himself into a ball against the belly of Shadow.

"At least that put a stop to your stupidity," his father shouted. "Get out of here, Liam!"

He scowled at his father. "Come with me, Sophie."

"Get lost!"

"Please yourself!" Liam growled and walked away.

"I haven't done it yet, Sophie," said Dan. "Thought you might like to hold her."

After the second gunshot, Edward remained in the same position, murmuring something to himself. Dan crouched near to him.

"I won't leave you, Gerry," Edward was saying. "I'll get you fixed."

"Eddie, it's Dan here. Righto?"

"I have to get Gerry some help." He unfurled himself and leant against Shadow. Edward's nose was dripping blood, but he took no notice. Sophie pulled out a handkerchief and moved towards him, but Dan took her arm. "Take a mo, love. He's in the war again, like Ross told us."

"How do we help him?"

"We tell him that we're not in the war anymore, and we're all friends here, but slowly. Just keep talking."

"Hey Eddie, you know me. It's Sophie. No soldiers here. We're all safe. Can you stand up?"

Edward slumped to one side and was motionless as Sophie repeated her comforting words.

Gradually, he turned, blinked a few times and stared at her. "Oh, sorry, was I ...? I heard gunshots."

"Yes, but nothing dangerous. Liam was an idiot again, and he's made your nose bleed. Take my hanky."

He wiped his face and started to get up. "Oh, crap! Shadow. I'm so sorry Sophie."

"Never mind that now," said Dan, "let's get you cleaned up, and I need words with that son of mine."

***

It was customary for the family, including Nora, Danny and Liam, to exchange presents after supper on Christmas Eve. They all gathered on the veranda as the day cooled down. When it was Edward's turn, he gave Ross a framed coloured drawing of Hot Socks; Oliver a multi-tool penknife and Sophie a sketch of Shadow. The candlesticks went to Nora and Danny, and he gave Liam a handmade cigarette box.

From Nora and Danny, Edward received a couple of new shirts and a leather water bottle with a strap. The burnt initials on the front were very fancy. Nora said they were from all the family. There was nothing personal from Liam. Ross and Oliver presented him with a new leather hat and belt which fitted him better than Oliver's cast-offs. Sophie gave him a set of drawing pencils and a pad of paper. He grinned at her, and when she returned a smile, he noticed her eyes were a mixture of green and blue with a hint of brown around the pupils. The thoughts mulling around in his head were not selfish nor lustful. Their friendship had been a real bonus, and the way she had looked after him on the day Shadow died. Maintaining his gaze, however, he was sure she should do better than Liam.

Edward's chair jerked backwards, and he dropped his bottle of beer. It spilt down his trousers, and the bottle rolled away.

"Look who's peed his pants," scoffed Liam, before landing an upper thrust on Edward's chin, sending him reeling down the veranda steps.

There were shouts of disapproval from everyone, but Liam was squaring up for a fight. He lunged at Edward, who side-stepped the blow, but returned a hard jab, with his right, to Liam's cheek. As Liam came at him again, Edward remembered his boxing training, at the end of the war. He blocked and parried several incoming punches until Liam kicked him.

There was shouting, but Edward wasn't listening. Leading with his right again, he gave one almighty uppercut to Liam's jaw, who fell instantly, landing on the beer bottle, which broke under his head. Blood began to ooze at the side of his face.

Only a second of silence followed before Nora screamed. "Look what you've done!" and she ran towards Liam and knelt beside him, caressing his cheek. There was no stirring him. "Come on, son. We'll get you fixed." He did not move. Edward glanced at the others and saw a frozen tableau of dismayed faces. He looked to Ross for guidance and watched him gesture with his hand to stay out of the way.

Edward stepped to one side as they all rushed to towards Liam.

"I'm sorry. I didn't mean," Edward called. No one was listening.

Ross, Oliver and Dan lifted Liam. Sophie looked concerned, while Nora examined Liam's head. "You'll be dinkum, son. Just get you bandaged," she said, but her voice was tearful.

Edward watched the group move inside, and was uncertain whether to follow. Looking away from them, the broken bottle and patch of blood glared at him. For a while, he just sat on the veranda steps staring at the blood red. He told himself that the sticky shape, turning maroon, was just from Liam's cut and nothing more. The viscous mess had already excited some flies. The blood, however, was like an accusation. Again, he forced his thoughts to be reasoned. Liam had attacked first, and not for the first time. Was Edward just supposed to stand there? He went to fetch a shovel and brush from the stables.

Having removed all traces, he decided to take one of the horses out. Choosing a bridle and saddle, he walked down to the paddocks and found Samson. He held the harness over the horse's muzzle and guided the bit gently past the incisor teeth. Then he placed the saddle over the wither and slid it back to its natural resting place. Making sure it was balanced, he fastened the girth.

He trotted Samson around the paddock once, then out to the open land, and was soon cantering. The warm evening prompted him not to push Samson too hard. The release of energy helped Edward to rationalise what had happened. He had deliberately used an expert blow, but only after being brutally punched by Liam, who had shown no signs of desisting. Edward had not looked to where the bottle had landed. There had been no time before Liam struck him. Once they had patched up Liam, everyone would agree it was just bad luck that Liam landed on the glass.

Ross was waiting for him at the stables. Samson needed grooming before returning to the paddock.

As Edward dismounted, Ross moved nearer. "We'll get him sorted together, eh?" he said.

"Is Liam all right?"

"He's awake but groggy. Dan and Nora have taken him to Martin Street. He probably needs a couple of stitches.

"You know I was only defending myself?" Edward said.

"Yes. But... Look, I know he's a drongo, Eddie, but he's family. We all grew up together. He's almost another brother, and without Nora and Dan, when our folks passed, we'd never have managed. I love them all. We all do."

"What are you saying, Ross?"

"I'm really sorry but I'm afraid his parents want you to leave."

Edward dropped the brush and stumbled backwards. He felt sick and could not find words to respond.

Ross came around to him. "I'm sorry Eddie, I'd just like to straighten him out, but the truth is he's never going to leave you alone, if you stay here."

"But where would I go?"

"You'll do well on any farm or station. You get stuck into everything and do a good job. Johnno always knows where there's work. What d'ya say?"

"I thought they liked me"

"It's not about that."

"What about the nightmares?"

"Come on, Eddie; you're tons better."

"Maybe. But I'll have to explain, all over again, to people I don't know."

"Yes, but you are getting better at spotting the triggers. Be upfront with people. I think folk will understand. Everyone here did."

Samson whinnied, and Edward picked up the brush and started grooming again. "When do you want me to go?" he asked.

"I'm not happy about it, Eddie, but I think you shouldn't be here when Liam comes home. Get some space between you. I'll come down with you to Johnno's tomorrow. We can stay at the hotel for a couple of nights."

"So soon? I can't believe it. It's been wonderful being here."

"You've done well. Eddie. No matter what Liam says, you've been an asset to us."

Edward leaned into Samson's neck and wrapped his arms around the horse and let his tears fall.

"It's a mess Eddie, I know, but we'll stay in touch. Yes?"

"Sure."

"Get back to the house. I'll take Samson down to the paddock."

Rather than going through the house, and meeting anyone, Edward went to his room via the veranda. He packed and sat on his bed thinking about Elsie and James and regretted yet again, not bringing them. They had missed everything Edward had loved about being at Wollabungo. Moreover, he believed that Liam would not have bothered with him if he'd seen him as a family man.

The clock in the living room struck midnight, and he wondered about Christmas Eve in Stockport. What would be wrapped up to surprise James? His mother should be preparing her Christmas feast. It was weird having a summer's day at Christmas; it might be snowing in England. Would they be thinking of him?

He wished he had some of Ross' excellent rum when he heard a tap on his door. It was Sophie, with puffy eyelids and red cheeks. "I'm so sorry, Eddie. It isn't fair." She stepped forward and wrapped her arms around him. Edging her back to the door, he shut it quietly behind her.

Her head rested on his shoulder. Sophie's golden hair, hanging loose for once, felt as soft as warm silk against his neck. Her scent reminded him of freshly made lemonade. The comfort of being held by a woman was irresistible. Sophie pressed into him. He kissed her hair then her cheek. "Please don't marry Liam," he said.

"I won't. He's a pig!" She lifted her head and looked into his eyes.

"I still have to leave," Edward said.

"I know." She raised her slightly parted lips to his.

Their love making was urgent, passionate, then tender, and he felt no guilt in the moment. They fell into a deep sleep until stirred by the dawn chorus and bright light of the opening day. Sophie dressed. They embraced once more, and she crept away.

Edward washed, dressed and tidied his room. He was hungry now, but wondered about showing his face in the kitchen. Notwithstanding, he wanted to say goodbye. He moved out to the veranda for a smoke. A couple of Kookaburras flitted from branch to branch on a eucalyptus tree before their fiendish laughter irritated him. As he turned away, he saw Ross approaching along the veranda and waited for him.

"Thought you might be up early," Ross said. "Let's walk down to the paddocks."

"Yes, I'd like to see the horses one last time."

"I am sorry it has to be this way. I feel I've let you down."

"I've had the best of times, Ross. Being here has brought me back to life. You've been so generous."

"You can have good times anywhere now, Ed. The nightmares are much more under control. Just don't let them be a shock to someone."

"You're right. I won't hide it any longer. I'm going to have more adventures, and we will keep in touch."

"Always, me old choom!" and he slapped Edward on his back and pulled him into a hug.

"Whoa!" Edward called. "You'll have the old tears flowing. Thanks for everything. Can I say goodbyes?

"Course. Come and get some grub. They don't hate you. It has to be for the best."

Breakfast was uncomfortable. Thankfully, Liam wasn't there, but he couldn't look at Sophie, and Nora seemed to be paying extra attention to what was on her plate. The conversation was limited to jobs to be done at the station that day. No one brought up the fact that Edward was leaving until Dan said, "We're sorry Edward. You're a good man and you've been a great help around here, but we can't let..."

Edward knew everyone's eyes were on him, and stood up before he made a fool of himself. "You've all been the best. Thank you for everything. I won't forget you." He began to leave the room, but Nora rushed to him with a box of food. Dan had wrapped some whittling tools in a leather pouch. Oliver shook his hand, and Sophie said, "Stay safe."

"I've got a tent you can have," said Ross, "might be useful if you wander around for a while."

Clearing the Way

Johnno did have notion of a prospective farmer, further north-east, who was looking for another labourer to clear the land for wheat. He did not have the exact address, just the nearest station.

"He needs everything completed by the beginning of July, or it reverts back to state ownership," Johnno told Edward.

"I'm not afraid of hard work," Edward nodded. "It'll suit me fine."

"We'll sort out trains to get you as close as possible," Ross said, "Though, you might have a walk at the end. The folk at that town will know the man because he'll be doing his shopping there."

Edward shrugged his shoulders. There was no need for further discussions about the situation. In fact, he wanted Ross to go back home. His friend should be with his family on Christmas Day. The suggestion of Ross staying in Martin Street with him for a couple of days did not interest him under the circumstances. Ross was typically being kind till the last minute, but Edward felt queasy in his stomach and there was a lump in his throat. It was almost as bad as when he left England. He couldn't talk pleasantries any longer. "I'll need plenty of my tablets to take with me," he said to Ross and Johnno. "The nearest doc could be miles away, if the farm is remote. I'll go and see if the doc can see me this afternoon."

"On Christmas Day?" Johnno asked.

"Of course. Well, I'll poke around the store," Edward said. "See if there's anything I might need to take with me, while you two search the map and train timetable."

Edward bought a small oil lamp with some oil and spare wicks, soap, extra pairs of socks, underpants, another pair of boots and a knife – like the one he had bought for Oliver. He chose mint humbugs, aniseed candy and a stash of cigarettes with matches. Then he slipped out of the store. He walked down the main street to a pub, where he didn't have a drink, but did buy a bottle of rum.

When he returned to the store, they told him that he would have to wait two days for a train because of it being Christmas. The train would terminate at Dolwolani, which was the nearest he would be able to get to the land clearance at Nimbuwa. With this, Edward insisted that Ross should get back to his family. The two friends shook hands, hugged, and slapped each other on the back. Edward promised to write with all the details as soon as he could, and Ross suggested he would visit in a couple of months. Johnno helped Edward pack his new purchases in his kitbag and went with him to the Grand Hotel.

Settling into his room, Edward slumped on the bed with the bottle of rum. At first, sips were satisfying, but soon, gulps felt more appropriate. He cursed Liam out loud but could not help smiling when he remembered making love to Sophie. It had been delightful, but would never have happened if Liam had behaved rationally. This was quickly followed by deep remorse when he thought of the day and his family back in England. He regretted being unfaithful to Elsie, even though he knew there could be no going back to her.

He slept for a while, but woke with a rumbling belly, and went downstairs to the dining room. Cold baked ham and potato salad were on offer, which was all at odds with his ideas of Christmas dinner, but at least there was steaming pudding served with lashings of cream. The chef set down a generous measure of rum in front of Edward then poured more over the dessert, and set it alight. He thought of his mum with her shining eyes, bringing in the lighted pudding to the parlour, and how they always cheered.

Edward took another glass of rum to his bedroom. Sleep soon overtook him, and he did not stir until after lunch the following day. Then, with unsteady legs and a sore head, he sat for an hour drinking water. Edward recalled snatches of his dreams. There were definitely war scenes, yet he was still in bed when he awoke, and had apparently not disturbed anyone in the adjoining rooms. Luck was on his side, this time. Nevertheless, he swore to himself that trying to obliterate the memories of Liam was not worth going on any more benders. He spent the afternoon walking around the town to clear his head.

The following morning, Edward made his way to Doctor Lane's surgery. Edward had seen him several times, during the year at Wollabungo, for his medication.

"You look down in the dumps today," he said.

"Just a bit unsure about the future," and he briefly related his new turn of events without mentioning the actual injury to Liam.

"I think it's a good idea to move on, for a while at least." Doctor Lane suggested. "Ross and his family have been good for you, but perhaps you need to see how things are without them."

"That's about it, Doc."

"You might be gone for six months, so we'll give you a stock of your tablets."

In the train, he chose an empty compartment. He flung his belongings up onto the rack before choosing a corner. Back against the window, he put his feet on the seat and lit a cigarette. Any awe and wonder he had felt for the landscape and its creatures, on his first train journey in Australia, had waned. He despised Liam, and closed his eyes to conjure up images of Christmas and his loved ones in Lord street.

By four o'clock in the afternoon, he had set off from Dolwolani station, and begun walking the ten or so miles to his destination. The stationmaster knew exactly where Edward was headed and scribbled a route on some paper. He told him to follow the stream, starting at the bridge in the town, and go north. There had been little rain, so there was not much more than a trickle, moving listlessly over the stony bed, for most of the way. The air was still, and Edward was aware of his own soft footsteps. Birds flurried at his approach; some cheeping carelessly and others shrieking as if in fright. A turmoil of flies, whirred and droned around the remains of a kangaroo's carcass. Lizards skimmed and skittered across the ditch. Under a cluster of trees providing shading and near a more generous stretch of water in the ditch, Edward stopped and erected his tent. He sat on a bleached log and bathed his feet in the water, before looking in the box of food Nora had packed. The cheeses and fruit cake were very welcome. He slept well that night.

He had not walked much further, the next day, when he saw some new fencing, stretching left and right, in front of a copse of eucalyptus. His path led to the right, but someone was shouting behind the trees.

"You useless jackass! Bugger off back where you crawled from. We should have been ready for burning off here today, and there are joeys at the top of the hill."

Surprised by the English accent, Edward moved closer and peered through the thicket. One man was carrying a rifle, and he jabbed it into the other man's chest so hard that the chap fell over. The rifleman aimed and fired towards the joeys, but failed to hit a single one. The little man on the ground scurried away, almost at the same pace as the now leaping joeys. Edward had to suppress laughter and decided that the man making all the noise was likely to be his new boss, Wilfred Redford. Thinking it might be better if the man cooled down for an hour, Edward crouched low in the trees as Mr Redford mounted a horse and rode away.

Eventually, Edward approached a dwelling. Two tough-looking children with pudding-basin haircuts and wearing matching brown dungarees were chasing each other with sticks. They stopped as soon as they saw Edward and stared for a moment. A cradle rested on a narrow veranda by the front door.

"A new fella, mum!" the taller of the two children called.

"Send him round the back, I'm hanging washing."

A large dog growled, showing its teeth, then barked and pulled forward straining on his chain. Another dog, that looked more like a puppy, came wuffling around his feet and tried to jump up to him. The children avoided the angry dog and followed Edward as he approached their mother at the washing line. It was strung from the back door to a tree some thirty foot away.

"Excuse me, ma'am," he said. "I'm looking for Mr Redford. Been told he wants land clearing."

Surrendering the clothes pegs to the taller child, she approached Edward. "You're in the right place. Red's up against time to get the land finished."

"I know that. I'm a hard worker. I'll do all I can."

She was a little plump, but she had a sweet face with a snub nose and dark auburn hair tied back in a bun. Her face lit up when she smiled and her eyes were bright, if a little anxious, as she held out her hand to him. "You're in luck. Red should be back for lunch today, so you can probs start right now. We haven't inside lodging, but there's a lean-to near the water butts, where a couple of other labourers sleep."

"Actually, I've a tent. I'll camp out of the way," he said. "Don't sleep too good always, so I like to chip away at a piece of wood or draw at night."

"Righto."

By this time, the children had gathered in close to their mother's skirts, one on either side. They stared at Edward. The younger one was sucking a thumb, but the other child asked, "What's your name, mister? You sound a bit like our daddy."

Edward smiled and ducked to their level. The prospective farmer being English might be a good omen, he thought, despite his ill-humour earlier. "Hello boys. I'm Eddie, I could make you some proper wooden swords if you like." They looked puzzled.

"Excuse my manners," the woman said. "I'm Bonnie, and these are my girls, Jack and Georgie; Casey is in the cradle."

"I am sorry," Edward said, "The dungarees and the short hair... "

"Easy mistake. Red wanted boys and chose the names – Jacqueline and Georgina He wants them to grow up tough and be able to take on the farm."

"I see," he said, but felt sorry for the kids.

"You can't take the girl out of them completely though. The sticks are wands, not swords."

"Shut it, Duke!" Bonnie yelled at the irritated dog. "You could make yourself useful, Edward, and chop me some wood," she continued, "until Red gets back."

"Red?"

"It's the only name he uses. You'll see why when you meet him."

The house looked temporary compared with Ross's place. The corrugated roof appeared stronger than the walls. The area where everyone washed, was outside near the kitchen and some water butts. Jugs were placed on a crude table. Separated from these, by a screen of sorts, was a shower that was fixed up over a tin bathtub. On the shower side, to give a modicum of privacy, an old curtain stretched across from the screen then nailed at the top to the tree. This also held the tank of water that fed the shower. It was wedged higher in the branches and supported with wooden struts. Edward liked the idea but it was not in the least sophisticated. There was no electricity. The toilet, in a separate outhouse, consisted of a plank of wood placed over a pit. A hole had been cut out of the board. It was so different from Ross's long-established home.

Bonnie took Edward to the wood store on the opposite side of the cabin. Here, there was also the beginning of a small vegetable patch, surrounded by a low fence. A dozen or so chickens clucked and pecked around but scattered away as he began the chopping. The younger dog came and lay at a distance, watching him. It stretched out now and again and inched forward. After a while, perspiration demanded Edward remove his shirt. He was still swinging the axe when he heard,

"Who the bloody hell are you? What are you doing here half-dressed? My wife and children are about."

He was the same man Edward had seen briefly, earlier in the day – at least six feet and stocky. He was undoubtedly good-looking, clean-shaven and with chiselled features. The skin across his cheekbones looked stretched with slight hollows beneath. The flaming hair, which was obviously what Bonnie had meant about his name, was cut very close to his scalp. Edward glanced around to look for the family, but there was no one else in sight. "I beg your pardon," he said. "B... Mrs Redford asked me to chop some firewood while I waited for you."

"Looking for work? Where do you come from?"

Edward slipped on his shirt and explained briefly about coming to Australia at the behest of a friend with a sheep farm. "I had a great time and learnt a lot, but I don't want to join a union to become a shearer yet, until I've tried other things."

"True enough. There are a lot of ruffians amongst that lot who can cause trouble. That's why I chose wheat."

Edward recognised the voice of a Londoner. "Have you been in Australia long?" he asked.

"About a dozen years now. Got here when I was sixteen. Done plenty of other work, but I always wanted to be a farmer."

"Did you come with your parents?"?"

"No," he said. His voice was stern and Edward took the hint that it was a subject not to be discussed. "Right, you've come at a most opportune moment. Had to fire someone this morning. Lazy and soft. Won't tolerate namby-pambies. What are you like with a rifle?"

"I'm a good shot and a hard worker. I won't let you down. I've got a reference for you in my kit bag."

"You were in the war?"

"Yes, sir. Two years. Egypt and France."

"Good man. I did Gallipoli and the Somme."

Edward nodded and wondered if he should mention the shell shock at this moment, but decided against it.

"Let's get washed up and go in for lunch," Red said, "then I'll see how you get along this afternoon."

Inside was unsophisticated but immaculate. The kitchen and living room were combined. A table was set with a cloth, plates, cutlery, cups and saucers and crisp linen serviettes in silver rings. Some bread had been cut neatly and placed in a basket next to a plate of sliced cheese. Rolls of butter rested in tiny dishes near each place setting. Bonnie added apples, homemade pickles and sweet biscuits to the table, before setting down a large pot of tea with a milk jug and sugar bowl at one end of the table. This was where the only chair with arms was located. Apart from the silver serviette rings, the well-prepared table reminded Edward of home, when they ate in the parlour.

The children were standing silently behind their chairs, looking down. Edward followed suit, as did Bonnie when she had finished laying the table. The baby's cradle was at the other end of the room, near a couple of comfortable chairs, a small bookcase and a box of toys.

"You may sit," said Red, and he took his place at the head of the table. "What have you two been up to this morning?" he asked the children.

"We fed the chucks, sir."

"They're great. I saw them strutting about this morning..." Edward tailed off, suddenly aware that everyone was staring at him.

"You speak when you're spoken to at my dinner table," Red said.

"I beg your pardon," Edward said for the second time, feeling his cheeks flush.

"I hope you've done your reading," Red said to the children, "and not been chasing around foolishly outside."

"We always read," Bonnie answered for them. "We started Swiss Family Robinson today."

"It's exciting," said Jackie, "but a bit hard for George. I'm helping..."

"Anything else?" Red asked

"We brang water in for mummy," said George.

"Brought, George, and mother, not mummy," Red corrected.

The child's bottom lip extended and she bent her head. She did not eat a morsel of food for several minutes. The meal continued in silence, apart from the clatter of knives on plates.

"Said you were good with a rifle?" Red turned to Edward.

"I am. Did some sniper training when I first joined up."

"Excellent. I've a patch of land that seems to interest the roos. Can you saddle a horse?"

"Sure."

"Good. That's where we'll start," and Red drew back his chair to leave, so that Edward, still with his mouth full, had no option but to follow.

***

Red worked at a feverish pace, but Edward kept up with him. They finished clearing a section of scrub that Red was concerned about and created a damp ditch all the way around it, before tracking the kangaroos. Edward felt sure it was a test but easily bagged four roos to Red's two. When Red started the burning, Edward realised there had been no need to shoot the animals, who would surely have gone of their own accord when they heard the crackling and snapping and saw the flames.

Burning was painstaking and had to be prudently controlled. It was more of a quick smoulder. Fortunately, it was the right weather for the job, with a minimal breeze. A large metal container full of water with a pump and hose, sat at the edge of the field. They followed the burning, on either side of the field, each carrying a bucket of water and running back to refill quickly or turning on the hose if flames rose up. The whole area was doused again before they left for the night.

"I think you'll do," Red said as they untied their horses. "You're not shy of hard work."

Back at the house, by the time they washed, it was past eight o'clock. The children had gone to bed. Bonnie had eaten with them, so there was less formality than at lunch, and two other men joined them. Dishes of stew were put on the table and thick slices of cake.

"We'll have a beer this evening," Red said.

Bonnie had moved away to see to Casey, whimpering in her crib. She looked back at Red as if uncertain whether she should fetch the beer or see to the baby.

"Let the child snivel," Red answered for her. "You bother about them too much."

Red introduced Edward, who was too tired for much conversation and still needed to set up the tent. He excused himself as soon as he could. There was a flat area about thirty yards from the back of the building, and sheltered on one side by some tall bushes. The ground was impenetrable, and as Edward tried to insert the pegs, Bonnie arrived with a post maul.

"Red's very intense about this farm business," she said. "Put most of his savings into it. He's not always so short with everyone."

"I get it, Bonnie. I'll do my best."

"Woman! What you doing out here whispering with the new fellow?" Red yelled before he reached them. "Get back inside."

"Just brought the post maul for the pegs, or he won't get them in the ground."

"Thank you, Bonnie," Edward said as she darted away.

"Mrs Redford, to you," Red said, coming up very close to Edward. "Be up with the dawn."

***

Edward worked as hard as Red, and it was gruelling. Red had boundless energy and was determined to meet his deadline at the end of June. There was no faulting his constant resolve and Edward became caught up in it. A field full of wheat would be such a reward.

Edward did not, however, warm to Red. A threatening air hung about the man, with his ever so slightly narrowed eyes and pursed lips. He showed no friendship towards his employees and Edward did not have much opportunity to get to know the other two labourers, Red had taken on.

They all met at breakfast and the evening meal, and if the children were present, there was little chatter. Red gave orders at breakfast, and checked on progress at dinner unless there had already been time to inspect for himself. Whatever the case, he rarely praised anyone for their hard work, but often had a niggle.

"I don't think you two doused your section thoroughly. Go back out after you've eaten."

"The clearing looks OK, but you are behind with the fencing."

One of the labourers, Kit, was agreeable but they exchanged little more than greetings and nods and a few details about where they had worked previously. Like Edward, he was happy to get on with his work. The other labourer, Striker, was a different matter. He was short and thickset with bulging muscles and reminded Edward of a stock horse pulling a scrub roller. Tattoos covered Striker's arms and his hair was longer than the norm and tied back with a grubby piece of rag. Unfortunately, he also often had an unpleasant odour.

If the children were still up at dinnertime, they exchanged glances and stared at Striker rather too long, as if they were waiting for the jack to jump out of its box. He slavered over his food, wiped his mouth on his sleeve or arm and sniffed loudly between mouthfuls. The girls would look down and try to suppress giggles and then be reminded to get on with their food. As soon as Striker finished eating, he pushed back his chair. "Be off for me beer now," he'd say and strut out without any thank you to Bonnie. It was not his poor hygiene or lack of manners, however, which bothered Edward so much.

***

One evening, a few weeks after Edward's arrival, Striker came to his tent. "Wanna have a beer with me?" He thrust a bottle towards Edward.

"I don't drink much, thanks. I get migraines," Edward said. "That one Bonnie gave us with the meal was enough."

"Oh, it's Bonnie, is it? Think your luck's in there? I could do her alright."

"Get out of here. That's foul."

"Well I'd give her a go, any day."

"Find a bawdy house next time you're in town, man. Now get lost!"

Every other week, Red gave the labourers a different day off, according to his plans. It was easy to get back to Dolwolani by horse. Striker always went to buy beer and visit an establishment called Lu-Lu's. Kit went for something to do, but Edward often remained at the farm and did some whittling or sketching for the girls. He drew dogs, horses, birds and lizards, but their favourites were the kangaroos. Edward put funny expressions on the faces of the animals to make the children laugh. He made them wands and swords, cars, trains and building blocks.

He kicked a ball about with them, played hide-and-seek and taught them how to skip.

Bonnie seemed grateful for his interest in the girls, but he kept his distance. There was no point in raising Red's hackles and after the trouble with Liam, he was reluctant to become too familiar. His interest in the girls meant Bonnie could get on with her jobs and give more attention to the baby. Over the months, however, she always brought him a sandwich at lunchtime, and if Red was not expected to be home at midday, Bonnie might invite Edward to come to the house for his lunch. He insisted that it was not necessary, but as the weather grew colder, he was glad of the warmth of the kitchen. Over the kitchen table, they gradually opened out to each other.

One day she told Edward that Red had worked for her father at his sandalwood sawmill, which was near the docks in Perth. Red had started by just sweeping up, but showed a lot of interest in the business that exported all over the world. "He had a good head for figures, better than my brother, Ken, and within a couple of years he was a supervisor."

"So, how did the two of you meet?"

"My brother met him as he was boarding a ship from England. They were both about sixteen then – about 1915, it was. Ken had been visiting rellies out there. They became best buddies, and Ken snuck him into first class a couple of times. When they docked in Perth, Ken took him straight to Dad's sandalwood sawmill near the port."

"That was a lucky break!"

"Red slept there for a few months; did a spell as a night watchman, but dad grew fond of him. Red was always quick at learning, wanting to please and polite in those days. Dad felt sorry for him and brought him home."

"What about his family?"

"He didn't have a family."

"Was he an orphan?"

"Not exactly. I'll maybe tell you another time."

"Oh?"

"What about you, Edward? How come you're here on your ownsome?"

Bonnie was more than understanding, explaining that Ken had suffered in a similar way when he came back from the war. "He was in a dreadful state when he first returned," she continued. "My dad knew that Ken didn't want to go into the sandalwood business, so he set him up with a store near the docks and asked Red to help him run it, but really to look out for Ken."

"Did he accept?"

"Oh, yes. Red would do anything for Ken, and Ken won't hear a bad word said against Red."

"How come Red ended up in farming?"

"It was always his dream to own a plot of land and make a living from it."

"What happened to Ken?"

"He still has his moments. But he married his sweetheart, Jenny, from before the wretched war, and she's wonderful with him. My chosen one was killed in the conflict, and as time went by, I accepted Red's advances. We've been married nearly nine years."

"When did you move out here?"

"Just over twelve months ago. Ken and Red came out first to build this temporary house, till Red earns some money, then he's going to build us a proper home."

"If you don't mind me saying," Edward said, on a future occasion, when he felt more familiar with Bonnie, "I can't imagine Red having fun with anyone. He's very abrupt and stern with the girls."

"He's a perfectionist and has high expectations of everyone."

"Has he always been like this?"

Bonnie sighed, then said quietly. "He was charming at first, and he's quite well educated. We'd chat and discuss issues of the day. He was interested in politics and told me a lot about England. And he was handsome, of course."

"Is it just the threat of losing the land that has made him like he is?"

She said nothing for a few moments.

"I'm sorry, but he gets cross so easily and hates anyone even talking to you."

"I told you he wanted boys."

"But they are beautiful kids."

"Actually," and she paused again, "I don't think he likes girls at all."

"Why would you say that?

"I don't think he loves us," and Bonnie had tears in her eyes. "We're his possessions, like the farm, and we have to be and do whatever he wants because he believes that's right."

He wanted to hug her, comfort her. She deserved so much more, but instinct stopped him. These were the same feelings he'd had about Sophie. He reached across the table and rested a hand on Bonnie's arm. She looked up at him.

"There's something else." She struggled for a moment.

"You don't have to say any more, Bonnie."

She shook her head and looked at him for several seconds before blurting out, "His mother was a high-class prostitute in London."

He managed to stifle a gasp.

"One of her rich fellows paid for Red to go to boarding school, but the money ran out. Back home, he was an inconvenience to his mother. At the school, he had learnt to play tennis, and an opportunity came for him to enter a tournament when he won some money. It was enough for a passport and carriage class to Australia."

He had just withdrawn his hand when Red entered. "What the bloody hell is going on here? Get out, Edward!"

Edward was already on his feet. Red grabbed Bonnie's arm and dragged her out of the chair.

"We were just having a sarnie," she said grimacing at the same time.

"Why would you invite any man in here when I'm not around? He was shouting and shaking her at the same time. You women are all the same!"

He turned to Edward, "Why are you not in town on your day off?"

"I'd no need to go."

"Look, Red," Bonnie said, trying to extricate herself from his grasp. He's made the girls some building blocks."

"He'd be better teaching them how to hold a rifle."

"Jackie's barely eight and Georgie six!" she protested.

"It's Jack and George, you soft mare! They'll learn what I want them to learn."

He turned on Edward, who was worried for Bonnie and reluctant to leave, "I'd sack you on the spot, if you weren't such a good worker."

"What for? Having some lunch?"

"Get the fuck out of here! And don't let me catch you again, talking to my Mrs, ever!"

Over the months, Edward's migraines remained, but his nightmares gradually became less extreme. He might wake in a sweat and feeling miserable about having yet another haunting dream, but at least he did not sleepwalk nor attack people.

The headaches, par for the course, often followed a lousy night. On these mornings, he tended to avoid a full breakfast and just take tea and a slice of bread on his way out. Pulling the brim of his hat down tightly, to keep out as much light as possible, he focused on the ground rather than the trees, birds or sky. If there was to be culling of rabbits and roos to do, he left it to someone else. Anyhow, the others needed more practice.

Red was so impressed with Edward's shooting that he entered him for an annual competition that took place at the beginning of May. It was a whole day event of tracking and culling kangaroos, and chaps came from far and wide. Edward had the highest score and the largest roo. He had to pose with the carcass for a photo, which appeared in the Western Mail. Maybe Ross might see it. Edward had never written to Ross, partly because he did not want to encourage him to visit Red's set-up. There would be nowhere for Ross to stay, and he did not want Ross to meet Red. Edward knew Ross well enough to know that Red would irritate him, and there would be an unpleasant scene. He planned to write when the inspection was over, and meet up with Ross in Martin Street for a few days.

On the evening of June 21st 1928, a letter was waiting for Edward at the dining table. Red had collected it in town that day, but it looked well-travelled. There was a frank he could not make out, and a postmark showed that it had been to Martin Street before the final stamp in Nimbuwa. It did not look like Ross's writing on the front, and he could not imagine who else would be sending him a letter. He pretended to ignore it, but took sideways glances at the marks and writing as he placed his serviette on his knee. He dithered but was about to pocket it when Jackie asked, "Aren't you going to open it, Mr Edward?" He smiled at her and slit open the envelope with his knife.

May 24ᵗʰ, 1928

Dear Edward,

I have some bad news. Ross has had a terrible accident. He was taking part with Hot Socks in a point to point race in Perth. We all went to watch. He was thrown, and kicked by other horses following him. Ross was taken to hospital but passed two days later.

It has broken all of us, as I'm sure you can imagine. He was such a good fellow and well thought of by all who knew him. We hardly know how to carry on.

I'm writing on behalf of Oliver and Sophie, who want you at the funeral. I know everything got out of hand with Liam, and I'm sorry about all that business, but please come. It would be such a comfort to have his friend with us.

The funeral was delayed because of the investigation, but it will be here. Ross will be buried in the family plot on the morning of May 31st. A minister is coming out from Martin Street, and many people who knew Ross will attend.

Yours truly,
Nora.

Edward heard a muted voice but not the words. He could not even look up to trace the speaker. Icy prickles started at the nape of his neck. They ran down his spine, and his body felt numb. He saw a hand reaching for the letter and yelled, "Get off!" Strong arms either side, pulled him up and away from the table. Someone was shaking him.

"You're scaring the children," he heard.

"Bad news, hey?"

He had no words. They walked him outside, where Red grabbed the letter out of Edward's hands, letting him slump at his side. Kit hauled him up and supported his weight.

"This the bloke you told me about?" Red asked.

"I have to go and see the family," Edward aid.

"The funeral's all done," Red snapped. "Little point in going now, and I need you here," and he was shaking his head vigorously. "Only two weeks now before the inspection."

The chill wrapping Edward's limbs squeezed tighter, but a wave of nausea rose like bitter broth in his mouth, and he spewed it out over his boots. Pushing away from Kit, he snatched back the letter and ran.

For the next half hour, Edward filled his time with the *thwock* of an axe as he chopped logs, followed by the *tch, tch, tch, tch* as he reduced the logs to tinder. He did not stop when the sweat pouring down his face, rolled down his neck and soaked his shirt. He had perfected a rhythm and needed to carry on.

"Stop that now!" shouted Red. "No one will sleep."

Edward saw Bonnie standing a few feet behind her husband, holding a plate of food and a drink. It was so kind of her to bring his untouched meal, but he could not face it and shook his head in her direction. Red turned to see who Edward was looking at. "What are you doing woman?" he called. "Get back inside. I'll see to this."

"I'm OK," Edward said. "I'll get a shower and go to bed."

"Yes. Best to face these setbacks head-on. You'll have had worse in the war, I'm sure."

Edward had the urge to run straight at the man and floor him, but Red was much the taller and more muscular.

"A good night's sleep is all you need," Red added. "Put your back into work tomorrow. It will all soon be forgotten."

He avoided Red's eyes and walked around to the washing area. When he reached his tent, he found the plate of food and a glass of whisky. Only Bonnie would have left them. The gesture brought on his tears. He was grateful, but struggled to put a portion of the food in his mouth. It felt like eating sawdust. The whisky went down well enough, but he threw the remains of the food in the bushes.

Sleep eluded him. All his lost friends from the war years and now Ross too. Why, of everyone, was he, Edward Holmes, still alive? He would go to visit the family, he resolved, as soon as the inspection was done. Then, it would be time to move on again. He did not want to stay on Red's farm. Edward rocked himself to and fro, hugging his knees and trying to ignore his thumping headache. He was unable to hold at bay the conviction that life was no longer worth living.

Some Things to Sort Out

The following morning, Edward woke as the dawn was struggling to break through a sullen sky. Something sharp was stabbing into his back. Was he wounded? Why was it so quiet, and where was everyone else?

Becoming fully conscious, he realised that he was the other side of one of his episodes and leaning against the vegetable enclosure in his underwear. He swore and slapped himself across his head. Twisting around, he found the protruding knot in the fence post that was causing his discomfort. A gash above his left ankle caught his attention. It was still bleeding, so he could not have been sitting there for long.

He should have moved, but he was beached. Apart from some scuttering in the bushes and a few chirruping birds, everything was still outside. In his head though there was a humming noise like a busy insect. Somewhere – he caught a shimmer of bright light. Not the sunrise. The grey dome gave no hint that the sun would break through that day.

His thoughts stumbled into one another. Why should such a great bloke die in a fucking stupid accident? To survive the war for that? He had never properly thanked Ross for all his friendship and support, as far back as Egypt. It should have been me, he thought. I'm no better now than ten years ago. Nothing has changed.

Look at me, slumped against this goddamned fence.

He had to visit Ross's family. He could write a letter first to alert them and explain about missing the funeral. They surely wouldn't mind him staying a few days. He would not expect a room in the house this time.

Another penetrating glint and he knew it was his head playing tricks as a migraine took its grip.

He wanted to leave straight away, but he accepted that he should wait till Red's farm was ready. He couldn't let Bonnie and the kids down. They might lose their home if the inspector was not satisfied. He'd tell Red that he was leaving at the end of June and send a letter to Wollabungo in the meantime.

A snake of smoke crept up the sky. Bonnie must have already set the fire. The children shouldn't see him like this. He pushed himself up to standing, but his legs were wobbly, and he was dizzy. He grabbed hold of a fencepost. The familiar stabbing pain was above his eye. It circled his head, going behind his ears and into the nape of his neck. His shoulders were rigid.

In his tent, he took a drink from the bucket of water and swallowed three aspirin before submerging his head. There was enough water to wash and clean up his leg, and he wrapped a rag around it. Without thinking, he flipped his head back to shake off the drips out of his hair, and beads of light, like a string of popping stars in a firework, ran across his eye and gathered in the corner. He tried blinking them away then rubbing. He put on his hat carefully as if adorning a fragile object, but the rim felt like a vice, so he left it behind. He put a few bullets in his pocket, picked up his rifle and made his way to the kitchen.

"I'll not stop this morning Mrs Redford," he said. "One of my headaches. Tell Red I've gone to the far end. There's some fencing to finish, and I'll do my best with the roos and bunnies."

"Now just you stop there a mo," she said. "I know you're not right. Have a cuppa, and I'll pack you some tucker to take with you." She placed her hand on his arm, encouraging him to sit awhile. Putting a mug of tea in front of him, she stirred in two teaspoons of sugar and hovered, "Anyone would have been upset, Edward, but I know more than Red how much that chap meant to you. I'm so sorry."

Just as Edward was thanking her, Red entered and lunged at Bonny. "What the hell are you up to now, woman?" He pulled her away from Edward's chair and gripped Bonnie's blouse at the neck.

"The man's grieving, Red, don't be silly."

He towered over her, "You're the silly cow always fussing over the men. Enough!"

Edward had scraped back his chair as quietly as he could, ready to make his exit. "Red, nothing was going on."

"Get out of my bloody sight! This little whore might be willing," and he let go of her blouse at the throat, "but don't even think about it!" His voice rose again, and he wagged his finger at Edward.

"What on earth are you thinking?" Edward asked, but instead of an answer, Red took a swing at Edward, forcing him to dodge away. The quick movement made him nauseous.

"Just go!" Red demanded.

Edward's head was about to burst, and his eyes were blurry. He wanted to try reasoning with Red, but all he could manage was to stumble outside where he was sick. Kit was approaching the building.

"Don't go in," Edward said. "They're fighting in there, and it's pretty bad."

"He's a dog, isn't he? What's up with you? Too much beer after your bad news?"

"A migraine. I'm going down to the bottom end to finish fencing," Edward told him. "I'll be working under the trees so it will be shady if the sun gets up. That will help. What about you?"

"Ah. I'm taking the horse up to the first fields. Red says they haven't been looked at properly since it was sown. He's coming up later in the day. I probably won't be back till tomorrow, but Bonnie gave me tucker last night for today." Kit began to rummage in the bag. "There'll be summat in here for brekkie."

"Where's Striker?" Edward asked.

"Day off. Already left for town."

"Good. No one to disturb me."

Edward had made his way slowly to the bottom enclosure, about half a mile away. His head throbbed, and he could not bear even the sunless light. Praying that Red would not bother with a visit before going up to Kit, Edward lay down under the trees and was soon asleep. When he woke, the day was as quiet as a graveyard with not a breath of wind. The sky was still a watery grey. He had no idea of the time, and he was cold, but the headache had dwindled.

He had put in three sections of fencing when a couple of roos appeared about a hundred yards away. He reached for his gun. But he had left the kitchen in such a hurry; he had forgotten to collect it. Thinking the roos would linger a while if he moved away from them, he decided there was plenty of time to return to the house and come back with his gun.

The day had no voice until a flock of birds rose as if they had been waiting in hiding. Their clamouring and flapping were startling, and he stopped walking until they settled again. As he approached the house, he heard crying.

In the kitchen, Bonnie was kneeling on the floor, gently rocking Casey in her arms. Jackie leant against her shoulder, sobbing. There was blood at the corner of Bonnie's mouth. Her lip was swollen and she had the beginnings of a black eye. Georgie was crouched under the table whimpering. A gash was visible on her forehead.

"Who did this?" He went towards the baby. "Is she all right?"

"She's still breathing but all limp and sleepy, but I'll put her down now."

As she moved towards the crib, Jackie clung to her arm and looked terrified.

"Let mummy settle Casey," Edward said to Jackie. "Come and sit down and tell me what happened."

She sniffed a few times before being able to speak. "Daddy was madder than ever today," she blubbered. "After lunch, he sent me and George to the veggie garden to dig up spuds and collect the eggs from the chucks." She broke down again and wiped her nose with her hand. "We could hear shouts so we came back. He was hurting mummy. We shouted at him to stop, but he walloped us. Georgie fell down, and won't come out from under the table, and he threw Casey on the floor." She cried again.

"Hush darlin," Bonnie said, "We'll clean up now. Edward will help us." She was giving Edward odd looks. He wasn't sure what to make of them, then she said,

"Will you lift Georgie for me, Edward, and carry her to her bed?"

He reached under the table and smiled at Georgie. "Come on sweetie, let's get you to your room. I can carry you." She reached her arms out towards him.

Bonnie hugged her eldest daughter once more. "You go and have a wash in the yard, honey. Your daddy won't come back today. Bring a fresh bowl of water to bathe your sister's face then sit with her till I call you."

When Edward returned to the kitchen, Bonnie was kneeling by the crib and singing a lullaby; *Close your eyes now and rest, May these...*" but her voice cracked, and tears rolled down her cheeks. He felt helpless.

Bonnie looked shattered. Her hair was hanging down, and the blouse was torn. "She's still breathing," she whispered. "I'll keep a close watch."

"I don't understand, Bonnie." As he looked in the crib, he saw a purple bruise forming on the child's brow. "Did Red attack all of you?"

She made an attempt to speak but only sobbed louder. When she caught her breath and nodded before she managed, "I did love him once," then dissolved once more. "Big strong, handsome man, he was" she added, after a few moments, "and so capable; so full of dreams – it's why I fell for him."

Edward knelt down in front of her. "Where is he now?"

She shook her head; her lips tightly closed. "How could he?"

"What?" asked Edward, but she made no reply. "I'm so sorry. I saw Red grab you. I should've stayed."

"He'd have set about you as well."

"Why?"

"Thought you and I were fooling around." She sniffed and tried again to wipe away her tears.

He sank back on his heels. "But why? And why did he hurt the children?"

"He was furious when he found out you don't always go to town on your day off," Bonnie rushed on, almost breathless.

"So, you're telling me that he attacked you and the girls because of me?" Edward was shaking his head in disbelief. "Should I try to sort it all out with him?"

She held her head in her hands. "He said horrible things to me - that the girls were probably not his. That's when he pulled Casey from the crib and just dropped her." She leant into the crib and kissed the child and stroked her cheek. "Jackie and Georgie screamed out and went to get her, but he thrashed them then dragged me to the bedroom, where he hurt me some more."

"Where's he gone? Edward gasped. "I'll straighten him out. I'll tell him I'll leave here straightaway."

"There's no point."

"But you can't go on living like this."

Her head sank over the crib, and her tears flowed freely. It seemed best to let her cry. "My girls need a doctor, "she said eventually – "but they'll take me away - and my children will be orphans!"

Jackie came running into the kitchen and looked anxiously at Edward.

"It's all right, honey," Bonnie managed. "I'm a mite worried about getting you all to the doctor, but Edward is going to help now."

"There are just a few things to sort out," he interrupted. He spoke calmly. "You be the best girl for mummy, and go and sit with your sister again until we have decided what to do next." He smiled at her and handed her two buns from underneath a net covering. "I'll make us all some sweet cocoa. I know it's your favourite." Bonnie nodded.

He made the drinks and took them through to Georgie's bedroom. On returning, he shut the kitchen door.

"What do you mean, they'll take you away?" he asked and took their cocoa over to the crib.

She wiped her tears. "You left your rifle this morning in the corner by the door."

"Oh, God!" Something in his chest lurched, and put aside the drink.

"I was only going to threaten him with it," Bonnie said, "tell him we were all going to my parents."

"What have you done, Bonnie?"

Getting up from the floor, she pulled a shawl down from the rack above the range and wrapped it around her. "I told Jackie I was going after him to tell him off. I sat the girls down under the table and gave Jackie the baby to hold. I said they should stay put there, where they'd be safe until I got back. I told them I'd lock the door." As I ran out, something made me grab your rifle at the back door."

Edward was silent for a moment. "Is he dead?" he asked quietly.

"I don't know. I ran up the lane. I knew he wanted to see to a stretch of the road, where there's still a stubborn tree stump, on his way up to the first fields." She paused and looked Edward in his eyes. "There he was, standing with his back to me, by the tractor. He was a little hunched over. I didn't stop to think, I swear. I was so mad with him about the children. I pointed the rifle and shot twice." She stopped, putting a hand over her lips. When she spoke, it was through her fingers. "His whole body arched. His arms flew out, and he fell forward."

"Did you approach him, see if he was...?"

"No. I couldn't. I dropped the gun and ran back here; in case the children had heard the shots." She was calmer now. "I was shaking all over but trying to act normal. I made us drinks, but Georgie wouldn't get up from the floor. Then you came in."

"I didn't hear the shots either; maybe accounts for some birds that were disturbed though," he said, and looked at her red cheeks and puffy eyes. "Look, I'll have to go and find him, Bonnie. See if anything can be done." He moved to the door but turned back. "Is there some brandy or the rum? Have a little; it'll keep you going."

***

Red lies face down. A bullet has entered below his left shoulder blade, and as Edward turns him over, he sees a further bullet wound to his head and another deep gash. The rifle and a blood-stained axe are close by. One of Red's eyes is closed and matted with blood. The bullet in his back has gone straight through creating a ragged hole in his shirt. Blood has oozed across his chest and seeped into the earth. One of Red's fingers is also severely cut. He must have had an accident with the axe, Edward thinks. Perhaps, as Red was attacking the tree stump. Maybe this accounts for the bloodied axe, and why he was standing still as Bonnie approached. Edward hears a bird's shrill cry and spots a wedge-tailed eagle circling. "Ah, Christ!" Edward says out loud. "She's really done for you, man."

Edward is not distressed by the wounds and has no pity for Red, but he recalls Bonnie's comments about orphans. Walking around the body, he wonders if he should hide or bury it or even take it back to the house. That would be too disturbing for the girls. But a man can't just disappear, even on a farm which is miles from town.

He stares at the body and sees the faintest flutter from Red's open eye. Edward drops to the ground, to look more closely, and hears a definite death rattle. He remembers that sound from the war. Looking at Red, Edward knows he cannot survive the injuries, and he stares for while at this most hateful man.

There's a hammer in Edward's tool belt. He takes it and raises his arm, but watches as Red's face becomes slack; the mouth falls open; his eye is frozen. Edward sighs with relief. He drops the hammer and drags the body to a ditch; drops in the rifle and axe, frantically covering everything with stones, branches and bundles of leaves. Taking more branches, he scuffs up the heel marks on the ground and kicks around the patch of blood, throwing more soil over it and a few small stones.

***

Bonnie is pacing in the kitchen. "Did you find him? Is he...?"

Edward nods.

"The girls are asleep, and Casey's had a drink." It's hard for her to speak above a whisper as if she has a sore throat. "I put her back in the crib." She looks at Edward, her eyes full of panic.

"Make me a cup of tea, and I'll think it all through," Edward says.

"But it's going to be dark soon, and I've got to get help."

"Yes, I know. Listen to me, Bonnie... I murdered him - not you."

"What on earth do you mean?"

"You cannot be charged with murder."

"But neither can you!"

"Remember I told you about why I sleep in a tent?"

"Yes. I do."

"A doctor told me once that my condition meant I was insane. Bonnie, your children are not going to an orphanage!"

"I don't know what to say."

"I'll claim I don't remember killing Red, but I'm sure it was me."

"They'll think you're crazy."

"That's the point."

"Are you sure it will work?"

"Why not? There's no doubting that I have absurd episodes. Lots of people know about them now."

"You're a good man."

"You tell the police that I wasn't making much sense, but I told you I'd done it. Say anything that will keep you safe."

"I can't believe you'd do this. You don't know me."

"You're a good mother. I'm going to spruce up a bit. Get the pony and trap ready. Bundle up the girls with blankets. I'll drive us all to Nimbuwa. You go to the doctor; I'll hand myself in. You come afterwards to the police yourself."

"I don't think I can let you do this."

"Make arrangements to go home to your folks," he said and smiled at her. You'll be able to contact them in town. Don't tell them the truth. This is our secret, always."

"I've to say you told me you had one of your bad nightmares, and found Red when you woke up."

"That will do. Just don't tell them which field I was working in. The police will come looking for the body. I've hidden it in the ditch near the tractor, so the children don't see it."

**

Edward leaves the family at the doctor's, but the police station is locked up. He takes a room at a bar nearby.

At eight o'clock the following morning Edward walks into the police station and reports the killing of Mr Redford.

"Sling your hook, and stop wasting police time," Constable Jenkins scoffs. "Too much grog was it, last night? No one hands themselves in for murder!" He scribbles out Edward's name in the daily log, but Edward refuses to move on.

When the sergeant arrives, Edward is put in a cell. A couple of hours later the constable drags him out.

"Mrs Redford's been. We'll have your statement now."

**

23ⁿᵈ June 1928

I am sure it was me who shot Mr Redford. I've hurt people before when I've had a nightmare. I've not killed anyone since the war. What happens is that I have a bad dream and when I wake up, I don't know what I've been doing, until someone tells me. I have no memory of killing Mr Redford. I had no reason to kill him.

The night before last, I had one of those bad nightmares. It's shell shock. Dr Lane in Martin Street knows I have the condition. I woke up with a dreadful headache, which is what happens after a bad night. I went to check some fencing, but I was struggling, so I lay down to have a kip.

When I came to, I found myself sitting in a ditch. My rifle was lying beside me, and two bullets were spent. I counted the bullets in my pocket, and two were missing.

Mr Redford was lying face down, further up the road, beside the tractor. When I looked at him closer, there was a bullet in his back, and he had a deep gash in his head. One of his fingers was nearly hanging off, but I think he'd done that himself when he was chopping a tree stump. There was blood on his axe.

I didn't want the children to see, so I rolled him into the ditch, with the rifle and covered the body as best I could. I went to tell Mrs Redford what I thought had happened. Then I got ready to come down here and hand myself in.

I had no reason to kill Mr Redford. We always got along. He liked my work. I must have thought I was back on the front line again, like the previous times.

The sergeant reads the statement slowly. He pauses every so often. There's a glaring frown on his face, as looks directly at Edward. "How did you really get on with the Redfords?" he says as he sits back to hear the reply.

"Very well. Like I've said."

"What about the Mrs?"

"What about her?"

"Were you attracted to her?" and he leans forward searching Edward's face.

"She's a lovely lady and a great mother. Good cook too, but no, I didn't want relations with her."

"So, tell me why," the sergeant said slowly, "she says you went for her, after killing her husband."

Edward moves back in his chair. Something cold skids in his belly and flips. He feels breathless.

"Perhaps you forgot to mention that," the sergeant suggests waving the statement in Edward's face.

"I didn't touch her nor the girls. Made toys for them."

"Then why the hell is she saying these things?"

Edward struggles.

"I suggest you were attracted to her." The sergeant nods and winks. "But she resisted, and that made you angry!"

They had not rehearsed what to say about her cuts and bruises nor the girls' injuries.

"You went for her and the kids. Do yourself a favour. Make it nice and tidy and just admit it."

"I didn't do it."

"So, why did she make this up?"

"Her husband is dead. I did it. She's hurt."

"Lock up this animal!" he calls to the constable.

Edward is trundled down a corridor, hands tied behind his back, until he is pushed into the cell. "You won't be out of here till we say. Piss and crap in that bucket."

For more than a week, food is passed to Edward through the small shutter in the door. Sometimes the policemen drop the food on the floor and at other times they make him wait and watch them spit in it, before allowing him to take the dish.

∗∗∗

At four o'clock in the afternoon of July 5th,1928, Edward arrives at Freemantle prison, where he is to stay for the duration of the trial. It looks like a fortress, with four storeys. He is shepherded through iron gates, which clang resolutely behind him. The guards rattle the keys and shut each door they pass through with a firm push and heavy click of the lock. In a small room, they stop, and he is given a sack to deposit all his possessions. He fingers the tattered photo of Elsie and James for a moment. He wants to kiss it, but feels foolish as he is watched so closely. It goes in the bag, followed by a handkerchief, a notebook, some pencils, a few coppers and some of his tablets. He has to strip naked and is searched before a warder hands him a bottle-green jumper, trousers - minus a belt - and shoes without laces. Passing through the next door, he is supervised while he has a bath and puts on the prisoners' uniform.

Two guards march him across a vast courtyard with rectangles of grass. The prison looms over it – a long row of connected four-storey buildings. He is handed over, without ceremony, at the third block, and shown to cell eighteen on the ground floor.

"I'm Mr Carrick," a guard says, "but you call me boss at all times. Can you read?"

"Yes, boss."

"Here's the timetable. Be ready to come out of the cell on time for all roll calls when you hear the bell. First thing in the morning, bring your bucket out. Collect breakfast and return to your cell. Lunch outside, if we feel like it. Most of the time, you will be in here. You've missed the last meal of the day – we call it tea here. Keep your nose clean, and everyone will be happy." He leaves, slamming the metal door with a hefty clunk, which echoes in the high hollow hallway with three further floors of cells on each side. As the key turns in the lock Edward stares up at the grey patch of light visible from the mean barred window. The other prisoners create a cacophony of banging on their metal doors. Stamping, yelling and whistling follows, until three shrill blasts on a whistle are heard, and the rousing welcome gradually fades away.

The cell – barely three strides across and four deep - holds a stained hammock with one blanket, a battered small wooden table and chair and a red tin bucket with a lid. The walls are lime-washed and crumbling with a variety of scrawls and drawings - some lewd. The flagstone floor offers no warmth. Edward knows the single blanket will give little comfort. Thinking about his nightmares, he considers it foolish to sleep in the hammock. He wraps the blanket around him and sits in a corner and studies the snatch of grey sky.

***

The following afternoon, Doctor Dempster, the prison medic, comes to the cell. Edward is told to strip.

"What's this fresh scar on your leg?" the doctor asks.

"Don't know," Edward replies. "I got it during the nightmare I had a couple of days ago."

"In a nightmare?"

"I dream I'm in the war again. Everything is as bad as it was – all around me there are dead or dying soldiers. I sleepwalk. Sometimes I hurt people and have to be controlled."

"How does that work?"

"People hold me. Keep me still. Tell me where I am."

"But it's ten years since the war ended."

"I know."

Doctor Dempster tuts and shakes his head. He listens to Edward's breathing and examines his eyes and teeth. Edward has recollections of the recruiting sergeant's office. The doctor makes him do some basic exercises in the confined space. It's all humiliating, and Edward believes the doctor is enjoying the situation.

"You're not a big man, but strong I'd say," the doctor comments.

"I've done physical work this last year or so. Given me muscles."

"Did Mr Redford do something to anger you?"

"No... what's that got to do with my health?"

"Smart-aleck, are we?"

"Pardon?"

"Do you easily lose your temper?"

"Not often."

"But you sometimes do?"

"Don't we all," Edward suggests, "when something's plain wrong, unjust?"

"Hmm. So, you think you have a mental condition because of these nightmares?"

"Yes. That's why I was given tablets to help me sleep when I was in hospital in Egypt in 1917. The others are for my kidneys and headaches. I've had all the tablets ever since I was in the war. There are letters from a couple of doctors, and Doctor Lane in Nimbuwa knows about it.

"Where are these letters?"

"In my kit bag, at the farm where I've been working."

"Does the medication you take at night not help?"

"Usually - It gets me off to sleep, but I still sometimes have a bad night. I'm better than I was, but I reckon it's been the difference between life in England to here that's helped me the most. I thought I'd lost the sleepwalking till the other night. Certain things trigger the nightmares."

"Did you have a nightmare last night?"

"Yes."

"Well, what's triggered that one?"

"It's the cold and sleeping on the floor – reminded me..."

"What's wrong with your hammock?"

"I might fall out when I have a nightmare."

Doctor Dempster's mouth turns up at the corners, but his eyes are full of scorn, and he stares at Edward in disapproval. "Did the guards notice you biffing about in your cell?"

"No one has said anything, but I do have a bruise on my head." Edward lifts his hair to one side.

"What have you done? Banged your head on the wall?" Doctor Dempster speaks as if addressing a small child.

"I've no idea."

"Indeed. Well, I've looked at the tablets you handed in. I'm prepared to continue them for the time being, including the sleeping aid, but if the nightmares haven't gone by now, I'm inclined to think the sleeping tablets should stop."

"I've tried without them, but I soon get worse."

"We'll see," he says casually and gets up to leave. At the door, he turns, fixing Edward with a steely look. His mouth opens as if he is about to say something, but just as quickly he changes his mind. He raps loudly on the door to let the guard know he has finished.

***

Edward's defence lawyer, a Mr Chambers, appointed by the court, is puzzled. "Mrs Redford has stated that you assaulted her, and attacked the kids."

"No, I didn't! I swear on the bible, I didn't hurt the family," Edward grasps the edge of the table then clasps his hands, as if praying, and leans his head against them. If only there had been more time.

"My job is to bloody well defend you! I have to ask awkward questions. Did you see any evidence of injuries to Mrs Redford, when you went to tell her about her husband?"

"I was in shock – confused, ashamed. I didn't actually look at her properly. It was a terrible thing to tell a wife. I avoided her eyes. I was distraught

and so was she, but I could hardly comfort her."
Edward paused. "The whole situation was dreadful.
I left as quickly as I could; went back to my tent,
changed into clean clothes and came down to
Nimbuwa to the police station. It was shut, so I
stayed at the pub.

"How did you get to Nimbuwa?"

"I walked. It's less than a couple of hours."

"Are you positive that you have not concocted
this whole story about your medical condition to get
off on the grounds of insanity? I need to know."

"I've told you, I hurt my own mother and wife."
He looks up at the lawyer. "It's why I left England
and came out here."

"Can they corroborate this?"

"I've not been in touch since I came to Australia,
but there are letters in my kit bag."

"Sorry, Edward...there are no letters. Mrs Redford
burnt your tent to the ground."

Edwards breathes deeply. "Oh, God!" he mutters,
slumping in the chair.

"The prosecution is going to push you hard about
the injuries to Mrs Redford and the children."

Edward looks up at his lawyer. "Murder is much
worse than assault, isn't it?"

"Absolutely."

"That's what I thought, so why would I lie about
the other stuff?"

"Somebody hurt Mrs Redford and her daughters.
I've seen the family. They were either injured before
you shot the husband, but you didn't notice, or

maybe later, and you have forgotten. There was no one else on the farm that day was there? I've spoken with the other labourer, Kit. We can't ignore these details. The prosecution won't."

Edward sifts through his story again. "I'm prepared to say that I have no memory of any events surrounding the death of Mr Redford, including these assaults. The first thing I recall is telling Mrs Redford I thought I had killed her husband. We sat for a few moments. She was crying, but she made a cup of tea, and I put rum in hers. Then I left. That's all I know."

Mr Chambers relaxes a little and nods his head. "That makes a little more sense. I can see you are confused about something. I'll get an expert to examine you, to establish if you were insane at the time of the murder. I think there might be a slim chance there."

***

Mr Royce-Smyth, the Inspector General of the Insane, visits Edward three times in prison and insists on the meetings taking place in a more neutral room than the cell. A man in his fifties, Edward guesses, with white hair and a handle-bar moustache. He wears glasses but often removes them, and chews the end of one of the arms. His face is open and kindly with laughter lines. Edward trusts him. The inspector asks about Edward's childhood, school days, his relationships, the war years, his headaches and medication. He encourages Edward to recall any occasions when he has injured someone. It takes time because Edward is ashamed and distressed, in particular when he recalls the incidents with his mother and Elsie. The Inspector questions Edward's replies which indicate that he is reporting what someone else has told him. "Yes. I don't actually remember hitting out at my mother or trying to strangle Elsie. My brothers or parents would tell me what I had done each time." Mr Royce-Smyth probes into the possible triggers that caused some of the night time horrors. "Anything that might prompt a memory of the war," Edward tells him. "Very bad weather; fireworks – I hate them; blasting; really, any sudden loud sound." He recollects that Elsie was so good at helping him avoid situations that might bring back the war.

The final round of questions concerns the actual day of Mr Redford's demise. Edward wants to shout out that he did not kill Red. His throat is dry. He puts his hands under his chin and around his neck to hide the pumping pulse, which feels like it might jump right out of his skin. Asking for water and a break to stretch his legs, he is allowed to walk around the quadrangle for a few minutes with a guard.

"This is distressing for you," Royce-Smyth acknowledges, "but we must be absolutely clear about the events."

During a Nightmare

On Monday morning 6th August 1928, the courtroom falls silent at once, when Edward is escorted to the dock by two prison officers. Every seat is filled; all eyes on him. He feels like the figurehead at the bow of a ship. He looks down until everyone rises for the entrance of Honourable Justice Dolan who is wearing a ornate wig and a scarlet robe.

Edward can only take shallow breaths. The room is stuffy compared with prison, but he still feels cold. In the second-hand over-washed ill-fitting prison garments, he knows he looks unkempt. He thinks about the suit his dad bought him when he joined up then has a moment of relief that at least his family cannot see what has become of him. A rivulet of sweat wrinkles between his shoulder blades causing him to shiver. He grabs at the metal bar around the dock to give him stability but the handcuffs create a clacking sound. It startles him, and he bows his head to avoid all the eyes.

"Good morning, your Honour, ladies and gentlemen. My name is George Wilson. It is my pleasure to represent the city of Perth and serve as the prosecutor in this critical case." His voice is polished, with a delivery like that of a well-rehearsed actor. Edward peeps from beneath his fringe and sees that Mr Wilson is tall and lanky with a box-shaped face and a hawkish nose.

"Ladies and gentlemen, this case concerns a man who is actually claiming insanity while carrying out heinous actions." He points at Edward, who lifts his head at these last words. He sees Mr Wilson adopt a puzzled expression, raise his eyebrows and make a hand gesture that suggests he is puzzled by what he has told the court. Edward looks down again.

"It is alleged that Mr Holmes murdered Mr Redford on 22nd June and went on to assault not only Mrs Redford but also her three young daughters. The defendant has claimed temporary insanity at the time of all these incidents. He maintains that he is still suffering from shell shock from the war that ended ten years ago." The prosecutor's tone is marked with incredulity. "I will prove that this is in fact a lie," he continues and he smirks as if he has superior knowledge. "On occasions, Mr Holmes says he has no recollection of what he has done." Mr Wilson's voice rises at the end of this sentence and

Edward sees him looking from side to side at his colleagues and shrugging. There is some burbling in the room. "Although Mr Holmes handed himself in and admitted to the murder of Mr Redford," he rises to a shout, "the prosecution believes this confession to be a ruse!" Edward feels winded. "Yes, gentlemen of the jury, Mr Holmes maintains that after the murder of his employer, he cannot recall attacking the rest of the family. I intend to prove that his insanity does not exist, and you will find against the defendant on all counts."

"Your Honour, and gentlemen of the jury." Edward's defence lawyer, Mr Chambers, rises. His voice is calm without any dramatic effects. "The defendant was barely sixteen when he bravely offered to serve his country." He looks directly at the jury. "Mr Holmes does indeed still suffer from shell shock and has been on medication for this infirmity since fighting for his country in1917. In the same year, he was hospitalised in Egypt, where he almost died." He returns his gaze towards the dock. "Edward Holmes went on, however, to fight again in the slaughter-house of France, throughout 1918. He was no coward. There was indeed some confusion when he first handed himself in, but this is symptomatic of his condition and not the charade, my learned friend suggests. I am sure our expert witness will erase any misconceptions you may have, and you will find my client not guilty."

***

Bonnie is the first witness for the prosecution, dressed in mourning clothes, her face ashen, underneath a black bonnet. She looks thinner with shadows under her eyes. Edward wants to reassure her, but she does not look at him. He cannot blame her for adding assault to his admission of murder; he had told her to say anything that kept her safe.

When Mr Wilson addresses Bonnie, he has a supercilious grin and is almost slouching to one side as if he is totally relaxed. "Do you recognise the man in the dock today, Mrs Redford?"

She nods and whispers, "Yes."

"There's nothing to fear Mrs Redford. He cannot hurt you now."

She clears her throat. She sniffs. "I'm not afraid of Mr Holmes." Her voice is dry but clear, and she coughs again. "I don't think he meant to hurt anyone, my lord." She focuses on the judge.

The prosecutor is surprised. The smile slips from his face, and he strides towards Bonnie. There is some murmuring, and a voice from the gallery is clearly heard, "I think you are confused, Mrs Redford."

"No comments from the gallery!" the judge calls out.

"I believe the observer speaks the truth," Mr Wilson says, like a head teacher who has been rudely contradicted. He points to Edward. "Did this man inform you he had shot your husband?"

"Yes, but it was his condition."

"Yes, or no, please."

She nods, but the chatter in the gallery prevents Edward from hearing what she says next. The prosecutor spins around to face the people up there. Silence is regained.

"What condition?" he continues.

"Shell shock," Bonnie replies "he has nightmares where he's still in the war." There's a definite crack in her voice. "He didn't know what he was doing, my lord."

And was it also because of his condition, that he attacked you and your children?"

"I think so. Mr Holmes was not himself."

"How do you *know* he was not acting?"

"After the war, my brother came home with something similar. It was upsetting and a little frightening. Mr Holmes explained his condition when we hired him, and my husband knew of shell shock too. Mr Holmes brought his own tent to sleep in so he would not disturb anyone at night with sleep walking, and we kept the door locked."

"On the day in question, what did Mr Holmes do to the children?"

"He grabbed them, shook them and pushed them around. He let the baby fall to the floor, but fortunately, she was well swaddled."

"How did you react to all this?"

"I tried to grab him to fight him off, but he was devilish strong."

"He should hang!" the same voice from earlier exclaims.

"Another outburst and you will be removed," the judge states plainly.

"Mrs Redford," the prosecutor continues, "do you have any medical knowledge to support your assertion that the accused has shell shock?"

Bonnie sighs. "No, but I saw him on days when he wasn't well and the tablets for his headaches. I got to know him." She rushes on. "He has to take medicine all the time. The migraines - and to help him sleep." There is a brittleness in her voice. "Edward's a good man, really he is. Wonderful with my girls. He made them toys." Her eyes are shining in her pale face, and there's a pink tinge to her cheeks. She reaches in her handbag for her handkerchief.

"Mrs Redford." The prosecutor stands up straight. He glares straight at Bonnie, and does not blink. "You have seen some tablets and heard some stories, and compared the defendant with your brother, but do you have any proof that this man suffered from shell shock?"

She looks from the judge to Edward then back to the prosecutor. She looks baffled and barely shakes her head.

"For the court please, Mrs Redford."

"Not exactly, but why would a real murderer hand himself in?"

"Precisely to convince us he's insane," he replies almost as an aside. "Thank you, Mrs Redford, that will be all."

She looks down and rubs her eyes.

***

Edward's defence lawyer approaches to cross-examine.

"Are you ready to continue, Mrs Redford?"

"I am."

"Were there ever any cross words between your husband and Mr Holmes?"

"No, sir. Red always spoke well of him and trusted him."

"Are you able to tell the court what happened to Mr Homes on the night before the accident?"

"Some accident!" a voice calls out. A man is standing up in the gallery. "Why are you defending him, love?"

Bonnie is also looking up to the gallery. "Dad, no," and her eyes glisten.

Edward watches the man who spoke being dragged back down to his seat by the people on either side of him.

"We will continue without further comment from the gallery!" The judge's voice booms out across the court. He scowls and wags his finger.

Mr Chambers nods to Bonnie, "Please continue, Mrs Redford."

"Mr Holmes had a letter, and it was bad news."

"Can you explain?"

"Well, his best friend here in Australia – they were in the war together in Egypt – had died in an accident. The family wrote asking Mr Holmes to the funeral, but the letter arrived too late. He was grief-stricken. He collapsed."

"Can you describe that?"

"It was obvious Edward was in shock. He went blank, couldn't speak or walk. My husband and Kit – one of the other farm hands – had to drag him outside. My husband gave Mr Holmes some rum."

"Just give us the main facts please, Mrs Redford. What happened next?"

"I didn't see him again until the next morning?"

"Was this the day of your husband's death?"

"Yes." She looks on the verge of tears once more, but shakes her head and sighs. "At breakfast, Mr Holmes was unwell and wouldn't have anything to eat. He complained of a migraine and just wanted water, then he was sick outside. He wasn't steady on his feet for a while."

"Did you think he was drunk?"

"Oh, no. He wasn't a drinker, sir. Only had an occasional beer at dinner."

"Did he do some work that day?"

"Yes. He had some fencing to finish."

"How do you know he did this?"

"I had to check that all the jobs in Red's diary had been completed before the farming board arrived. We're leaving the farm, going back to my family." Bonnie looks down and seems to brush tears away from her cheeks. She keeps her head bowed for a moment.

"Are you able to carry on, Mrs Redford?" She sits up straight and nods her head.

"On the day in question, when did you see Mr Holmes again?"

"About half-past two. Ed... Ed..," Bonnie crumples in her seat and uses her handkerchief.

"Would you like a break, Mrs Redford?"

She takes hold of a glass of water. There are furrows between her eyebrows, and she closes her eyes. "I'm all right. Mr Holmes came dashing in like a madman. His eyes looked like he'd seen a ghost." She squeezes her eyes even more tightly shut as she frowns deeply. "He couldn't answer any of my questions. It was like he couldn't hear me or didn't understand. Then he attacked me and the girls".

Loud exclamations from the gallery resound across the court. Someone shouts, "Monster!" Edward looks down and grips the bar so tightly that his fingers burn. A metallic taste flooded his saliva – he has bitten the inside of his lip.

The judge nearly rises from his seat. "Remove that man!" It takes a few minutes for everyone to settle.

"We can pause for a while if this will help, Mrs Redford."

She shakes her head, vigorously. "No. I've got to finish this." Her eyes are shut again. "After he'd attacked us, Mr Holmes calmed down," she begins, "He looked more normal. I asked him where his gun was, and he was puzzled that he didn't know. He ran out of the house and was gone for about twenty minutes. When he returned, he sat me down and told me he thought he had killed Red earlier, during a nightmare. He said he was going to hand himself in. He didn't register that he had hurt the children and me. I let him go, and brought us down to the doctor in Martin Street." She sighs deeply and opens her eyes. Her mouth is slack, and she stares at the judge once more as if expecting a response from him, but he is writing notes.

"Thank you for your testimony; no further questions."

Following this, an adjournment is requested because the expert witness for the defence, Doctor Royce-Smythe, is unavoidably detained. The judge grumbles but allows a commencement to be set for the following week.

***

Back at Fremantle prison, Edward asks to see the Catholic chaplain. "I am not guilty of the charges, Father," Edward tells him, "but I have not practised my faith since the war. God disappeared out there."

"That's not such an unusual thought, but now you want to make your confession?"

"I might, but I need to be reminded of the faith and the process first."

"Sounds like a good start." Father Bernard smiles. "Let's read some of the penitential psalms together."

They share his prayer book, and the first Psalm has comforting words: *"Thou art my refuge from the trouble which has encompassed me: my joy, deliver me from them that surround me."*

They read four of the seven psalms, and although Edward still has little change of heart, he is consoled with some of the words: *"Restore unto me the joy of Thy salvation, and strengthen me with a perfect spirit."* and

"In what day soever I shall call upon Thee, hear me speedily, For my days are vanished like smoke."

"My mother would be pleased I am doing this," Edward tells Father Bernard. "I wouldn't go to mass with the family when I got home from France."

"Are you doing this for her or for yourself?" Edward does not answer immediately. "I'm not sure. I'm not ready yet for confession, but I'd like to do some more reading. Can you bring me in a Bible?"

Father Bernard calls every day of the adjournment week, and they talk about what Edward has read. "Do you believe in miracles, Father?"

"I believe that sometimes events conclude in ways that confound what we think of as natural, and are beyond our understanding."

"Have you ever seen a miracle?"

"In John's gospel, he refers to signs rather than miracles and I believe I have witnessed signs that prayers have been answered, but not always in ways that might have been wished for. I've not seen a lame man walk nor anyone rise from the dead, but I have seen people gain gradually better health or have a change of heart over what at first was an unreconcilable situation."

"Surely that could be just the passage of time?"

"Possibly, but I have seen things I thought would never happen and I believe it's because God works in mysterious ways and is beyond human understanding?"

"You can say that again, but is there any point in praying for a miracle?"

"What miracle are you looking for Edward?"

"To regain my faith. I'm so bitter about what happened in the war. Why did God not stop it?"

"There are two issues here. Mankind began the war, and I think God lets us work things through sometimes, in the hope we all learn from our mistakes."

"Sounds like a cop-out to me."

"Then your bitterness, I think, has a firm hold on you. I'm sure those who decided on war never conceived the destruction and misery it would cause. No one can take away the sadness and regret you have for your lost pals, but you can try to forgive the instigators and perhaps yourself. I think you are carrying guilt for actions you were ordered to carry out, and, if I may say so, for surviving."

"I don't know about forgiving those bastards, but I do feel guilty."

"We'll talk about it again. Write down the names of as many pals you can remember. Pray for them and say goodbye to them, and try to find some peace."

Afterwards, they exchange stories about their backgrounds and families. There is a friendly banter between them, but Edward is still not ready to take the sacrament of penance.

***

When they return to court, the prison doctor is the prosecutor's next witness. Doctor Dempster is slim, clean-shaven with a sheen to his tanned face. He looks smart in a well-tailored suit and yellow necktie with blue stripes. Edward thinks he looks very pleased with himself and could be dressed for a wedding.

"Doctor Dempster, tell the court your observations of Mr Holmes during his remand at Fremantle."

"I examined him initially, and found a very healthy young man, who, nevertheless, complained of migraines and nightmares."

"Did he tell you about these nightmares?"

"Yes. Mr Holms claims that he has suffered with them since the war and could sometimes hurt people as a result of these dreams."

"Did you believe him, Doctor?"

"I gave him the benefit of the doubt, to begin with."

"To begin with? Did something change?"

"One morning, I was called to evaluate his condition. The guard told me that Holmes was disoriented, complained of a severe headache and did not know his whereabouts. When I arrived, he knew who I was, and was able to talk to me straight away. His main concern was getting some breakfast. He said he could not remember what had happened in the night, but I found him calm and perfectly rational."

"Have you witnessed such loss of memory in prisoners previously?"

"Yes. I've also seen prisoners feigning forgetfulness when they think it will get them out of trouble." The doctor looks towards Edward and wrinkles his nose. "Mr Holmes did not even act as if he had forgotten something."

"Doctor Dempster, are you cognizant of men suffering from shell-shock?"

"I have met men afflicted in this way. They arrived at Fremantle with clinical records and were more obviously unbalanced than Mr Holmes. They were quickly referred to a mental asylum."

"Can you describe their symptoms?"

"Hysteria, talking to themselves, muscle contractions that were uncontrollable, or the complete opposite – the inability to move or talk and unfocused eyes."

"Objection!" Mr Chambers shouts, "Shell shock manifests in variable ways. It cannot be valid to compare my client's mental condition with others who did not suffer in exactly the same way."

The judge pauses for a couple of seconds as he looks up. He nods then addresses Doctor Dempster himself. "Mental problems are tricky and diverse. Have you any other reason to believe the defendant might be pretending insanity?"

"There has been no demonstration of remorse. Furthermore, as you know, my lord, there have been three previous cases this year of successful pleas of insanity at the time of a crime. The suspects were all prisoners at Fremantle and displayed irrational behaviour. The prisoners talked about these men frequently, and the cases were reported freely in the newspapers."

"Objection! The suggestion that my client maybe aware of these cases is supposition."

The judge turns to Edward. "Mr Holmes, I will remind you that you are under oath. Were you aware of these cases?"

"I have not heard of similar cases, and we did not get newspapers at the farm, my lord."

"Thank you, Dr Dempster, that will be all."

The prison doctor begins to stand, but Mr Chambers approaches quickly.

"Just a couple of questions, Doctor Dempster. Have you read any of Siegfried Sassoon's Poetry?"

The doctor frowns deeply, "What?".

"An English poet," Mr Chambers explains. "Served in the war and spent months with sufferers of shell shock in an institution that was aiming to help the soldiers. He wrote of *'Their dreams that drip with murder'*. Am I right in suggesting that your knowledge of shell shock is based on witnessing only physical symptoms?"

The doctor thinks for a moment, still looking puzzled. "That's not wholly true. I saw how physical impediments affected the mind."

"So, you would agree with me that shell shock is much more complex than corporeal demonstrations of distress?"

"I can only repeat what I have already testified to," he replies, looking puzzled. "In my opinion, it is likely that Mr Holmes was feigning insanity. After all he must have been passed as normal by a doctor before gaining passage to this state."

The judge nods in agreement.

***

The following day, Doctor Royce-Smythe, the defence's expert witness is called to testify.

"Please tell the court first how you qualify for this title?"

"My studies in psychology were in Germany and England, after which I worked here at Claremont Mental Hospital until the outbreak of war. During that time, I served as a medical officer with the Australian Army Medical Corps in both Gallipoli and on the Western Front. I returned to work at Claremont Mental Hospital for six years, where I became chief medical superintendent before being appointed to my current post. I am now the Inspector General for the Insane and responsible for the mental health services in Western Australia."

"Thank you. How long did you spend with Mr Holmes?"

"Three days."

"Please tell the court your expert findings concerning the accused, Mr Edward Holmes."

"In my opinion, this is a sensitive man from a loving family. He volunteered to fight for his country when he was just sixteen, and I think this has been one of the contributing factors to his mental state. He had not fully reached adulthood, and had countless shocking experiences, as many of our lads did. Having served myself, I know how important your pals were, and Edward lost every single one of his comrades."

"Was this unusual?"

"I'm sure it wasn't, but Edward was also compromised by an almost fatal illness in Egypt. Blackwater fever is a severe complication of malaria and affects the kidneys and the brain. Patients fall into a coma, and death is usual. It can leave survivors with forgetfulness and severe migraines."

"Could this situation have caused shell-shock?"

"I don't think we will ever know the diverse causes of shell-shock, but I think his history and a few other circumstances, I would like to add, go some way to explaining Mr Holmes' behaviour."

"Please continue."

"There was evidence of some uncustomary actions, which are now associated with shell-shock, while he was in Egypt. Furthermore, at the end of the war, Edward was one of the last to be repatriated. As I have mentioned, all his friends were killed in ghastly ways. Many of these deaths, Mr Holmes witnessed personally, including those of his sergeant and lieutenant. There was too much time to dwell on it all before he went home. His spirits were very low, and he had a disappointing experience with a French girl. Mr Holmes was in grief and suffering from abandonment long before he reached the safety of his home."

Are you saying that a combination of factors contributed to continuing mental problems for Mr Holmes?"

"I've witnessed many similar cases since the war. At first, we thought shell-shock was evidenced with tremors, confusion, rigidity and catatonia. But we now know that hundreds of men have suffered from night time horrors, like Mr Holmes. Many have failed to recover since peace was restored."

"So, in your experience, does Mr Holmes still suffer from shell-shock?"

"Oh, undoubtedly, and he has had very little help with the condition. He has never spent time in an asylum."

"How does the condition affect Mr Holmes?"

"We do not yet understand the operation of the unconscious mind, but I believe that he has never been able to bury his wartime experiences deeply enough, and they catch him off guard when he sleeps. There's no mercy. The war literally terrorises his thoughts – gives him nightmares - and when these are combined with somnambulism, he may act as if he is still fighting the enemy. When he awakes, he has little or no memory of his actions, which is common to sleep walkers."

Mr Wilson is on his feet before Edward's lawyer has thanked Doctor Royce-Smythe. They cross paths as Mr Chambers returns to his seat.

"Is it your contention that Mr Holmes' unsuccessful tryst with a French floozy made him unwell?"

"I beg your pardon?" The expert witness speaks as if he is incredulous. "The loss of his girlfriend was just another small factor."

"Have you ever witnessed the accused having one of the episodes you describe so vividly?" Mr Wilson asks.

"I do not have to witness every symptom of insanity to analyse the condition of a patient. Mr Holmes has had more than ten years of living with his condition; I believe his accounts and descriptions because I've seen the same in other sufferers."

"But, - not in Mr Holmes?"

"Well, hardly! I would have to have watched him while he slept!"

"Is it possible to fake the symptoms you have described?"

"Are you calling into question my skills and experience."

"Please answer the question," the judge intercedes.

Dr Royce-Smythe glares at the prosecutor. "I imagine it could be possible."

"One further question. If Mr Holmes was unaware of his actions until after his assault on Mrs Redford, why did he hide the body and the instruments of murder?"

"Objection! Supposition!" Mr Chambers shouts.

Whispers flutter through the gallery. An elderly juror, whom Edward has noticed has been asleep for several minutes, is startled into consciousness. Others are staring into the distance, while a few are leant over paper, scribbling. Bonnie catches Edward's eye. She looks forlorn and gently shakes her head.

"I'll allow the question," the judge says.

Dr Royce-Smythe raises his eyebrows. "It is my understanding that Mr Holmes only found the body after Mrs Redford asked him the whereabouts of his gun. Upon discovery of Mr Redford, Holmes hid the body, as you say, to protect the children."

Silence falls immediately, as if all the breath has been sucked out of the room. George Wilson, the prosecutor, is standing there with a broad grin. After a moment, he announces, "That, I propose, is supposition or hear say. Mr Holmes could very well have already disposed of the body before he returned to the farmhouse in the first place, when he attacked the family. No further questions."

Dr Royce-Smythe is red in the face. "May I remind you that I am an expert witness, giving my professional opinion with due diligence, following a lifetime's work and study of mental conditions."

"Thank you for that reminder Doctor, but it cannot be definitively proven that Holmes was insane, can it?"

"What on earth is the point of an expert witness, if you just ignore my deductions?"

"Dr Royce-Smythe, refrain from further provocation, or you will be in contempt of court," the judge interrupts.

The Inspector General for the Insane steps down from the witness box and walks straight out of the courtroom.

***

Mr Chambers announces that he is calling Edward as his next witness, but that he will remain in the dock. An usher approaches with a Bible for the necessary oath. Edward releases his intense grip on the bar and reaches out, but his fingers are stiff and his wrists still handcuffed. The book clatters to the floor. Edward's cheeks burn, and there are further murmurs from the gallery. The usher retrieves the Bible and ensures that Edward has a firm hold before releasing it.

"At what point on the day of Mr Redford's demise, did you become aware of your actions?" Mr Clement asks.

Edward's mouth feels like he has swallowed sand. He tries to clear his throat. "When Mrs Redford asked about my rifle." His voice croaks as he begins.

"What happened next?"

"In my head, I saw the gun in a ditch with a man. Bonnie had said Red was out with the tractor, up the road. I ran to the tractor, which was further along from where I had been working. Mr Redford lay with my rifle in the ditch."

"Murderer!" someone shouts. "Butcher!" comes from another. These are followed by a raucous jumble of shouts and protests from the gallery.

Edward's knees buckle, and he reels to one side. The prison officer holds him up. The judge demands that everyone in the gallery must leave. There is a lot of mumbling and rasping of chairs.

When calm finally resumes, Mr Chambers continues. "Did you assault Mrs Redford and her daughters?"

Edward's stomach is slip-sliding; his temple is pinging. "I knew nothing of this until the sergeant told me at the police station in Wubin."

"You had no recollection of attacking the family?"

"No. I went to the police only because I thought I had killed Mr Redford."

"Thank you, Mr Holmes."

***

Mr Wilson announces that he would like to re-call Bonnie.

"On what grounds?" the judge asks.

"Some new information has come to light."

"What new information? Have I had notice of this?" Mr Clement stresses.

"Council will approach the bench."

They huddle in front of the judge, but no one can hear what they are saying. General chatter breaks out around the court until the lawyers move away from the judge. Edward cannot imagine what else can possibly be revealed. As she enters the court room, Edward sees Bonnie is blanched, and moves slowly, as if struggling to keep her balance on the floor. Her once smart mourning attire is creased.

"I have noticed, Mrs Redford, that you have referred, on occasion, to the defendant as Edward."

She shrugs her shoulders.

"Have you a question to ask?" interjects Mr Chambers.

"Indeed. Were you on such friendly terms with all your workmen?"

"Well, yes. We all ate together every day and the children. Red wasn't much for chit-chat, but I like to be sociable. Striker was a bit different, but Edward and Kit were grand lads."

"So, you thought you knew them pretty well?"

"Yes, I did."

"Did you know that Mr Holmes abandoned a wife and child in England?"

There are gasps all around the courtroom. The judge lets it go; looking astonished himself. Bonnie's eyes are wide. She looks stunned.

"So, Mr Holmes lied to you?"

Bonnie does not reply immediately. Edward is on the verge of tears and cannot look at her.

"Would you agree that the defendant lied to you?" Mr Wilson repeats.

"It was none of my business. It wasn't a lie. Mr Holmes could tell me what he wanted..."

"Exactly!" he takes a stride forward, clasping his hands as if clapping.

"I put it to you," he says, raising his voice, "that he is capable of cruelty and lying!"

Bonnie says nothing, "Thank you, Mrs Redford, that will be all."

Mr Chambers is on his feet before the prosecutor has regained his seat. "A word with Mr Holmes, please." The judge nods.

"Mr Holmes, will you tell the court why you left your family in England?"

Edward has to take a drink. His cheeks are sizzling. It feels like the whole world is waiting for his answer. "In one of my nightmares, I hurt my wife," he struggles to get the words out clearly. "I wanted to keep them safe. I left them so they could have a new life."

Wilson and Chambers return to their seats and are shuffling papers. There is the scraping of chairs as people readjust themselves. The jurors begin to glance at one another, then at the judge who is busily writing again. Everyone is waiting for the final comments from the lawyers. Edward is exhausted and wants it to be all over.

Mr Wilson begins his closing statement. "I am sure," he states moving up close to the jurors, "that you will have the measure of the defendant today. There is no evidence – only an estimation from Doctor Royce-Smythe – that this man ever suffered from shell shock. We've heard of his bravery in the war, but again, who is here to verify this? I advocate it is all smoke and mirrors. What has been proved is that this man is capable of dishonesty and cruelty. What decent man leaves a wife and young son to run away and hide on the other side of the world? What was he running from? Why did he keep these facts about his family from everyone, yet so readily talk about his shell shock? I suggest that it is easy if you put your mind to it, to fabricate any story about your life and stick to it. You must find him guilty on all counts."

Mr Chambers rises and approaches the jury. "The prosecutor has suggested that you have the measure of the defendant concerning his state of mind. I will remind you, however, that it is the prosecutor's job to prove, beyond all reasonable   doubt, that Mr Holmes' mind, at the time of the incidents described, was sane. Moreover, Doctor Royce-Smythe is a highly esteemed expert in his field of study, with many years of experience. How can he have made a mistake? It's improbable. There have never been any complaints about Mr Holmes' behaviour during his time at the farm and he has never been in trouble with the police in the time he has been in Australia. Mr Holmes' private life has nothing to do with the possible charges against him. It is obvious from the testimony of Mrs Redford, that the defendant is telling the truth."

The judge announces a short adjournment until three o'clock that day, while he makes his deliberations. The court empties with plenty of chatter as Edward is returned to the basement. Two guards remain, after locking him in the cell. They pay no heed to Edward, but play cards at the desk, laughing and joking.

***

Honourable Justice Dolan coughs before beginning the final summing up.   "Terrible events happened on June 22nd this year. A faultless man was killed; his good wife assaulted, and their innocent children cruelly hurt. The defendant has accepted responsibility for the death of Mr Redford. The question you must answer, however, is whether or not the defendant was insane at the time of these actions. You must neglect none of the evidence but decide which you can accept as reliable and what conclusions to draw from it. You must reach your decision based only on the evidence and any common-sense conclusions that you deem right to draw from the evidence. You must ask yourselves if you are convinced beyond all reasonable doubt that the defendant is guilty. Do the actions that have been described seem like those of a sane man? If the answer is yes, then Holmes is the devil incarnate."

Bonnie has crumpled again, sobbing. The jurors are all staring at Edward. Mr Chambers has sunk in his seat, head bowed. Edward feels faint and has to concentrate on his bowels. The prison officer pushes him up straight and leans him against the barrier with one hand firmly on Edward's back.

"In this case," Honourable Justice Dolan continues, "I can accept only a unanimous verdict. If you return a verdict of insanity, Mr Holmes will spend the rest of his life in an asylum. If your unanimous verdict is guilty, then I must pass the sentence that the law requires."

Edward is to be remanded in the cells at court until the jury return their verdict. As he is escorted down the metal spiral stairs to the cells beneath, Edward can barely put one foot in front of the other. The drop between each tread seems vast. A prison officer in front, and one behind, prevent him from falling as they clomp slowly down. The clangour of their steps reverberates in Edward's head.

It's My Turn

Edward stumbles at the bottom of the spiral staircase. His legs don't coordinate. Relief comes as he sits on the raised wooden planks, that will serve as his bed if he has to stay the night in the cell. There are no other prisoners, so the guards toss a coin to see who will remain on duty. This is the basement, and there is no heat and only early spring weather outside. The cell smells of damp earth. He jiggles like a kid needing to pee – then jerks his legs up and down, to distract himself from the frigid air. His handcuffs are removed, and he is given a cheese sandwich and a cup of water.

Within minutes Father Bernard is there carrying a thick woollen jumper, a pair of socks and a book. The officer examines the book, a G K Chesterton story – The Paradise of Thieves - and allows Edward to have everything. "The jumper will have to be removed if the verdict is called," he says.

"How did you know I was here?" Edward asks the priest.

"I've been following the trial. It's not been easy on you."

"I don't know what I ever did to make Doctor Dempster dislike me."

"He's certainly hostile."

"Right from the start, we didn't get on."

"I'm sorry. He's not done you any favours."

"You believe I'm innocent?"

"I've got to know you a little," the priest smiles. "I think that if you did do these things, you would not have been your normal self at the time."

"Thank you, I'm glad about that, but it doesn't matter anymore."

"What do you mean?"

"If I am found guilty, well, I should by rights be dead anyway, like all my mates."

"That's an odd way of looking at it."

"No. My fate will be much quicker than most of them had. I'm alive, but not living, with this bloody shell shock. I know it's never going to stop. I've given up my family in England because of it. I could never go back. I've lost everything here as well. Call it my penance for surviving and for leaving Elsie and James." He breaks down at this, and Father Bernard puts an arm around his shoulders and lets him weep.

"You can't think like this Edward."

"I do, though. I could never figure out why I survived. There was no reason. I'm ready to accept whatever happens."

Father Bernard takes hold of Edward's hands. "Let's remain hopeful. We'll pray together." He reaches inside his cassock and brings out a bag of biscuits. "I don't think you get much food down here. I'll leave you a bible again and this book. It's a detective story with a priest, who solves the case. My sister, who lives in London, sends me all sorts. It's a good tale. I once wanted to be a writer myself."

The officer ignores them and sits at a desk near the stairs. Edward is comfortable with the priest. They spend a couple of hours swapping more stories about their earlier lives, munching the biscuits and praying together. "You're not a bit holier-than-thou," Edwards tells the priest. "You haven't preached at me at all. You've been a good friend."

"What I wanted to ask, is whether you would like me to write to your family if the worst happens?" Father Bernard says. "You could write to them yourself, but it would be censored."

"I thought it would be best to just disappear."

"I think all those back in Stockport, could have some comfort if they knew the whole story. You've not been gone so long that anyone will have forgotten you."

"I'll think about it. My parents won't have moved, but Elsie could be anywhere."

"You know, your mother, even more than Elsie, will grieve your loss for the rest of her life. Not knowing what happened will consume her; make her ill. She will always love you. It's her I'd like to write to."

Another officer arrives for the night shift. "Nothing from the jury yet, but you'll have to go now Father."

Father Bernard makes sure his back is to the guard. "We'll talk again. I'll bring a notebook," he whispers to Edward.

***

On the fourth morning, Edward is escorted back up the stairs to the courtroom. It feels like going over-the-top once again, and he wishes he had a tot of rum. The gallery is packed with more reporters than during the trial– all with cameras or sketch pads. One reporter has balanced himself in the corner with his equipment, which includes a lightbulb on some sort of contraption. Several have pushed their way to the front, forcing some of the observers to stand on chairs behind them, which is not customarily permitted. The officials are all seated waiting for the judge, and the whole court is as silent as growing snowdrops, until someone coughs and several people show surprise. People are beginning to fidget and look around, whisper to each other. After ten minutes the clerk finally requests everyone to stand as Judge Dolan shuffles to his dais.

"Foreman of the jury, has a verdict been reached?" a clerk asks.

A white-haired man wearing thick glasses stands. His hands shake as he holds the piece of paper. "We have, my lord."

"On the count of the death of Mr Redford – do you find the defendant was sane or insane at the moment of his actions?"

The foreman turns and looks at his fellow jurors. Some of them frown at him. He returns to his piece of paper. "Sane," he replies.

"Hooray!" someone yells in the public gallery and this is followed by clapping and hugging as if people are celebrating an award.

"We must have silence," the clerk shouts, and Judge Dolan sits like a statue until everyone settles.

"Is that a unanimous verdict?" he asks the foreman.

"Yes, my lord, sane."

"On the matter of assault of Mrs Redford and her three daughters, how do you find?"

"Guilty!"

People are jumping off chairs in the gallery, and a babble of comments praising the verdict and the jury follow. The judge allows this for a few moments as he waits for the clerk to hand him the foreman's piece of paper, which he studies as if there is something puzzling about it.

Despite the hubbub, Edward can hear his own breathing, feel the drive of his heart. The crowd of onlookers and reporters has lurched forwards from the pressure of people pushing from the back. There are people hanging over the edge of the gallery. Edward is startled when the judge finally speaks.

"Very well," Judge Dolan says. The gallery calms down quickly hanging on the judge's final words. "The only question to be determined in this case was whether you were sane or insane at the time of your actions." He pauses and looks directly at Edward, "and the jury has found you were sane."

A flash from the lightbulb, and definite cheers and a yelp of "Yes!" batter Edward's ears. Judge Dolan gives the gallery another of his scalding looks, and silence is recovered as he dons a black cap. "The sentence of the court is that you will be taken hence and returned to the place from whence you came," he says in a monotone voice, "where you will remain in close confinement until 3rd of September 1928. Upon that day, you will be taken to the place of execution, and there be hanged by the neck until you are dead, and may God have mercy on your soul."

Camera shutters click furiously, and several cheers erupt again. Edward catches a glimpse of Bonnie with her hands clasped as if in prayer – fingers against her lips. Her eyes are closed, but tears roll down her pale cheeks. Edward is hurried away to the transport and back to Fremantle.

Sitting between the two officers, in the transport, Edward tries to avoid even the merest touch of their bodies. A tingling like pins and needles fizzes in his head. Holding himself rigid, he barely breathes, and an icy film envelops him. The guards chatter about the football at the weekend, and it reminds him of

Joseph. He hopes his little brother is playing football for Stockport and is happy. Maybe, he has girlfriend, he thinks – must be growing up now. Other motors are tooting; there are church bells in the distance and a snatch of laughter as the police vehicle comes to a halt for a moment. They are waiting to cross the bridge over the estuary. He thinks about seeing the sea. Even on a cold grey day, like this, he loved to watch and listen to the breaking waves. The salty air would make him lick his lips and the driftwood in the strand line could be marvellous for carving. Fish and chips with lashings of vinegar, and walking the prom at Blackpool – such a long time ago - with Elsie. He wishes he had said goodbye; made Elsie understand why he had to leave.

***

Edward is taken to the cells for a condemned prisoner in Division 4. This section of the prison is the closest to the gallows. His new confinement consists of three cells knocked together and providing three separate areas. There are a table and two chairs in one section, where he can sit to eat or meet a visitor. A metal bed frame with a mattress in the next, that looks better than the old hammock. Finally, the third area has a wash stand and new bucket, which he no longer has to empty himself. Further comforts are afforded by the provision of a more varied diet, and extra windows giving better light for drawing. Edward is not permitted any contact with other prisoners, and has to exercise in a separate yard.

When Father Bernard is not visiting, Edward carries on reading the novel. He is allowed some charcoal and paper and begins to draw Wollabungo from memory and some horses. Father Bernard spends several hours a day with him making notes about Edward's life. Edward agrees that the priest should write to his mother.

"Maybe the judge is right; I am a devil." he says one afternoon. After all, I killed without any mercy in that wicked war. Was I more vicious than my pals? They were slaughtered, and I wasn't. Was it only because I ran faster? The priest, back then, said we could kill without sinning in combat, but it's still taking a life. I read that part in Genesis - 'Whoever sheds the blood of man, by man shall his blood be shed.' I became like a wild beast, when I went over the top. I thought of nothing but the kill, or be killed. Then there was the firing squad. That terrified boy. God help me, it's my own brutality that haunts my dreams."

"Edward, you were conditioned to fight to kill, as were the enemy," Father Bernard says. "The only difference between you and thousands of other soldiers is that you survived – albeit with shell shock - and have had time to reflect,"

"But I must have been vicious to survive, and now this is my lot."

"Enough of this, Edward. I have no reason to believe that you have cause for guilt or shame about the war or these recent events. Very little was made of the fact that there was no motive for the crimes you are accused of. Tomorrow, you will meet your maker, and I am relieved that you are so calm about it, but your desire for death worries me."

***

"I'm not longing to die, Father, but it's my time, my turn, and I accept it. I belong to another world. Wouldn't life in a lunatic asylum be hell on earth?

"They are not happy places, that's certain."

"Father, you will write to my mother, won't you.?"

"I will tell her everything; the highs and the lows and all of your bravery."

"Thank you. I'd like to pray now and make a confession."

"We'll say the Glorious Mysteries of the Rosary together." He hands Edward a set of beads, "Fill your mind with thoughts of salvation and heaven."

Twenty minutes later, Father Bernard brings out his purple stole and drapes it around his neck. Edward kneels before him and begins, "Oh my God, I am sorry and beg pardon for all my sins, because they deserve thy dreadful punishment..." and Father Bernard starts,

"Deus, pater misericordiarum,
Qui per mortem et resurrectionem Filii sui
Mundum sibi reconciliavit et Spiritum Sanctum effudit in remissionem peccatorum, per ministerium Ecclesiae indulgentiam tibi tribuat et pacem."

Edward recalls events from his entire life. There is no mention of the occurrences of June 22nd. He hears

367

Father Bernard's absolution, "Et ego te absolvo a peccatis tuis, in nomine Patris et Filii et Spiritus Sancti," answers, "Amen," and sinks back on his heels. "Where will I be buried?"

"Not here, at the gaol. There's a cemetery on the other side of the city."

"Will you be there?"

"Of course. It will be an unmarked grave, but I'll make a record of the place."

"Maybe, in years to come, James or his children will find me."

"I'll pray for that."

***

...At five o'clock on the morning of 3ʳᵈ September, Edward was woken and given his last meal. He chose steak and kidney pie to remind him of home, he told me. We shared the meal, as we had done many times in those last few weeks. He showered and was given clean clothes. Then, I had to leave him, for he was taken to solitary confinement for the remaining two hours. The guard told me he was given brandy, but honestly, he was not agitated. He continued to be calm right to the end; firm in his faith once more and accepting his fate.

Just before eight o'clock, he was released from solitary, and we walked down the narrow passageway, with sunshine blessing our steps, to the final moment. Edward was asked if he had any comments to make and he replied, 'I have nothing left to say, thank you.'

The end was seconds long, and he would not have felt pain. The chapel bell rang out once.

I truly believed him to be innocent right to the end. At his grave, I read from Wisdom 4:7-11, and I continue to remember Edward in my prayers. 'But the righteous man, though he dies early, will be at rest. For old age is not honoured for length of time, nor measured by number of years; but understanding is grey hair for men, and blameless life is ripe old age. There was one who pleased God and was loved by him, and while living among sinners he was taken up. He was caught up lest evil change his understanding or guile his soul.'

Fremantle Prison

Today

Acknowledgements

I have to start by thanking my awesome Thursday morning writing group and our very talented and insightful tutor, Jo Browning Wroe. John, Edwin, Val, Joyce, Martin, Sophie, Kate, Ann, Lizzie, and Joan, I cannot thank you and praise you enough for readdressing my pages several times over the last four years; for your support, questions and ideas. I would have been nowhere without you, and especially John, the polymath of our group, for all his attention to details, and helping to get my head around formatting.

Also thanks to Major General Julian Thompson who gave me his time, in the early days, to explain how the army functioned in World War One.

My husband deserves thanks for putting up with my exasperation at times and never giving up on me. I thank my three wonderful daughters, Siobhán, Victoria and Josephine for keeping faith in me and Victoria needs a special mention for creating the astonishing cover. I love you all to the stars and beyond.

My extended family; each and every one of you, for asking constantly how I was getting on – thank you.

For Gail Murphy, in Perth Australia, for locating my grandfather's grave and Kathy and Brian Narbett for introducing me and Steve to Perth, and driving us to wonderful places. Thank you.

Christine Eccles grew up in Cheshire but now lives in Cambridge. She was educated at Loreto convent schools in Altrincham and Llandudno. Graduating from Manchester University with a B. Ed in 1972 and subsequently a BA from the Open University, she went on to teach English for many years but spent the last eight years of her teaching career in Primary education. She retired in 2010. She is married with three daughters and four grandchildren. Christine loves family gatherings and is drawn to the sea and visits the Norfolk coast as often as possible.

Printed in Great Britain
by Amazon